Gu Hua

Pagoda Ridge
and Other Stories

Translated by Gladys Yang

Panda Books

Panda Books
First edition 1985
Copyright 1985 by CHINESE LITERATURE
ISBN 0-8351-1335-3

Published by CHINESE LITERATURE, Beijing (37), China
Distributed by China International Book Trading Corporation
(GUOJI SHUDIAN), P.O. Box 399, Beijing, China
Printed in the People's Republic of China

CONTENTS

Translator's Preface

GU HUA, born in 1942 in a small mountain village in South Hunan, took up writing in his spare time while working on a farm and published his first story in '62. There was pressure in those days on Chinese writers to gear their writing to the current political line, and his earliest works were fairly stereotyped. In the late seventies, after the fall of the "gang of four", Gu Hua like other writers felt free to express himself more truthfully and to deal with a much wider range of subject matter, to attack social abuses, describe backward superstitious practices and to introduce romance.

Gu Hua has written two novels, ten novellas and over fifty short stories as well as articles on writing and accounts of his travels in Egypt and Morocco. The four stories in this collection were written between '81 and '83. "The Log Cabin Overgrown with Creepers" was voted one of the best short stories of 1981, while his outstanding novel *A Small Town Called Hibiscus* won a Mao Dun Literary Award in 1982. "Pagoda Ridge", though not a prize-winner, is one of his representative works. Its theme is not too original. Many Chinese writers have written about the hardships of the peasants during the "cultural revolution" and how, to survive, they defied the ultra-Left policies in agriculture. But Gu Hua's handling of this theme is gripping because of the local colour which pervades all his work. "Ninety-nine Mounds" and the other stories presented here also illustrate his familiarity with the folk-lore and customs of his native place.

We have amalgamated and slightly abridged Gu Hua's two articles "How I Became a Writer" and "About Pagoda Ridge" to help our readers understand the background of these stories.

Gu Hua is too modest to say much about his language, a treat for Chinese readers but losing much of its flavour in translation. He tells us that his Chinese teacher at school was always critical of his compositions because he kept straying from the subject, being interested in everything under the sun, and because he flouted conventions. In this respect some purists may still fault him. Born and bred in the Wuling Mountains, unlike some writers from cities who go to the countryside to experience life and enrich their vocabulary, Gu Hua comes out naturally with the idioms, local sayings, graphic figures of speech and crude swear words of the Hunan mountaineers. But he refines them to some extent and also uses classical expressions. He has made a study too of such Chinese stylists as Zhao Shuli and Shen Congwen. The result is a fresh, distinctive style of his own, colloquial and popular yet literary. Hunan has some of the loveliest landscapes in China, and so evocative are his descriptions of the Hunan countryside and the characters peopling it that film and TV producers reading his stories at once visualize them as pictures. Six films based on his work are being made.

Gu Hua has been called the Hardy of Hunan. He has not attained Hardy's stature. But though a century apart and living in totally different societies at opposite ends of the world, both men are regional novelists with a passionate love for their native place, its people and folk customs. They evoke these sometimes lyrically, sometimes with caustic humour, describing stark reality with deep feeling or with romantic or burlesque exaggeration. Both like to comment on the social scene. Both have given us unsurpassed portraits of country women, seemingly gentle yet strong enough to rebel against convention. Gu Hua has been criticized for dwelling unduly on the physical charm of some of his alluring heroines and for certain suggestively sensual passages, though Western readers are unlikely to take exception to this.

Where he differs completely from Hardy is in his approach to life. The English novelist generally saw human life as an inevitable tragedy, while Gu Hua is an optimist able to describe the nightmare of the "cultural revolution" with flashes of earthy humour in the best tradition of Chinese satire. He has infinite faith in ordinary people, convinced that sanity will prevail, and they will win through to the better life they deserve.

Gu Hua, now a well-known and popular novelist, has recently left his old home and moved to Changsha, the capital of Hunan. As a professional writer, attending many conferences and meetings and able to travel widely, his horizons are broadening. It will be interesting to see what effect this new style of life will have on his work.

Gladys Yang

September 1984

Pagoda Ridge

— A Song for Our Mountaineers

I

A "public road" paved with stones passes Our Lady's Temple on the way to the Wulin Mountains. Officials of earlier times are said to have conscripted labour to build it, to have sent government troops up there to mop up bandits. It still shows the imprints of their horses' hoofs. Sometimes it rears up like a snake to scale the heights, then plummets like a vigorous vine down precipices, or thrusts like an arrow into densely gullies. This stone track climbs peaks wreathed in white clouds or rosy mist, coils through chasms which even monkeys dread, and penetrates virgin forests as murky as night. As strong and tenacious as the mountaineers here, it is clearly marked on the military maps of the Wuling Mountains from different dynasties.

Past Our Lady's Temple and beside this stone track flows Guanyin Brook, clear as jade yet headstrong. This brook, too small to be traced on the map, is too out-of-the-way and insignificant to be known to any but a few. But just as the stone track, after leaving the temple, joins the highway to the commune and county town, then links up with the railway to the provincial capital and Beijing, Guanyin Brook flows to the Chunling River which joins the Xiang River, Dongting Lake and the Changjiang River. Since the brook's ripples spill at last into such vast expanses of water, why should she belittle herself? Month after month, year after year, glinting through the valleys of the Wuling Mountains, she decks herself with reflections of wild flowers, is caressed by lustrous green creepers, embowered by old trees, courted by goats, monkeys and pheasants. . . .

Guanyin Brook and the stone track diverge and then join up again like the two fluttering strings of a mountain girl's apron. Too small for boats or rafts, the brook irrigates the emerald paddy fields on her banks and waters many households in the hills. A few young mountaineers thought of building a small power station in her upper reaches, to decorate her with luminescent pearls. But, alas, they never succeeded, because she is too capricious and fluctuates too unpredictably. She brims her banks in spring when the plum trees blossom, at the Dragon Boat Festival in summer and the Moon Festival in autumn, when she thunders like a cataract through the pass. But then she subsides and dwindles to appear like a jade girdle, gentle as a small girl in the hills. Once past the temple, the stone track and brook diverge and go their different ways.

No offerings have been made for many years in Our Lady's Temple. Just after Liberation, the two nuns who remained there used to place two buckets of tea by the temple gate, so that passers-by could rest and quench their thirst. To lay up virtue in heaven they might also leave alms. But during the Big Leap Forward a steel-smelting army was billeted in this temple. They pulled down the side halls, using the bricks and tiles to make a furnace and boost the production of steel. Although the next year this nationwide campaign was halted, the temple was taken over by the commune for a huge pig farm, and the goddess and her attendants had to give way to thousands of hogs and sows, Chinese and foreign. In those days, of all livestock pigs were the most prized. But during the hard years when the commune members had no meat, this pig farm was disbanded. In 1966, at the start of the "cultural revolution" to sweep away everything old, the tumbledown temple was razed to the ground. All that remains of it now are the bases of a few pillars, and the slogans written on them — "In Agriculture Learn from Dazhai*" and "Never Forget Class Struggle" — so eroded by wind, rain and frost as to be almost indecipherable.

But the name "Our Lady's Temple" has come down. Its site was a strategic one, the stone track there, too narrow for more than one horse at a time, being hemmed in by two cliffs. Year in year out, that track was gloomy and dank, and passers-by used to whistle or sing a folk-song to keep up their courage, or warn people going down to wait for them to get up it. Once through this pass they were among the mountains shrouded in mist, with only a crack of sky overhead, far-stretching hills beneath their feet.

> Beyond Our Lady's Temple, beneath the soaring sky,
> Monkeys rule the heights, the emperor has no say.
> Beyond Our Lady's Temple various trees and wild flowers thrive,

---

* A production brigade in Shanxi Province.

The men there brandish clubs, the women brandish
knives.

It was early spring, before the peach trees in the
mountain had bloomed, willows burgeoned, or bamboo
shoots thrust through the ground, yet someone singing
a folk-song was climbing up to the pass. Had this been
in the years when everything was viewed from the
angle of class struggle, his loud, defiant singing would
have been thought counter-revolutionary, requiring in-
vestigation. But now that the "gang of four" were on
the shelf, fewer people lived off struggles and political
campaigns.

Beyond Our Lady's Temple lie
Fine hills and streams beyond compare,
While life on our Pagoda Ridge
Is leisurely and free from care.

The singer, a burly man of medium height in his
thirties, was wearing a faded army cap and old PLA
uniform, sloppily patched and held together in two
places with sticking plaster. His lantern-jawed face
was bronzed, his skin roughened by wind and rain, and
the fierce looks he flashed from his big eyes made him
seem at first glance rather vicious. On his back he was
carrying a blue batik bedding-roll, in one hand a brown
canvas hold-all. In rubber-soled sandals he strode
along with a heavy tread, kicking up dust, as if to leave
deep footprints on the track.

"Old Man Heaven has opened his eyes! Sent Tian
Faqing back. I'm back!"

When he reached the crumbling steps of Our Lady's
Temple he halted and let out a deep breath. As he had

announced, his name was Tian Faqing. But was he a frustrated demobbed soldier? A cadre from some production team who had been studying in the county town or commune? A trader who scoured the hills for mushrooms and mountain products? He might have been any of these, yet didn't look too much like them. A few years earlier he had gone every winter to meetings in the prefectural or county town, returning with big silk banners, big framed prize certificates. But he had broken the law — quite knowingly too. So now he was on his way back from labour reform. He, a Communist, had been in a labour camp! That reflected badly on his ancestors and was a black mark against him, nothing to boast about. Yet he was singing.

He sat down on a broken tablet inscribed with the names of the faithful who had contributed funds to build the temple. He was perspiring. The matted grass, which did not shrivel in winter, had been buffeted for so long by the wind from the pass that it bent eastwards, rustling, making the place seem more desolate and wild. His feet resting on rubble, his hands on his knees, he stared raptly at the misty mountain track ahead of him. He was not the sort to cringe after a beating, especially as now he was all on his own, with no mother, wife or children depending on him. What had he to hold him back, to be afraid of?

Why had he come back? It was like a dream, yet something he had never dreamed of. Ten days ago he had been on the labour reform farm by Dongting Lake. Suddenly the director had summoned him to the head office. He announced, "Tian Faqing, since you've toed the line here for three years, the authorities have reviewed your case and decided to shorten your sentence. You're now to be released."

Tian shuddered as if his blood had stopped circulating and his heart ceased beating, impairing his sense of hearing and his sight. His skin smarted and he had to shut his eyes, as if dazzled by bright sunshine after a long confinement in the dark. But he shed no tears of gratitude. He was used to life in that camp. He had been a team leader there too, in charge of forty-odd felons and the cultivation of two hundred *mu* of dry land and over three hundred *mu* of paddy fields. He had farmed in accordance with the Eight-point Charter for Agriculture, paying attention to soil improvement, rational application of fertilizer, water conservancy, good seed strains, close planting, plant protection, field management and improvement of farm implements. So they had raised more than a thousand catties of grain per *mu*, going all out to "learn from Dazhai". But, separated from his wife, there had been no warmth in his life.

"Well? Are you deaf? Didn't you hear what I said? Your sentence has been commuted, you're being discharged!" said the director loudly, when he saw how blank Tian looked. Anyone else would have bowed to the ground, shedding tears of gratitude.

Tian shook himself and shuffled his bare sunburnt feet. A sudden fantastic notion flashed through his mind. He demanded gruffly, "May I ask you, director, if this means I'm in the clear now, rehabilitated?" Even in this labour camp each brigade had a copy of the provincial paper, and so they had some inkling of policy since the fall of the "gang of four".

"In the clear? Rehabilitated?" The grim-faced direc-

tor had to smile. As Tian had never seen him smile at
any of the camp's inmates, this smile struck him as
unusually friendly. "Well, never satisfied, are you?
We've had no notification to that effect. ..." The director was looking irritated now, ready to launch into one
of his tirades: You were simply the leader of a production team in the mountains, not on the state pay-roll,
without even a personnel file, at most listed in the
register of your local security office. You'll be going
back to farm work, swinging a hoe or driving an ox;
so there's no question of clearing you or implementing
any policy. What he said, however, was:

"Take this identification slip and this chit to the accountant's office to draw a hundred yuan for travelling
expenses."

Tian left the labour camp without bowing or expressing heartfelt thanks. Hard as nails, he could sell his labour anywhere and make enough to feed and clothe himself without bending his back or cringing. Though not
branded on the forehead or tattooed as a criminal, he
was marked for life as a counter-revolutionary — and
people would never forget that! They were likely to say
behind his back, "He was sentenced to hard labour. Now
the policy is to be lenient — he's been lucky."

"How long was his sentence?"

"Seven years! For seven years he ran Pagoda Ridge
as an independent kingdom; so they gave him seven
years hard labour, but let him out after three!"

And if he quarrelled with anyone, the fellow might
point at him and swear, "Watch out. Back from a labour
camp! Even if they've taken off your cap, you're still
a marked man."

He sat on that broken tablet till his sweat dried, his

back felt chilled, his feet numb. A cold wind was blowing through the pass straight at him. He stood up, slung his bedding-roll over his shoulder, picked up his almost weightless canvas hold-all, and looked up at the stone track ahead. After three whole years in the broad plain by Dongting Lake, now that he was back in the mountains, this steep track through the mist and clouds amazed him.

Three years ago he had been marched off down this track; now he was going back up it. Well, he must get even! For three years he had been treated as a counter-revolutionary and was now labelled for life as a stinking ex-convict. He wasn't going to take that lying down.

2

Deep in the mountains beside Guanyin Brook, ranged over fifteen *li*, were four small hamlets: Gong Flat, Oxhorn Hollow, Muffin Cliff and Monkey Rock. The nineteen households who lived there, comprising at most a hundred souls, made up Pagoda Ridge Production Team. The name Pagoda Ridge reflected rather badly on their forbears. But we may as well explain why, as we have long been in the custom of writing the genealogies of our families and clans, and a few years ago believed in checking up on people's antecedents for three generations.

In the old days, so the story goes, bandits hid away in the primeval forest on Pagoda Ridge. Murderers from north Guangdong, south Hunan and southwest Jiangxi, they had taken refuge here high in the mountains far from the imperial court, and built themselves these hamlets. Later, some philanthropist took pity on these outlaws and wanted to build a seven-storeyed pagoda there to subdue evil influences and save their souls. But the mountaineers were too savage and benighted to be moved by Buddhist beneficence, and so the pagoda never did get built. Only the empty names Guanyin Brook and Pagoda Ridge were handed down. As to why the nineteen households there lived in four different hamlets, there were two theories about that. One was that the gully was so narrow and the small fields opened up in the hills above the brook were mostly little hummocks. When the old team leader Liu Jiejie opened up one *mu* he found forty-nine hummocks. He dug for three whole days, but then could count only forty-eight of them. Dammit! Where had the missing one gone? And how had it got away? To hell with it! If it was lost it was lost. Not till he went down to the brooks to wash his feet did it occur to him: I forgot to count the mound I was standing on. Since the fields were so small and scattered, the mountaineers did not need to live together to till them.

The other theory was: Since most of the men up there had criminal records, they had to be on their guard against the government troops sent to capture them. Luckily the road into the mountains was over thirty *li* long, and there was only that winding stone track up it. Gong Flat stood closest to the bottle-neck pass. If troops were spotted, they at once sounded a gong, whereupon oxhorns were blown in Oxhorn Hollow opposite. As hills and valleys resounded, all sprang into action. Then men rushed with knives and spears to Gong Flat to hold back the enemy, while the women and children grabbed some provisions and valuables and slipped away into the forest. So even if the troops captured Gong Flat they wouldn't find a soul in the mountains.

After Liberation and Land Reform, mutual-aid teams, co-operatives and communes were formed, and farming became more collectivized. Life improved even for the mountaineers on Pagoda Ridge among their green forests and emerald fields on the banks of Guanyin Brook. But towards the end of 1958 a steel-smelting contingent spent the whole winter burning charcoal here, denuding the mountain of its old trees and leaving nothing for the local people but poverty, pillbox-shaped furnaces and tree stumps. Pagoda Ridge was reduced to living on relief rice and credit. Luckily it was a small team, over thirty *li* away from the brigade, more than fifty *li* from the commune headquarters and about a hundred *li* from the county town. Its tiny fields, seemingly scattered at random by some immortal on the heights, were hidden in mist and clouds.

Tian Faqing strode up the mountain track, no longer singing at the top of his lungs. As he approached Pagoda Ridge he grew preoccupied by his personal problems. Tian Faqing, Tian Faqing, how did all this happen? You made one false move, then everything went wrong. . . . If a man loses his way he can turn back, all the way to the ends of the earth. But if he goes astray at a turning-point in his career, he can never make up for it.

In fact Tian's troubles had started when he got to know a girl at the foot of the mountain. That was in the autumn of 1965 when he, just twenty, went thirty-odd *li* down the mountain every morning to attend a forestry course organized by the commune. The young commune members who studied there assembled each morning and dispersed in the evening, having their mid-day meal in the forestry station. Guanyin Brook flow-ed into Guanyin Stream, considerably wider but not too deep, so that people could wade across its rocky bed. Near this ford, in Rich Flats, lived vivacious Liu Xiuxiu, who rolled her trousers up over her knees each morning to cross the stream, her satchel on her head, her cloth shoes in her hands. A large smile on her face, she would mince across. Sometimes she halted abruptly in the middle to look at the mottled rocks or admire her own lovely reflection in the clear water, and then she would chuckle to herself. Tian forded the stream here too every day, sometimes ahead of Xiuxiu, sometimes behind her. They never spoke to each other, as in the country men and girls who had not been introduced had to keep their distance. But every day the young moun-taineer kicked up foam, not caring whether it spattered her face or wet her pretty clothes. He may even have done this on purpose. Liu Xiuxiu changed her clothes almost every day, and put on airs, for ever giggling to herself for no reason. The sight of her provoked him. And how could a well-to-do, delicate girl from Rich Flats be impressed by a young man from Pagoda Ridge? Month after month he wore the same dark blue nankeen jacket, yet there were no sweat stains on its back — he must wash it every night to wear the next morning! His bare feet were sturdy and good-looking. Bah! He must have been born with them, and had never worn water-proof boots, gym shoes or army shoes.

Before long the youngster from Pagoda Ridge had a chance to laugh at her expense. For five days and nights that autumn Guanyin Stream was in spate. The lively girl from Rich Flats squatted on the bank in tears. The first day Tian ignored her, took off his pants and slung them over one arm to wade triumphantly over. The next morning his heart softened when he saw her on the bank again in tears. She looked more attractive laughing. But since she didn't ask for his help, he paid no attention, and just started splashing across. In any case, what could he have done for her? Thinking of this, his heart beat fast, his cheeks burned. He had reached the middle of the stream when he heard a soft cry "Hey there!" He turned round and saw her watching him intently, beckoning. That meant she wanted help. For a second he hesitated, then went back to the bank. However, the girl from Rich Flats said not a word, just looked at him with smiling, expressive eyes. Wasn't that maddening? She wouldn't condescend to talk to him! Still, the young mountaineer was an honest fellow. Red in the face, he stuttered:

"You, if you're not feudal-minded, I'll see you across. . . ."

He himself was too feudal to say, "I'll carry you."

"All right, if you promise not to bully me. . . ."

Xiuxiu, still smiling, kicked at the pebbles on the ground, looking as if she were doing him a favour. Tian was tempted to go off and leave her in the lurch. But he found himself rooted to the spot. She had such a pink and white face, such soft cheeks, such a sweet roguish smile, and her big black eyes seemed to see into his heart! With her willowy waist, her high breasts, she was altogether entrancing.

"If I bully you I'm a pup!" he swore like a little boy.

"Swearing like that, watch out! You'll be a horse in your next life!"

Spluttering with laughter, she eyed him with a show of annoyance.

The young fellow from Pagoda Ridge bent down in front of her, his hands on his knees to steady himself while Xiuxiu climbed on to his back. For the first time she held his broad shoulders, trying not to let her breasts touch him, her heart racing. When he gripped her legs with his strong hands, she found this so ticklish that she couldn't stop giggling. Once across the river she jumped down, speechless with embarrassment. Tian had beads of perspiration on his forehead, presumably because the girls of Rich Flats were so delicate and plump — the result of good living.

Guanyin Stream remained in spate for four more days, and Xiuxiu had to ask him to carry her across. She took a fancy to his thick eyebrows, big eyes, his strength and his whole appearance. They stopped treating each other as strangers. As few people forded the stream here, no one saw them. Later, when they were used to this way of crossing the river, they chatted together.

"I hear you do pretty well at Rich Flats."

"I hear your Pagoda Ridge is poor!"

"Poor we may be, but we have guts."

"You have a pretty bad reputation."

"What bad reputation?"

"They say the place is a bandits' lair. You used to come down to rob Rich Flats. Our old people still hold that against you. Ha! Don't pull a long face and glare like that. That was before Liberation. . . ."

"Wipe that smile off your face! They're full of crap! We're all poor or lower-middle peasants on Pagoda Ridge. Not a single middle peasant among us."

"What's it to you if I smile? Your fathers before you were brigands, like in the story books. . . . They were highwaymen."

"They were good men, heroes of the greenwoods. Don't keep harping on bandits, have you no class stand?"

"All right, all right, I won't smile. Tell me honestly, Faqing, what did your father do before Liberation?"

"What is this, a political interrogation? Dad died when I was two. If he was a bandit — so what?"

"So what?" She giggled again. "As long as you aren't one, that's good enough. . . . Help!"

Either through carelessness or to teach this cheeky girl a lesson, Tian slipped on a stone and the two of them fell into the muddy water. They climbed out like drowned rats, drenched to the skin. Laughing and pouting, Xiuxiu pummelled his shoulders and back with her small fists. They stayed away from the forestry class that day, hiding in a willow grove till their clothes had dried.

From an exchange of blows a friendship grows. The forestry course lasted for three months, and every morning and evening these two young lovers crossed Guanyin Stream together. No matter whether the weather was fair or foul, or whether the water was only ankle-deep, Liu Xiuxiu made Tian carry her across, not taking off her socks and shoes.

Two young lovers by Guanyin Stream. . . . Was he looking for trouble? He loved Xiuxiu and she loved him. Three days apart seemed to drive them to distraction. What business was this of anybody else's? But Xiuxiu's parents disapproved. They wanted her to marry the son of the brigade Party secretary.

The next spring Tian joined the army, hoping in this way to win credit and stop the Rich Flats villagers from regarding him as the worthless son of a bandit. There was nothing more glorious than being a PLA man, and Xiuxiu had agreed to marry him. Unknown to her parents she went to the county town to see him off. Not smiling, her eyes full of tears, with so much she wanted to tell him. She was afraid that once her young man was in uniform and saw more of the world, he would be dazzled by the smart girls outside and stop loving her. Tian was intelligent enough to guess what was on her mind. He took her to a quiet spot and produced from his pocket a silver heart-shaped amulet which his mother had left to him. He put this in Xiuxiu's hand. Though primitive and smacking of superstition, it was a pledge of his love, a sign that nothing would make him give her up.

Tian served in the army for three years on Hainan Island. Every month Xiuxiu smiled over the letters he wrote her. The sea must be as blue and vast as the sky over the Wuling Mountains. Brother Faqing must be standing guard under a coconut palm or patrolling a beach strewn with conches. Were his bushy eyebrows and big eyes reflected in the blue water? Was he salty from the brine? They said there were many rainstorms on that island; had they drenched the clothes of the soldier under the palms? Every evening Xiuxiu went to stand in the wood by Rich Flats, smiling foolishly as she gazed up at Our Lady's Temple and the towering Wuling Mountains. Blast that temple and the mountain peaks for blocking her view, or she might have had a glimpse of Hainan Island, of Brother Faqing with his rifle under the palms. She could imagine the place from pictorial magazines and films she had seen.

Then suddenly the soldier under the palms received a letter from the Wuling Mountains. The laughter-loving girl from Rich Flats had written it with tears of desperation. Her parents and the brigade secretary did not recognize their "marriage". She hadn't moved to his house and he had sent no betrothal gifts, so how could they count as married? Her parents had accepted betrothal gifts from the secretary's family, and ordered her to marry his only son whose left leg was shorter than the right. They'd fixed the marriage for the end of the year. . . .

Tian Faqing had made a good showing in the army, had joined the Party and was to be promoted from squad leader to platoon leader. But having read this letter he sent in three applications to be demobilized. As if possessed, he shouldered his haversack with a pair of new army shoes stuffed on the top, and made off at full speed for the Wuling Mountains.

The first thing he did when he got back was to hurry to Rich Flats with three hundred yuan — his demobilization pay. He gave this to Xiuxiu's parents and asked them to return the betrothal gifts from the brigade secretary. This caused a great uproar in Rich Flats. It was absolutely unheard of, one of their girls choosing to marry a man from Pagoda Ridge, so poor that their hens laid no eggs, their goats left no droppings. But with a brash smile Xiuxiu said, now that we're learning from Dazhai to battle with Nature, even Pagoda Ridge will be better off. Still her father and mother refused. They locked her up in the attic with the three hundred yuan. Late at night she climbed out and ran to the wood to find Brother Faqing, her eyes all swollen from weeping. She wanted to elope with him to Pagoda Ridge. However, he wouldn't agree to this. A demobbed soldier and a Party member, he must not do anything underhand. He must find a go-between to propose the match, not let himself be accused of being a bandit who had abducted his bride.

The crippled son of the brigade secretary limped round Liu Xiuxiu's house with a stout cane, threatening to "break the legs of that bandit son of a bitch from Pagoda Ridge". But the thud of the demobbed soldier's oxhide boots sent him scuttling off into a dark corner of the lane. Tian Faqing, carrying nothing but his khaki haversack and army canteen, would come boldly to Rich Flats, not afraid of being shot down or getting an arrow in his back, much less of the cripple's cane. Most of the men of Pagoda Ridge, no doubt influenced by their formidable forbears, had trained since boyhood in the martial arts. If one of them took up his stand on a patch of level ground with a roar of defiance, seven or eight lesser fellows dared not go near him. Tian was tough, talked big and refused to back down. He announced to Xiuxiu's parents, for all the old villagers of Rich Flats to hear:

"Pagoda Ridge may be poor, but your daughter won't feel the pinch there. In two years I'll send a go-between and escort Xiuxiu up to my home with gonging and drumming."

3

Recklessness never pays. Only simpletons are reckless. If someone shrewd makes a show of reckless behaviour it is actually to attain some secret end. For most rash people come a cropper. Pagoda Ridge was desperately poor, yet now Tian had rashly sworn to send a go-between in two years' time to ask for Liu Xiuxiu's hand.

When tough young Tian arrived back from the army and spent a whole three hundred yuan to win a bride from Rich Flats, the Pagoda Ridge folk thought him a fool to leave himself no way out, but otherwise showed no special interest in him. What occupied their minds was their own dilemma. Spring was just round the corner, yet they were a flock of sheep without a bell-wether, unable even to choose a team leader. The old one, Liu Jiejie, had sworn that he would sooner lose his head than go on with that thankless job. In fact their production team was already bankrupt, heavily in debt. The brigade had gone to the trouble of sending someone to check their accounts. Well, the books hadn't been cooked, there had been no hanky-panky, no embezzlement of public funds. The team had no grain or oil, not a cent of cash. Everybody had to tighten their belts. Liu Jiejie still wore the padded coat issued him during Land Reform, now a mass of patches. His family's only two quilts, also given them at the time of Liberation, were riddled with holes. His sixteen-year-old daughter's shoulders were bare, his two young sons had bare bottoms. How could such a team leader be suspected of being a swindler?

Bare mountains, destitute people — who was to blame? Were they lazy gluttons, fit only to steal? Had Guanyin Brook refused to water their fields? Was Old Man Heaven against them? No, the people here were not idlers; since Liberation they had mended their ways, had given up thievery. And Old Man Heaven had sent them sunshine, rain, dew and frost in due season. So why was Pagoda Ridge so poor that no one would take on the job of team leader? It was not as if the higher-ups had shown no concern for the place. It received relief every year, state grain and credit. Every year, learning from Dazhai, it opened up terraced fields and grasped class struggle, awarded political workpoints and ate together. But Dazhai's priceless experience didn't suit the local conditions, didn't work here. Luckily everyone on Pagoda Ridge was a poor or lower-middle peasant (though their forbears might not have been up to much), so they need not worry about the power being seized by landlords, rich peasants, counter-revolutionaries, bad elements, Rightists or the bourgeoisie. Their problem was quite the reverse. No one wanted to seize power, no one dared to take responsibility. Who was willing to be the unlucky team leader who had to trek scores of *li* to meetings in the commune or brigade, where there was never a word of praise for him and Pagoda Ridge was invariably cited as backward, a hard nut to crack? When the commune heads saw him they scowled, as if the sight gave them a headache. Other ruddy, well-fed team leaders eyed him askance as if he were a mangy beggar, afraid he would ask them for seeds, grain, insecticide or fertilizer. . . .

Still, even for a lion dance or dragon lantern display someone has to take the lead, so someone had to head Pagoda Ridge Team even though it was a shambles. However backward, however its name stank, it had to send someone to meetings in the commune, have someone to pass on the Central Committee's instructions, carry out the latest directives, lead them in shouting slogans in each political movement, and go through the motions of grasping class struggle.... As the saying goes, "Three cobblers with their wits combined equal Zhu Geliang the mastermind." Surely Pagoda Ridge with its nineteen households could do this too. The hunter Knock-out Wang of Monkey Rock came up with a bright idea — draw lots for the job. Slips of paper should be prepared, one of them with a red circle on it, which could be put in a bamboo cylinder and shaken up. Then all the men eligible to be team leader should draw one lot with the chopsticks and display it. Whoever drew the red circle would get the job.... How fantastic? At the height of the "cultural revolution" when people far and wide were combating feudalism, capitalism and revisionism, loudly singing quotations from Chairman Mao and dancing loyalty dances, here in this political backwater deep in the Wuling Mountains such a primitive election was to be held. Well, in a great country wonders never cease. They were really putting the clock back.

That evening bonfires were lit in Gong Flat where the new team leader was to be elected. Carrying pinewood torches, the other villagers trudged there from eight to ten *li* away, from Oxhorn Hollow, Muffin Cliff and Monkey Rock. Darkness falls early in the mountains and a cold wind was blowing, so all were wearing their old padded jackets. As they seldom had get-togethers, old friends called out greetings and chatted. Tian Faqing found himself a stone and sat down in an inconspicuous corner. He was appalled by the conditions here and already regretted having sworn to marry Xiuxiu. He had been in too much of a hurry to leave the army.... Next to him sat Jiang Shigong from

Oxhorn Hollow. A man in his early sixties, who before Liberation had posed as a witch-doctor, he was growing crankier in his old age and liked to mix with people who were in trouble, as if he could still exorcize evil spirits. Tian held out a piece of red charcoal to light his pipe, and as Jiang puffed at it he half-jokingly told his fortune:

"Don't you worry, Faqing! You're down on your luck now, but there's great happiness and honour in store for you. Don't laugh. If I'm not wrong, I can predict from your physiognomy that you've a long successful career ahead...."

"What kind of talk is that, uncle? Aren't you afraid of being struggled against for preaching feudalism?" Tian felt that the old man was making a fool of him.

"That girl in Rich Flats is cruel, leaving you to live all on your own.... You've set your heart on Liu Xiuxiu, but haven't we a girl in our team who's just the image of her?"

As the old fellow rambled on, Tian knew that he meant Liu Liangmei, their team's barefoot doctor, the daughter of Liu Jiejie.

"Watch out, or Uncle Jiejie will shut you up!" He glared at Jiang, ignoring his senior status. When he had just come back the previous year, on his way home one evening from Rich Flats he had heard a cry for help from the rocks by Our Lady's Temple. He found it was Liu Liangmei, the barefoot doctor of the production team, who had been set upon by some hooligans. He drove them away immediately and saw her back to Gong Flat. He gave her his word to let his tongue rot sooner than mention this to anyone. He had kept it a secret even from her father, because she still wanted to save face and get married.

Now Knock-out Wang clapped his hands and called out in a booming voice:

"Brothers, comrades! Quit talking and let's start our meeting! Come over here."

The men seated round the bonfires stood up and produced their little red books from their pockets. The old team leader Liu Jiejie presided over this meeting. Over sixty and rather flabby, unable to button his ragged padded coat because the button-holes were torn, he had tied them with bits of creeper and looked like a scarecrow. Still, he had learned from the commune cadres to hold his little red book in front of his chest and lead the way in wishing Chairman Mao a long, long life and Lin Biao lasting good health. After this evening ritual, they recited two supreme instructions, then all were told to sit down to hear his report on the revolution and production in recent years. Of course achievements were paramount, outnumbering shortcomings by nine to one. The situation, not just good, was excellent. Any problems were naturally ascribed to the "counter-revolutionary revisionist line" and the Five Categories of class enemies. Although Pagoda Ridge had no landlords, rich peasants, counter-revolutionaries, bad elements or Rightists, it was under their pernicious influence.

"Brothers! I've let you all down, I've bungled things," said the old team leader gruffly. "We all live by Guanyin Brook and, as you know, in the hard years to fill our bellies we undermined the collective economy by fixing output quotas for each household — we took the capitalist road. Other teams upheld the

Three Red Banners — the General Line for Socialist
Construction, the Great Leap Forward and the People's
Commune — but we upheld a white banner. That was
my biggest mistake. During the Four Clean-ups Movement I stepped down. Three years ago the rebels in
the commune hung a placard round my neck and paraded me in the street, not to accuse me of being a counter-
revolutionary but to educate me.... These last few
years as team leader I've tried to keep in step with the
higher-ups, to take the Dazhai road. Still, as you all
can see, their priceless experience won't work here....
The next team leader, whoever he is, mustn't follow
my example.... People have to eat.... Our kids are
in rags...."

The team leader broke down and sobbed. Liu Liangmei took his arm and cried, "Dad! Dad!" The rest
remained silent, wide-eyed, as if waiting to hear some
frightful news. Knock-out Wang sat motionless as a
stone lion, the bamboo cylinder in his hands.

Jiang Shigong, his back to the light, whispered to
Tian, "Pagoda Ridge is under an unlucky star....
What we need is a really able emperor with the guts
to find a way out...."

"Stop talking about emperors," Tian hissed. "What
times are we living in?" His mind was in a turmoil.
By insisting on being demobbed he had landed himself
in trouble, unable to marry Xiuxiu from Rich Flats or
even to fill his own belly. The whole team was eating
sweet potato vines. Soon they would have forgotten
the taste of rice. If only he could leave Pagoda Ridge
tomorrow and never come back!

Team leader Liu dried his eyes, then told them the
team's financial situation. They were six thousand

yuan in debt, for funds borrowed for farming, insecticide, fertilizer and relief. That meant that each household owed three hundred and thirty-two yuan, thirty-three cents, or sixty yuan per head. As for grain, they had borrowed from the state and other teams a hundred and twenty thousand pounds for food and seeds. Six thousand three hundred and fifteen pounds, six ounces per household! One thousand two hundred pounds per head! They'd been eating their corn in the blade. It was now 1971, yet they'd eaten their grain supply for '76.... They had never cleared these debts, just piled up new ones each year. And to penalize them for their backwardness, the commune and brigade refused to ask the state to remit their debts.

This fearful reckoning made it clear that the team was completely bankrupt. Liu Jiejie stood there limply, hanging his head like a criminal and weeping.... He had let down everyone, old and young in the team. The bonfires, left unattended, were dying down. The men eyed each other grimly, motionless as blocks of wood. The women took refuge behind their men, covering their faces to weep.... In the old society they had piled up debts which could never be paid in a lifetime, but in the new society how could they have run into such heavy debt? What sort of collective economy was this? What sort of election for a new team leader? It seemed more like finding a scapegoat to jump into a fiery pit or serve a prison sentence.

Liu Jiejie sat down by a bonfire, unable to look anyone in the face. Soon, as if his wits were wandering, he went to skulk in a dark corner. Knock-out Wang, who was in charge of the election, announced how the lots should be drawn. Each man was to take one and show it to the rest. Glowering, he held up the bamboo cylinder with a pair of chopsticks sticking out of it. One by one he called the men over to draw lots. He watched as each displayed what he had drawn, then cried, "A blank! A blank!" The "losers" heaved sighs of relief, but stayed there to see who would be the ill-fated "winner".

When a dozen or more blanks had been drawn, Knock-out Wang began to feel tense. Sweat broke out on his forehead, his heart pounded. If blanks were drawn until only one lot was left, that one with the red circle would be his — that would be the end of him! By the time only three lots were left his back was soaking. Now it was Tian Faqing's turn. Wang grinned at him.

"Young Tian, just demobbed from the army, you should have good luck!"

Tian glanced casually at old Jiang beside him and said, "My luck may be out, but it can't be that bad!" He took the cylinder and fished out a lot. Wang, hoping against hope, ordered him to show it. Tian felt a little nervous then, but said, "It just couldn't be me." With trembling fingers he smoothed out the crumpled paper. On it was a red circle!

Wang chucked the cylinder and chopsticks on to a bonfire. At the top of his voice he boomed, "He's drawn the lot! Our new team leader is Brother Tian Faqing of Gong Flat!"

Not only Tian but everyone there was staggered by the result of this election. Jiang Shigong smiled knowingly and urged the young fellow to stand up and say a few words. But before he could recover from his stupefaction Liu Liangmei came flying over, her hair dishevelled, looking completely distracted. She screamed:

"Quick, go and save him! My dad's jumped into Guanyin Brook! Dad! Poor dad!"

4

Tian Faqing's first job as team leader was seeing to Liu Jiejie's funeral. Hardly a lucky start! Would he follow in the steps of the old team leader, who had left the team a shambles, crippled with debts? How could he possibly tread in his steps? If he let his people go short of even sweet potato vines, would he too end up by jumping into the brook? It was too shallow to wet the back of his head!

"There must be some way out, Faqing. Must we drown in our own piss? First figure out a plan. If you need advice, ask Jiang Shigong, Old Crow Liu or me. We can give you some tips. . . ."

After Knock-out Wang had helped Tian to handle the old team leader's funeral and adopted Liu Liangmei as his foster-child, he gave the new team leader this parting advice before going back to Monkey Rock to his trapping and hunting.

Instead of inspecting Pagoda Ridge or painting a rosy picture of their splendid prospects if they learned from Dazhai, Tian paced his stone cottage for three whole days till he wore out his shoe-soles. No one knew what scheme he had in mind for making their poor team rich. However, he was as stubborn as an ox and feared neither men nor devils. He must make a go of things, save the situation. He decided to rope in the key men in the team. To make Jiang Shigong of Oxhorn Hollow his strategist, Old Crow Liu of Gong Flat his accountant and secretary, and Knock-out Wang of Monkey Rock his sergeant to keep an eye on trouble-makers. He would also ask Sister Mushroom of Muffin Cliff and the barefoot doctor Liu Liangmei to keep their ears open for news and pass it on. . . . Finally he stopped pacing the floor. Gritting his teeth he slapped his thigh and swore: "May as well be hanged for a sheep as for a lamb! Sink or swim! It's just as well I haven't married Xiuxiu, there's nothing to stop me risking my own neck."

His mind made up, he went to Oxhorn Hollow to see Jiang Shigong. Jiang was over sixty, white-haired but spry. Before Liberation he had always clung to his three "magic weapons": the oxhorn on his back, the charms in his pocket and his boxwood cane, which made him look rather like a Taoist immortal. So he was called Heavenly Commander Jiang, Jiang Half Immortal or simply Oxhorn Jiang. Unable to work big magic, he could only exorcize a few evil spirits to earn a little rice or cash to eke out a living. After Liberation he gave this up and turned to farming, keeping goats, planting pines and growing paddy. But during the hard years of 1961 and '62, he reverted to being a witch-doctor, deceiving both himself and other people. He and Tian Faqing had made friends after Jiang's "fight with a devil".

In the autumn of 1961, when Tian had just started studying in the agricultural middle school and had to make the trip there every morning, he often met Jiang on the misty mountain track coming back after spending a night casting spells. Once Tian asked:

"Uncle Shigong, walking alone at night aren't you afraid of tree spirits or ghosts?"

"No, I'm not afraid of any spirits, lad. I know spells and incantations and I can walk on the air," Jiang had boasted, patting Tian's head.

"You're honestly not afraid?"

"If I were, lad, I wouldn't be a witch-doctor."

Boasting in jest is easy, and not against the law. After this exchange they went their different ways, and Jiang thought no more about it. Why, during the Great Leap Forward the higher-ups had made all sorts of boasts, claiming yields of hundreds of thousands of pounds per *mu*, and that hadn't been illegal — they'd been promoted for it. So why shouldn't Jiang boast a little to a student?

But early one morning not long after this, the mountain was swathed in such a heavy mist that people walking through it felt as if they were swimming in milk. Jiang was on his way home after practising magic all night at the foot of the mountain. When he reached the graveyard by Guanyin Brook, a place dreaded by timid souls even in broad daylight, a black monster over ten feet tall suddenly appeared before him! On its head was what looked like the enormous helmet of some ghostly warrior of old. Jiang swore to himself: This time I've met a real ghost! He froze in his tracks, closed his eyes and recited an incantation to drive away ghosts. When this didn't work he used his cane to draw a charm in the air. But that didn't work either. Instead of retreating the monster came closer and closer. Help! Jiang fell back, blowing his horn as a last resort. But that monster had such magic power that this too proved useless. The faster he fled, the more it gained on him. He invoked Guanyin and all the deities to come to his rescue, to save their disciple. Then, frightened out of his wits, his legs buckling under him, he let out a cry of despair and fell unconscious.

When Tian Faqing took word of this to the three families in Oxhorn Hollow, they hurried to the graveyard to carry Jiang home and nurse him. For five whole days he could neither eat nor drink, just raving "Sacred General, spare your disciple. . . ." Chinese and western medicine were tried but neither could cure him.

The sixth day was a Sunday when Tian had no school. He went to see Jiang, taking with him a tapering wicker crate used for catching fish. Once over the threshold he asked, "Uncle Shigong, the sacred general you bumped into that morning — did it have this crate on its head?" He put the crate on his own head and swaggered forward. Heavens, in that big pointed hat with its broad rim he was the image of the "sacred general". From an exchange of blows a friendship grows. Jiang recovered. And instead of bearing Tian a grudge he admired his courage and resourcefulness. He predicted a fine future for him.

Now Tian went to Oxhorn Hollow and took Jiang with him to a quiet spot to consult him about his plan for "going it alone". Jiang gaped when he heard it, staggered. Then he scratched his white head, staring blankly at the new team leader. His silence made Tian frantic. His eyes flashed.

"Say something, uncle!" he urged him. "I'm not here to have my fortune told."

"Have you thought this through carefully?" asked Jiang finally, first nodding then shaking his head.

"I have. If anything goes wrong I'll take the consequences. I'll be the one to go to prison — none of you uncles will be involved." Tian stamped his foot on the rocks, his hands on his hips, as if unable to work off his energy.

"Good, spoken like a man. But with this millstone round your neck it won't be easy."

"Things have come to such a pass, Uncle Shigong, I can't see any other charm working for our Pagoda Ridge. I'm not going to follow Uncle Jiejie's example and jump into the brook."

"Ha, looks as if Pagoda Ridge has produced a man of parts.... But has it struck you, nephew, that this may land you in gaol?"

Jiang closed his eyes, his wrinkled face twitching.

Tian's face was pale, his mind filled with conflicting emotions: a sense of guilt, defiance and a fearless determination to win through. In a voice like muffled thunder he replied:

"Don't worry about me, uncle. I've no old folk, no children. If things go from bad to worse here, we shan't be able to bury our old people, when our boys grow up they won't be able to marry, we'll never pay off our debts.... That's why Uncle Jiejie drowned himself. Now that I've been made team leader I'll risk my neck to make a go of it."

"Fine! Our ancestors' graves must be letting off steam.... It's not enough to have guts though. First you must rope in the people here who count. With them on your side you'll have won half the battle."

"Which people?"

"First Knock-out Wang of Monkey Rock. He's your kind of man, with guts, afraid of nothing. And

he packs such a punch, everyone has a healthy respect
for him as a military talent. The second's Old Crow
Liu of Gong Flat, who can write, reason and keep accounts — he's a literary talent. The third. . . ."

"The third is you, uncle. I'd thought of both those
others. What I'm afraid of is that unless we're all in
cahoots, word may leak out."

"Don't worry about that. You know the history of
Pagoda Ridge, the times we've all lived through. We
may have no other good points but being poor we're
tough and we stick together. We'll take an oath, drinking liquor with chicken blood, to cut out the tongue of
anyone who blabs!"

The old man and the young one saw eye to eye. There
was no time to be lost. They decided to go at once to
Monkey Rock to consult Knock-out Wang and decide
when to assemble the whole team to make a pledge with
blood and announce the new rules, to prevent anyone
from selling out. They made their way down from
Oxhorn Hollow to the crossroads. There Jiang proposed:

"I don't think we need go to Monkey Rock to find
Wang. Let's try Muffin Cliff. Quite likely he's there,
bold as brass, courting Sister Mushroom!"

5

Knock-out Wang, in his fifties, was a rough diamond.
His native place was Peach Stream in south Jiangxi,
and he had become a good boxer while still young,
hence his nickname Knock-out. If anyone crossed him
or behaved like a bully, he struck out so hard and fast

that the fellow's left ear smarted, his right ear bled, and if he didn't die he'd be deafened for life. However, Wang only did this when goaded beyond endurance. In 1945, when the Japanese surrendered, he was just twenty-one, bursting with energy, ready for anything, when he found out that his new bride was promiscuous. That was not too strange as the Peach Stream girls were flighty and usually had two or three affairs before marriage. One day when he charged home drunk, he discovered her curled up with a young man. Wang let out a roar, at which the fellow fled; and failing to catch him he came back to see his wife packing up her things to run away. In fury he struck out and knocked her dead. That sobered him up, he knew that it spelt trouble, as she had many brothers to take revenge. So that same night he fled several hundred *li* to take refuge in Monkey Rock on Pagoda Ridge, where he opened up some wasteland and took to hunting and trapping. He had never remarried and lived for thirty years on his own, to atone, maybe, for killing his poor wife.... But now that he was over fifty he had fallen for Sister Mushroom, a thirty-five-year-old widow in Muffin Cliff. The barefoot doctor Liu Liangmei, whether by design or by chance, had brought them together. After the old team leader died, Wang had made her his foster-daughter, and she considered Sister Mushroom her foster-mother.

Today Wang had set out first thing for Muffin Cliff. Because two days earlier Liangmei had gone to Monkey Rock to tell him that a relative from Jiangxi, who was staying with Sister Mushroom, had told her that their province had produced a really able man. He had galvanized Jiangxi and given the villages two years in which to mechanize and use iron oxen! Now tractors large and small were chugging all over the place, shaking the earth. The old people couldn't wipe the grins off their faces, jumping for joy. They were killing their oxen or selling them off dirt cheap: a calf for a hundred yuan, a big water-buffalo for only three hundred. . . . When Wang heard of this new phenomenon, his hands itched. What farmers prize most are oxen. Pagoda Ridge was too poor to buy the iron ones which drank petrol and puffed out smoke. Couldn't have used them either. But they could keep calves and buffaloes and use them. Besides, the Jiangxi border where cattle were selling so cheap was less than eighty *li* to the east. And the slopes of Pagoda Ridge were covered with bitter bamboo and undergrowth, good fattening fodder.

Wang strode on up hill and down dale.

> Never three fine days on end,
> Three feet of level land,
> Three feet of water or three cents to spend.
> Above, a crack of sky;
> Below, vast ranges lie. . . .

In his excitement he sang at the top of his voice. The poor have their own way of enjoying life. His tuneless yodelling frightened away wild animals and made the birds take flight. Soon he reached Guanyin Brook, where he stopped to have a look round, as if trying to reach a decision. Gong Flat lay four *li* downstream, and Old Crow Liu's tiny store there had shelves filled with bottles of liquor. Liu had been up to Monkey Rock to chew the fat with Wang, in the course of which he mentioned that he'd pulled strings to get half a case of tiger-bone liquor specially for his old cronies. It was a famous old brand of liquor. A few drams limbered you up, half a bottle made you feel like an immortal; while by the time the best drinkers had downed a whole bottle, they were walking on air or dreaming wonderful dreams. . . .

"Old Crow Liu knows how to do business! With his silver tongue he can charm the birds out of the trees. And he talks as if he's buying the drinks!"

Wang spat, then cursing and laughing all the way, he headed for Gong Flat. He was longing for a drink. Of course it wasn't good to become addicted to anything, whether liquor, tobacco, card-playing or women. Scholars were addicted to reading, cadres to drinking tea, playing chess or getting promoted. So what if he, Knock-out Wang, sometimes liked a drink? When Pagoda Ridge had a wedding or funeral he drank maize spirit like water, tossing off ten cups without even turning dizzy or staggering. And when he lurched back in the dark, snakes took care to keep out of his way.

But instead of going to Gong Flat, Wang took off his straw sandals, rolled up his trouser-legs and splashed across the brook. A path on the other side led up two slopes and down two hollows to Muffin Cliff. That was where Sister Mushroom lived, and where his foster-daughter stayed if she was treating patients near by. Over two months ago he had summoned up the courage to ask Sister Mushroom to marry him. Sitting on the other side of the table, she had blushed, cast him a glance and hung her head. He had stared unblinkingly at the nape of her neck. She wore her hair in a bun, had a long neck, rounded arms and sturdy shoulders on which she could carry a crate holding a child. She neither shook her head nor nodded, just looking down. After a long pause she answered briefly, "Stop drinking."

Stop drinking? Heavens! That would be the death of him. Wang was a good boxer, who even now could carry a hundredweight for a hundred *li*. Didn't he owe his strength to maize liquor? But, confound it, ever since that day when he flopped down on his hard bed mat and shut his eyes, he could see Sister Mushroom, her hair in a bun, her sturdy, high-breasted figure. She didn't look thirty-five, should still be able to bear him a son. If Wang had a bouncing baby boy, his line would not die out. And even if she had no son, a young wife would be a companion for his old age, warming his quilt for him in the cold winter. . . .

Hell, what was he thinking of? Sister Mushoom hadn't consented. He mustn't make a fool himself at his age. Besides, Liangmei was already twenty-two, it was time for her to marry and have children. How could he contemplate marrying before getting her off his hands!

Wang walked along thinking and singing, so that the way seemed short. In no time he reached Muffin Cliff.

Muffin Cliff was a plateau of some fifty *mu*. From crevices in the rocks all around grew broad-leafed banyans, fragrant cedars, black cypresses, maples, bitter bamboos and chestnut trees. From a distance it looked like a green oasis set in the rugged mountains. There were no paddy fields and the dozen or so *mu* of dry land were not planted with grain, but each autumn mushooms were grown there, coming up after rain or snow. They also grew hibiscus and aromatic and other medicinal herbs such as the local ginseng. The mushrooms of Muffin Cliff were famed far and wide, and whenever any were marketed in the county or prefectural towns customers flocked to buy them. In the first two years of the "cultural revolution" when the policy was to "take grain as the key link", Muffin Cliff was ordered to grow grain. "What are mushrooms? Who ate them before Liberation? And who have they catered for since Liberation? Today two-thirds of our class brothers all over the world still live in want. What they need is revolution, not titbits like mushrooms grown for the landlords and the bourgeoisie." This had been solemnly announced by Liang Youru, head of the commune, at a rally the previous year to pledge to learn from Dazhai. So that was the end of the mushrooms of Muffin Cliff.

"Sister Mushroom! Sister Mushroom!"

Sister Mushroom was feeding swill to her pigs after breakfast when she heard a gruff voice calling from the steps below. Knowing who it was, her cheeks burned. She hurried indoors to wash her hands, smooth her clothes and brush back her hair before tripping down to open the gate for him.

Eighty-one stone steps led up to Muffin Cliff, and she had got someone to fix up a cedar-board gate twice the height of a man at the top. Visitors standing outside it had to call her to open this gate.

"So it's you, Brother Wang. It's been a long time. . . . My window's so small, it doesn't let in much light, and coming out I get dazzled. I wasn't expecting you. . . ."

Knock-out Wang laughed, rather flustered. He lacked her ready tongue and could only tag behind her, his eyes fixed on her bun. When they went into the cottage he was still laughing sheepishly.

"Come all this way so early, Brother Wang?" she pulled out a stool from underneath the table and offered him a seat, then poured him a bowl of tea.

"Yes, I started out early...." Wang held the bowl in both hands and bent over to gulp down the tea like an ox lapping up water. He was thirsty.

"Come for anything special or just passing by?" Sister Mushroom looked cool. She casually sat down by the door, picked out a long hempen thread from her work-basket and started sewing a shoe-sole.

"Special, yes, while just passing by...." he said, contradicting himself idiotically. Having put down the empty bowl he had no idea what to do with his clumsy hands.

Sister Mushroom suddenly felt rather amused. In her presence this big, hulking fellow seemed as dumb and docile as a buffalo.

"Well, brother, did you come to see Liangmei?" she asked.

"Yes ... but not just Liangmei...." Beads of sweat stood out on his forehead. He could have kicked himself for not handling the situation better.

"Is there anyone else worth seeing apart from your foster-daughter?" She stole a glance at him and pursed her lips.

"There is, there is!" Wang took the towel from his belt and mopped his damp forehead before taking the plunge. Holding his breath he finally blurted out, "I came specially to see Liangmei's foster-mother."

Sister Mushroom lowered her eyelids and hung her head, as if he had hit her, hurt her.

"Come now, sister, don't take offence. I came to-day... specially to ask for the news from Jiangxi." Seeing how put out she looked, he hastily changed the subject.

"What news from Jiangxi?" she asked, looking up.

"I heard that in our old home they're going all out to mechanize agriculture, giving up ploughing with oxen to use iron oxen. Water-buffaloes and oxen are out of date, so they're slaughtering them or selling them off for little more than the price of a pig.... It was Liangmei who told me she'd heard that from you. Is it true, sister?"

On this subject Wang could speak distinctly and clearly.

"My uncle from home told me, of course it's true. He was complaining how the times have changed, with everyone going crazy. Now he won't be able to farm the land...."

Wang's interest in this subject rather disappointed her, so she spoke drily and indifferently.

"Well, this time Pagoda Ridge's luck should turn!" Wang slapped his thigh, his face shining, his eyes gleaming. His burst of laughter nearly deafened her.

"Brother, they can mechanize, sell off their buffaloes and buy iron oxen, but what has that to do with a poor place like our Pagoda Ridge?"

"It has a lot to do with us, a lot!" Wang talked as if he had downed several bowls of liquor. "Ha, old Jiejie jumped into the brook, and now that Faqing's team leader our luck has changed.... Every family on Pagoda Ridge can make two or three thousand, ha! If he treats me to a pot of grog I'll give him this good tip, aha!..."

Wang stood up, swaying from side to side with joy, meaning to go and find Tian. But the ardent look in Sister Mushroom's eyes made him feel a bit odd. He sat down again. After a pause he said rather impatiently:

"Five times I've come to you, Sister. When will you give me an answer?..."

Sister Mushroom had been afraid he would up and leave. Now, flushing again, she lowered her eyes and was silent. Then she stood abruptly to fetch from her cupboard a bottle of spirits and a white porcelain bowl. She half filled the bowl and offered it to him.

"Taste this, brother. I bought it a couple of days ago from Old Crow Liu in Gong Flat, to make chilli sauce."

Wang took the bowl, his eyes flashing, his mouth watering. It smelt wonderful, this tempting brew, this nectar! How he longed to toss it back. But he closed his eyes and gritted his teeth, saying in a low, muffled voice:

"I haven't drunk a drop, Sister, not since you put your foot down. Not even when Old Crow Liu invited me to go and drink tiger-bone liquor.... Don't you believe me? I swear it."

"Why should you swear, a man of your age?" Sister Mushroom burst out laughing, showing two attractive dimples. She took the bowl back and emptied it outside.

"You're a real goddess, Sister!" Wang preened himself on having passed this first test.

"And how about your fist fights? Are you going to go on knocking people out whenever your palms itch?"

Sister Mushroom widened her eyes, interrogating him like a female judge.

"I mean to get Blacksmith Zhang at Gong Flat to make me a knife. Next time my palms itch I'll jab them with it!" replied Wang, half seriously, half jokingly.

"I don't believe it!"

"No? Then I'll give you the knife."

"I don't want your damn knife!"

For some reason she turned her back on him, shoulders shaking, and started sobbing.

Wang felt frantic. He went round to hold out his callused hands to her. "Sister, Sister...."

They faced each other for several minutes in silence, Wang still holding out his hands. Sister Mushroom's heart softened and slowly she raised her own hands to lay them softly on his. He forgot himself then and touched her high breasts.

"Mum, mum! Brother Faqing's come!"

Just at that moment in came Liu Liangmei, her first-aid kit on her back. Shocked to see them carrying on like this, she blushed and covered her face with her hands, then dashed outside to stamp her feet angrily.

"My, my! Shame on you both! Not even shutting the door!"

"Don't talk such nonsense, Liangmei." Sister Mushroom kept her head and went to the doorway to explain, "Your foster-father pricked his hand and asked me to pull out the thorn."

"Why not do it outside where it's light?" demanded the tactless girl.

"You silly girl! I'll give you a slap if you go on any more," she threatened.

"Has your Brother Faqing come? I must go and see

him." Wang squeezed out of the door, beaming all over his face. At a time like this he had better make himself scarce.

"Dad! Come back! Faqing and Jiang Shigong of Oxhorn Hollow are coming up the steps!..." Liangmei called out to stop him.

"Did you come together?" Wang asked. "How did Faqing know I was here?"

"The devil only knows! He's not like you, the way you carry on at your age...." Liangmei rolled her eyes, torn between amusement and anger.

"What are you talking about?" Wang glared at her.

"Well, well, what a fine pair you are! You only need someone to stir things up!" Sister Mushroom teased, going back into the cottage.

"You might be the one!" said Liangmei sulkily, like a spoiled child.

"Come on, Liangmei, let's make tea and fry some beans.... Look, here come your Brother Faqing and Uncle Shigong."

6

As Tian and Jiang came through the gate they saw Wang, Sister Mushroom and Liangmei waiting for them on the steps.

"You two tomcats must have second sight!" chortled Wang. "I was just going over to Gong Flat with big news for Faqing, and here you come of your own accord!"

"Let's get this clear, who's the tomcat with second sight? Would you have come all this way first thing in the morning if you hadn't known that there's fresh fish and salted fish in Sister Mushroom's kitchen?" Flaunting his seniority, Jiang walked in without being invited and plumped himself down on an easy chair.

"Stop joking, Uncle Jiang," said Sister Mushroom. "Liangmei's father came to ask about the sale of cattle in Jiangxi." Flushing, she passed on what her uncle had told her.

"That's a good omen! With Faqing as team leader our luck's in. Old Man Heaven has opened his eyes!" Jiang slapped his thighs, beaming all over his wrinkled face.

Tian seemed rather stunned by this unexpected news. He raised his eyebrows, widened his eyes and gaped, hardly able to believe it.

"We must figure this out carefully." Wang handed Jiang a spill. "Each household would need three or four hundred yuan. As it is, we can hardly keep body and soul together, we're so saddled with debts; so how can we raise so much money? Even if we managed to borrow it, how would we buy the cattle — in the name of the team or as individual households? And how would we raise them, collectively or privately?" He fired off these questions at Tian.

"So in Jiangxi they're going all out to mechanize agriculture, buying in tractors, selling off their oxen. . . . But suppose this is just a flash in the pan, like smelting steel in '58? I can't see us getting tractors up these mountains, much less ploughing our fields with them. And if we buy cattle cheap, won't we be taking unfair advantage of their movement? . . ." Though Tian raised these objections he found the prospect tempting.

"Why shouldn't we? In Jiangxi they're slaughtering

buffaloes and selling beef. If each family buys two or three head of cattle to keep up here, we'll be saving those draught animals. Of course that's not so up-to-date as using iron oxen. But when has Pagoda Ridge ever been advanced? Ever won a word of praise? You have to dirty your hands to make money, so let's get something going cheap. If we can buy oxen for one or two hundred, in two years we'll be able to sell them for one or two thousand.... It's not as if we were robbing anyone, all open and above board." Old Jiang pontificated, wagging his head, his eyes half closed as if drunk. "Brother Knock-out, Sister Mushroom, Little Barefoot Doctor, we can gain enough on these oxen to tide us over, but that won't solve our problem. To make Pagoda Ridge a going concern we must put in more time farming.... Nephew Faqing, tell Uncle Knock-out how you're going to set about things as new team leader."

Tian then explained in detail his plan for "going it alone". As the men were discussing business, Sister Mushroom and Liangmei went into the kitchen to prepare the midday meal.

Wang knitted his shaggy brows as he heard Tian out. Then, his face black, his eyes furious, he rounded on Jiang.

"Did you put him up to this, brother? Faqing is an honest young fellow, I watched him grow up. Now that he's demobbed, our team leader, you should help him go straight, not lead him astray to end up in a fiery pit, a counter-revolutionary."

Showing the whites of his eyes Jiang protested, "As Heaven is my witness, it was Faqing who thought this out! To stop our folk from starving. He's not going to tread in the steps of Liu Jiejie."

Tian was sitting opposite Wang, his arms folded. Fixing his eyes on him he said, "Yes, it was my idea. If it's against the law I'll take the blame. I've thought it over and this is our only way to get Pagoda Ridge on its feet again. It's not a new discovery either. Uncle Jiejie tried this out in the two hard years, parcelling land out to different families while pretending to be farming collectively."

"Heavens above! Times have changed since then! This is the red-hot 'cultural revolution'. Everybody's grasping class struggle, learning from Dazhai, shouting themselves hoarse to oppose a capitalist restoration. . . . Why not just give yourself up to the security bureau, or register for a place in a labour camp?" Wang was red in the face, his neck swollen, his fists on his knees.

Wang's attitude worried Tian. He hitched his stool closer to him, with a meaningful glance at Jiang. Keeping his voice down he reasoned, "Uncle, I just don't see any other way out! Here we are, nineteen families on four different mountains, dozens of *li* apart. If we insist on assembling every morning at Gong Flat to 'ask for instructions' and recite quotations, then march off together to work, before we've warmed up or swung our hoes many times we have to knock off for lunch. That's called marching in step, acting in unison, or militarized production. But where does it get us? It's camp and field training, not farming! It ties our hands and feet. . . . Our team went bankrupt long ago, we're head over heels in debt; men over thirty can't get wives, our teenage girls are in rags! Uncle Jiejie saw no way out, so he drowned himself. . . . If we go on like this we'll end up as refugees, beggars or robbers. So before we've lost hope completely, while we still have some guts, why not let each household farm the fields near by and be responsible for their own output and what they sell to the state. Then after the autumn harvest the team can deliver grain to the state, and sell off any surplus.... Think of that, Pagoda Ridge selling surplus grain!"

Tian's eyes were bloodshot, his voice was hoarse. Still Wang glowered at him in silence. Jiang, his eyes bloodshot too, now backed Tian up.

"Brother Knock-out, I didn't lead him astray. Faqing has guts and good sense. He dares stick his neck out for the rest of us. We're waiting for you to give the word. You have the final say."

Wang frowned at Jiang as if he were a scoundrel. But gradually his face cleared. He smiled grimly, then said with a sigh:

"Brother Shigong, I'm not deaf or blind, I'm no fool. But it was that business that killed our last team leader. In the Four Clean-ups Movement he was bashed for parcelling out the land in the hard years, had to spend two months in the commune thinking over his mistakes. Liangmei's mum was so frantic, she had a heart attack and by the time he came back was at her last gasp.... Three years ago, when the 'cultural revolution' started, the business of taking the capitalist road was raked up again and Liu Jiejie was hauled off to the commune to be struggled against and paraded wearing a placard.... And so our team piled up new debts every year, and the team members blamed him too.... Now you want to take that old road to a fiery pit — at this of all times!"

Hearing this, Jiang had broken out in a cold sweat. "How are we people to live then?" he demanded. "Young fellows can go off as robbers, but an old man like me can only starve to death.... The old higher-ups have all had to stand down, the new men in power don't investigate and won't issue relief funds or rice...."

Tian kept his eyes fixed on Wang, cracking his knuckles. His feet were so firmly planted on the stone floor, it seemed he wanted to dent it.

"Uncle Knock-out, this is our only hope! If you want me as team leader, you must try out my plan. If you don't, you can draw lots again. Besides, we'll still call ourselves a team even if we go it alone; and living at the back of beyond, if everybody agrees we can stop word getting out.... If we deliver our quota of rice each year, the state won't lose out in the least. If by any chance someone blows the gaff, I'll go to prison as team leader!"

Wang was impressed by Faqing's community spirit. Head lowered, he thought it over, then sprang to his feet and slapped the young fellow's broad back. "Good for you, nephew! Seems Pagoda Ridge is bound to buck up now that it's produced such a dare-devil.... All right, there's only one thing...."

"What's that?" The two others were on their feet now.

"Renegades!" growled Wang.

Tian shivered.

"Never mind," Wang went on. "I'll play the villain in this opera. First we'll draw up our rules. Anyone who sells out our team will have his stove smashed, his door sealed up!" Eyes wide, brandishing his fists, he looked like the god of vengeance. "Liangmei! Come out. Why hide away in the kitchen?"

"Dad. . . ." Liangmei's face was red. While getting lunch with Sister Mushroom she had overheard them and been horrified.

"Off you go to Gong Flat! Ask your Uncle Old Crow to come here. And to bring two bottles of liquor and a big rooster. Tell him the team leader says to charge it to the team."

"We're going to drink liquor with blood!" Tian added loudly, bracing himself like a fighter waiting for the signal to charge. "We must also decide today about buying cattle from Jiangxi."

"You men! Why didn't you ask earlier for a hen? I've just killed one and boiled it for soup!" Sister Mushroom had come out from the kitchen too. Her face flushed from the heat of the stove, she glanced at Wang.

7

Halfway down Pagoda Ridge on the way to Gong Flat was a shining dark rock which could seat a score of people. What had made it so shining? Most likely the backsides and the feet of all the passers-by had polished it year after year. For above it grew a spreading red bayberry, green the whole year round, providing welcome shade from the blazing sun in summer and shelter from the rain for woodcutters or shepherds. Round about the time of the Double Fifth Festival, if you stretched out on that rock, your head pillowed on your arms, looking up at the bright red berries, the wind might blow one down into your mouth. Those berries, so sweet yet tart, made you screw up your eyes. . . . In the old days a clear fountain had gushed out of the cliff beside this tree, where you could wash your face or slake your thirst. But it had dried up in '58 when so many trees were cut down to make charcoal. Still, this red bayberry had been spared. On the cliff beside it two slogans "Take the Dazhai Road" and "Beware of Class Enemies" kept tabs on the mountaineers.

Walking is less tiring than standing still. Tian, climbing steadily, took little more than an hour to cover the thirty-odd *li* from Our Lady's Temple to Pagoda Ridge. When he reached the red bayberry, he tossed his bedding roll and canvas hold-all on the rock and sat down. He was in no great hurry, and he had to watch his step. He had not come home as a hero or model worker with banners and prize certificates. No, he was newly discharged from a labour camp, under a cloud, cold-shouldered. Maybe the warm-hearted mountaineers might sympathize with him, shaking their heads, sighing or even shedding tears when they saw him. But he did not want their sympathy or pity. Since the fall of the "gang of four" big changes had taken place, but did that mean that people had stopped judging others by their social status? Suppose someone said, "So you're back. Mind you toe the line and turn over a new leaf." He'd tear the fellow apart! A man who has been to prison is not afraid of serving a second sentence.

He sat on the rock like a stone lion in the mountain wind at sunset. The sun, a ball of flame, was sinking slowly behind the opposite peak into the thick, soft, milky mist. The moon rose, casting a crystal light. The hills below seemed carpeted with silver, the mist concealing all their valleys and gullies. Tian was spellbound by the mountain in the moonlight. The hollows by Guanyin Brook reminded him of the white coral reefs he had seen on Hainan Island while in the army.... For a second he was tempted to close his eyes and plunge into that thick, soft mist, that sea of silver coral. It was on a misty night like this, years ago, that team leader Liu Jiejie had jumped into the brook....

Tian sat on the rock below the red bayberry oblivious of the cold wind, the dew wetting clothes. He relived the past, feeling stirred yet strangely proud. Obviously he was not remoulded, was still a rebel at heart. A man's nature is hard to change. But what was his nature? His father had not been a landlord, his grandfather a rich peasant, his great-grandfather a bandit. He was a demobbed soldier who had joined the Party in the PLA. But he knew what it was to go cold and hungry. He had wanted to make money, not to starve or drown himself. Had wanted a woman's tenderness and love....

Tian remembered that the old team leader's grave was not far from this rock. They had all gathered in front of it that year, he, Knock-out Wang, Jiang Shigong, Old Crow Liu and all the other householders and housewives. There they had taken an oath, drinking liquor mixed with blood in the time-honoured way. They had really been a band of desperadoes. Wang had sternly ordered the rest to go back and warn their children that if anyone let out a word of what they were up to, the people of Pagoda Ridge would banish his whole family to Water Hollow. That was how treachery had always been punished there. . . . That had been a solemn moment, an impressive ceremony. Their blood raced as they swore to sink or swim, go through thick and thin together. For better for worse they depended on each other. They raised no banner, sounded no drum or oxhorn, carried no glittering weapons. They were not out to plunder any village or town, to commit arson or murder. But what they were doing was absolutely taboo: striking out on their own to farm and raise cattle each household for itself. By this frenzied restoration of capitalism they were establishing an independent kingdom. And this blatant fraud was being perpetrated under the banner of the people's commune. No wonder the revolutionaries who later dealt with their case were furious. They swore, "Those bandits on Pagoda Ridge all deserve ten years' hard labour!" However, in the end they made an example of the chief offender, letting off his accomplices. Because in those days the prisons were too packed to accommodate them all; so the lesser offenders had to be left under mass surveillance.

Tian laughed, "Now he's back, the head of that independent kingdom. He's sitting on this rock on Pagoda Ridge. . . ."

He stood up in high spirits, bursting with energy after his rest. His stomach was rumbling though. He bent down to take from his hold-all some buns he had bought at the bus station, which he munched greedily. A man needs food. If not because they had to eat, Pagoda Ridge would never have become an "independent kingdom", scandalizing the whole province. He must hurry on his way while there was still moonlight, to put up with Knock-out Wang on Muffin Cliff.

Tian was a lonely bachelor now, a homeless cur. Would Uncle Knock-out take him in? Would Sister Mushroom be willing to open the cottage door? And what reception would he get from Liu Liangmei, the barefoot doctor whom he had rescued that year by Our Lady's Temple?

He was reaching for his hold-all to start downhill when he heard footsteps on the narrow twisting track. The next moment a figure confronted him. Both of them stepped back. Tian shuddered, his hair standing on end. Bald, with no eyebrows, his face splotched with red and his clothes in rags, this apparition looked like a devil or man-eating monster. As if terrified too, his wizened hands shook and he babbled incoherently. Then he bumped into a cliff and knocked his head on a rock.

Tian, the first to recover, stood his ground. Clenching his powerful fists, he strained his eyes to make out who this monster was. So they confronted each other for a while, casting black shadows on the rocks. The leaves of the red bayberry were rustling eerily.

"Aren't you Faqing? Nephew Faqing...."

The other man shivered as if he had malaria. His teeth were chattering.

Who was he? His voice sounded familiar. But he looked so wretched and furtive, Tian could not recognize him. He took a step forward.

"No, spare me, Faqing! Don't kill me...." The fellow covered his bald head with his hands, longing to squeeze into a crack in the rocks.

"Don't be afraid. I'm not a tiger, you're not a rabbit. I won't lay a finger on you. Our rule on Pagoda Ridge is not to hit someone who pleads for mercy."

Tian unclenched his fists and folded his arms. "Tell me who you are. Why are you so terrified?"

"I'm Liu, Old Crow Liu, your Uncle Old Crow.... You, you haven't changed.... So, did they send you back?"

Old Crow Liu! The keeper of that small store in Gong Flat, who had been Tian's secretary in their "independent kingdom". It was he who had faked all those false reports, then finally sold out and reported everything to the county committee! Well, he had paid for it. After Tian was sentenced to hard labour, the mountaineers cursed Liu for his treachery. And Old Man Heaven had eyes. The next year he came down with leprosy. His cottage was burnt, his stove smashed, and his whole family were driven off to Water Hollow. Forbidden to show his face! So he could only come out after dark.

"Old Crow Liu! Go back to Water Hollow," Tian said. "I'm letting you off.... But don't tell your family I'm back. From now on we steer clear of each other — have you got that? Well, remember, and be off now."

8

The seven families in Gong Flat lived in stone cottages, some with stone tiles on the roof instead of cedar bark, only the window-frames being made of wood. These squat cottages were so solid, no axe could cut them and bullets only left a white mark on the wall. They stood like seven old-style forts at different heights along the bank of the brook. The tranquil moonlight and shifting milk-white mist made them appear more mysterious and ancient, as if nothing could shake or erode them but centuries of thunderbolts, wind and rain.

When Tian Faqing reached home the other six households were sleeping behind closed doors. His arrival passed unnoticed. Not a dog barked. He stopped before his own cottage, which stood alone in a fold of the hills half a *li* from the brook. The doorway was clean, with no weeds or cow-dung in front. Had the wind blown the dirt away, or had someone swept it? This struck him as rather strange. The padlock was still on the door, unrusted even after three whole years.... Should he go in? How could he? In any case it would be cold and cheerless inside, covered with dust and maybe with cobwebs and mould.... Still, this was a home-coming! It was in this cottage that he had been born, had learned to prattle, to toddle. Here he had grown up then gone off to be a soldier, come back when demobbed, married Xiuxiu, been her husband and team leader for six years until his final arrest here....

Now he was back. The shame and resentment that had chilled his heart gave way to a feeling of warmth. But how to get in? Would he have to force a window like a burglar? With a wry smile he groped in a crack in one corner of the wall — Xiuxiu's hiding-place for the key. Heavens! To his amazement the key was still there! His pulse quickened, and his trembling fingers took some time to open the lock. Once inside he reached out to brush away any cobwebs in front of his face. It was pitch-dark but he had a torch in his holdall, having had the foresight to buy one as soon as he left the camp.

The torch shed a bright light on this cottage he had left for over three years. The inner room was a bedroom, the outer one a living-room with a brazier inset in the floor. He gave a start, staring round in astonishment. The place was spotless. No trace of dust, cobwebs or mould, no smell of mustiness — and it was warm! The table, still in its old place by the window, had on it the storm-lantern he had used every evening, and by this lay a new box of matches. He picked this up, his hands trembling, and struck three matches in a row, but a draught from the door blew them out. He had to close the door before he could light the lantern. By its light he saw to his amazement that the dresser was in its old place, the crockery and chopsticks set out neatly. The chopping-board was hanging on the wall, the cleaver stuck beside it. The water vat and buckets stood where they always had. When he raised the lid of the vat he found it brimming with clear water from the brook; and the buckets in the corner were still wet. . . .

All this warmed Tian's heart. Who was responsible? Who could know he would be back today? He shook his head. He had written no letter, sent no word. Was it Xiuxiu? Impossible. Before going to prison he had written her a bill of divorcement, and she was said to have married a man in distant parts. Who else could it be? He was puzzling over this when he smelt a baked sweet potato. His stomach rumbling, he strode to the brazier. It was hot. When he poked the ashes with the tongs he uncovered two big sweet potatoes in the red embers! He grabbed one, brushed off the ashes and wolfed it down, not troubling even to strip off the skin. Pagoda Ridge sweet potatoes, sweet and floury, tasted much better than the mushy ones grown by Lake Dongting. Not until he had finished off one sweet potato did he realize that he had burnt his tongue. Well, it had warmed him, taken the edge off his hunger. Mountaineers are so easily satisfied! Why, then, had he been sent to a labour camp?

Tian ate the second sweet potato more slowly. As he carefully removed the skin he thought back to his life with Xiuxiu. . . . However, those sweet memories reduced him now to tears. The brazier was unchanged, the bellows still hung beside it. But his wife had gone, leaving him lonely, a grown man who had lost hope, lost all interest in life. He wept until he felt limp, then stood up, not stopping to wash his face or feet and, picking up the lantern, lurched into the bedroom. It too was spotless with a mosquito net hanging over the bed. The batik quilt looked slept in. But what caught his eye was the woman's jacket hanging on one bedpost.

Crying "Xiuxiu! Xiuxiu!" he rushed to pull back the quilt. There was no one there. Holding up the lantern he walked round the bed as if Xiuxiu were shyly hiding herself away. There were signs of her everywhere, of her warmth, her consideration . . . but she had vanished. Tian charged wildly out of the cottage calling her name.

"Xiu — xiu! Xiu — xiu!"

The brook gurgled, the cliffs echoed back his cries, the wind soughed. Shafts of moonlight fell on the hills. Dogs in the distance were roused and started barking. . . .

"Xiuxiu! Xiuxiu! Where are you? Where? How can I live without you. . . ."

Tian stood by the brook as if rooted to the ground. The moon, sinking westward, cast its tenuous, lengthening shadow on the path. At long last, giving up hope, he dragged himself wearily back to his cottage. A surprise awaited him. There in the yellow lamplight Xiuxiu was standing! Where had the silly creature been hiding all this time to tantalize him? He sprang forward to hug and kiss her, stroke and caress her. Xiuxiu had been plump but now he could feel her ribs. Missing him day and night and feeling afraid for him had made her lose weight. She said not a word, simply shaking with sobs in his arms. Her tears trickled down his collar, wetting his shirt. Why cry, silly creature? You always used to laugh. Aren't I home again safe and sound? So why cry? But how did you come back? I heard that two years ago you went over the hills and far away to remarry, so what does this mean? Am I dreaming? Out of my mind? He held her close.... But how come you smell of herbal medicine, Xiuxiu? And your hair is in two plaits. You used to bob it.... Suddenly she pushed him away.

"Brother Faqing!" she sobbed. "It's me — not Xiuxiu. Don't get so worked up. Tomorrow ... tomorrow...."

Was it Liangmei? Liu Liangmei.... Heavens! The old team leader's big daughter. Tian sobered up as if doused with cold water. At once he let go of her. He had been in too much of a hurry to notice the first-aid kit standing on the table.... He rubbed his hands uneasily, as if they were to blame.

"Sorry ... Liangmei.... I'd no idea.... Took you for Xiuxiu, you always looked so like her...."

Liangmei's face was burning. Her heart pounding, she hung her head.

"I'm not blaming you, Brother Faqing. I know you mistook me...."

"How did you know I'd be back?"

"I've just finished my rounds. I've been staying in your cottage. Dad said, judging by the present policy, you'd be coming home before long. Told me to clean the place out for you.... I'd no idea you'd be back so soon. You didn't send word...."

"How is Uncle Knock-out Wang? Well?"

"He lives in Muffin Cliff... can still catch boars and kill tigers.... Brother Faqing, tomorrow, I've a whole lot to tell you. I'm going back now to spend the night in the clinic."

Liu Liangmei picked up her first-aid kit and went to the door. Silhouetted against the moonlight, her face lit up by the lamplight, she looked sweet and lovely.

9

"Remember, Brother Faqing, that year you came back from the army, how I scandalized Rich Flats by wanting to marry a man from Pagoda Ridge?"

Who was it speaking? Sobbing? Xiuxiu or Liangmei? Both, yet neither one.... Sometimes they were separate entities, but then they fused together ... and they could fly. Fly up to the roof, into the starry sky....

"Darling Xiuxiu, wait! Don't go. I'll get up, get up...." But Tian lay flat on the bed. No, it wasn't a bed but a pit as black as a grave. He could not move hand or foot, his whole body felt limp yet rigid, as if

crushed by a huge rock. . . . I'm fagged out, Xiuxiu,
after speeding home full pelt as if whipped along. . . .
I'm falling apart, can't get up. . . . Don't cry, Xiuxiu,
there's life in me yet. . . . I want to hear you chuck-
ling. . . . I'm not blind or deaf, I can see how unhappy
you look, can hear your sobs. . . . Tell me, quick, what's
upset you, why do you feel so wronged? . . .

Where to start? It's all past and done with, no use
crying over spilt milk. You know, after Xiuxiu let on
that she loved a man from Pagoda Ridge she got a bad
name in Rich Flats, as if she had lost face for them by
wanting to marry a bandit. What sort of place was
Pagoda Ridge? No daughter of a respectable family
had ever married into that bandits' lair. Even if they
were no longer bandits, they were paupers with no
pants to wear. Out of only nineteen households a dozen
men in their thirties were still unmarried, had to share
a woman. Disgusting!

There was so much dirty talk, Xiuxiu was afraid to
repeat it. According to her neighbours, the pigs and
dogs in Rich Flats were a cut above anyone on Pagoda
Ridge. The whole village was dead against her. Their
contempt for Pagoda Ridge dated from way back, from
the days when brigands from there came down to rob
them, burn down houses and make endless trouble. So
Xiuxiu's behaviour was seen as an attack on the good
name of Rich Flats. She was cold-shouldered. Girls gos-
siped about her behind her back; young wives laughed
at her derisively, raising their eyebrows; older women
sighed and shook their heads as if sorry to see her go
astray. Even her parents felt under a cloud, hearing so
much slanderous talk. This pretty daughter they had
raised in a rice bin wanted to jump into a bin of husks,

to marry into a bandits' lair where not even grass would grow or hens lay eggs. She had brought disgrace on them. When the demobbed soldier came back to Pagoda Ridge, they shut her up in the attic to starve her into submission.

"Slut! No sense of self respect! I should break your legs!" swore her father. "Haven't match-makers worn out our doorstep, proposing plenty of good young workers and cadres? Yet you shamelessly pick a bandit's son, choose to go to that den of thieves. You're no daughter of mine!"

Her father disowned her. Her mother wept when she saw her. She had spoilt Xiuxiu, the apple of her eye, and the girl growing up so happily was too naive.... She blamed that demobbed soldier who had stolen her daughter's heart. During this deadlock Xiuxiu's mother tried to reconcile father and daughter. And the old man relented when he saw how the girl was wasting away, white as a corpse.... He stopped swearing at her, but forbade her to see any more of Tian. Her parents were in a difficult position, as the lame son of their Party secretary was still sweet on Xiuxiu and kept prowling round their house or coming in to sit down and ogle her.

The Party secretary himself came to tell her, "Liu Xiuxiu, in choosing a husband you have to put politics first. Rich Flats is your home, but your heart's in the enemy camp. Proletarian dictatorship extends to the grass-roots. Rich Flats isn't open to the public. You can't just up and leave."

Xiuxiu and her parents were mystified by this talk, but realized that it was a serious warning. Sure enough, the next day the head of the Iron Girls' Team did not call Xiuxiu to attend the morning and evening rituals; and she did not dare go on her own for fear they might drive her away. She felt under heavy pressure. In those times you had to attend those daily rituals to count as one of the revolutionary masses. Still, she didn't knuckle under or ask forgiveness, just went to the fields as usual. She remembered Tian's promise: Within two years he would send a match-maker and marry her in style.

Soon a year had passed. Early in spring a girl in patched clothes with a crate of herbs on her back came to see Xiuxiu.

"Good news, Sister Xiuxiu! Good news!" she said, hurrying in.

"Who are you? Where are you from?"

"Oh. . . . I thought you knew me!" The girl from the mountains laughed bashfully and flushed. "Sister Xiuxiu, I'm Liu Liangmei, the barefoot doctor of Pagoda Ridge Team."

The words "Pagoda Ridge" were music in Xiuxiu's ears. She eyed the visitor more curiously. Strange, this graceful girl from the mountains looked very like her. They might have been twins. This other girl liked to laugh too.

"Sister Xiuxiu, I've dropped in on my way to the commune hospital to give you a piece of news. Brother Faqing's been made our team leader, the head of Pagoda Ridge!"

Of course Liangmei did not mention that lots had been drawn for this job, nor the pledge they had all taken.

"Team leader, eh? Can he make a go of it?"

Xiuxiu stared with shining eyes at the barefoot doctor, her expression rather surprised and sceptical.

"Of course he'll make a go of it! The men talk about 'special measures for special times'. Brother Faqing drank liquor mixed with blood and swore to make Pagoda Ridge rich or die in the attempt!"

After gaily passing on this information, declining offers of tea Liangmei hurried off.

So her young man was a team leader! This was something of which any village girl could be proud. Brother Faqing wanted to be a credit to her. This ought to put an end to people's gossip.

At supper that evening, afraid to look at her father, Xiuxiu hung her head and told her mother softly, with a smile, of this news from Pagoda Ridge.

"So you still hanker after him. . . ." Her mother sighed. She knew that no hill however high, no river however wide, could bar the love of a grown girl for her sweetheart.

"You fancy the head of that beggarly team? For shame!" Her father scowled and slammed down his bowl and chopsticks, then rapped his pipe on the table.

Her mother threw him a glance, not wanting him to hurt their daughter's feelings. Men think they have the right to settle a big thing like marriage offhand.

The old fellow clamped his mouth shut, and none of them spoke. Xiuxiu did not make a scene, for fear the neighbours would talk.

Before long Liangmei came back from Pagoda Ridge. Again she had good news.

"Sister Xiuxiu, Pagoda Ridge is in luck at last. Each family has bought two or three water-buffaloes from Jiangxi. They're going all out there to mechanize agriculture, selling off their buffaloes and oxen dirt cheap, using iron oxen instead. Brother Faqing has bought three buffaloes, one big one, two calves, for three hundred and twenty yuan. Before he fetches you as his bride his work keeps him so busy, he's left his buffaloes with Sister Mushroom on Muffin Cliff. By winter, they say, he'll be able to sell off two for a couple of thousand. Up on Pagoda Ridge everyone says that with Brother Faqing as team leader our luck has turned."

Liangmei spoke enthusiastically. But she kept two things back. One was that the money for the cattle had been raised by felling cedars from the state-owned forest, without so much as asking for a loan. The second was that she was helping to tend Tian's three buffaloes.

After this Xiuxiu smiled even in her sleep as she dreamed of going to Pagoda Ridge. But how could she raise the question again with her parents? How could they stand any more malicious gossip? Having set her heart on this marriage, she passed sleepless nights. She was annoyed with Brother Faqing too. As team leader he obviously had to go to meetings in the brigade and commune, passing Rich Flats on the way, so why hadn't he come to see her? Surely he couldn't be afraid of that cripple's cane? How long would it be before he sent over a match-maker? Men really had hearts of stone! He'd dropped her, forgotten her. Well, suppose I harden my heart and break with you, leaving you a bachelor, she sobbed. You shouldn't be so cruel. . . . Why didn't you send me word about the cattle you bought. . . . Think I don't know how to raise cattle? How heartless you are! If I harden my heart you can send a bridal sedan-chair with eight bearers, but I won't go to your damned Pagoda Ridge. . . .

Another six months went by. At the Mid-autumn Festival Liangmei brought her a final message. No longer wearing patched clothes, she had on a brand-new checked costume bought in town, and her two short plaits were glossier than before. She looked lovelier than ever. The Pagoda Ridge girls had always dressed in rags, yet here she was smartly turned out. Pagoda Ridge must really be looking up. Last time Liangmei had told Xiuxiu in confidence that she had a friend who worked in the state forest. . . . Now she horrified her by saying:

"Sister Xiuxiu, if you dilly-dally any longer, aren't you afraid Brother Faqing may have a change of heart? Big and strong as an ox he is, and though he's so busy with the work of the team he must still want a wife. . . ."

There is something a little selfish about love. These insinuations staggered Xiuxiu.

The days dragged by. By the time of the winter solstice Xiuxiu was frantic, unwilling to stay a day longer in Rich Flats. She spent the whole afternoon mending her father's work clothes and sweeping the house and yard. At supper she helped her parents to vegetables and rice. She had never behaved so dutifully before. Unnoticed by her father, her tears fell into the rice bowls. But she had determined not to make a scene or give the neighbours a chance to laugh at them. The next day dawned cold and frosty. She got up very early. Taking simply a red umbrella (red for good luck) she left a note on the table explaining where she was going.

That morning the mountain track was white with hoar frost, the pools had frozen over. Tian was just about to set off to work after breakfast when he saw a girl in red, holding a red umbrella, on the far side of Guanyin Brook. Her trouser-legs rolled up, she jumped nimbly over the stepping-stones, her feet crimson with cold.... Heavens! Wasn't that Xiuxiu? You've come on your own without waiting for me to send.... Yes, it's Xiuxiu, plucky Xiuxiu.... He bounded to the brook and clamped his arms around her. She was shivering, pale, sobbing....

"Brother Faqing! Brother Faqing, I was born under an unlucky star!"

"Don't say that, Xiuxiu. You mustn't!"

"They forced me...."

"I know, I know. Dear Xiuxiu, don't cry."

"I can't go back. I've no home now...."

"Pagoda Ridge is your home. We'll set up house in a way that will make Rich Flats green with envy!"

"I've come empty-handed, with no dowry...."

"Xiuxiu! Darling Xiuxiu! What nonsense you do talk! You're everything to me. More than all the gold or silver in the world."

For weddings or funerals on Pagoda Ridge the mountaineers keep up the good old custom of mutual aid. They pasted up couplets, sounded gongs and drums, let off fire-crackers, blew *suonas*. Each family brought red rice for this happy occasion, bamboo cylinders of liquor, salted pork, game and vegetables. They made it a really lively, boisterous wedding. Bashful Xiuxiu laughed elatedly, close to tears. The mountaineers were so warm-hearted, she felt completely at home. Their roars of laughter and drunken shouts frightened away the wild beasts. Like their forbears celebrating some successful foray, they drank till they passed out.

Xiuxiu, Liangmei ... how is it you came then left? Which of you? Are you two stand-ins for one spirit? No, this must be a crazy dream. Xiuxiu isn't Liangmei, Liangmei isn't Xiuxiu. Tian dreamed of finding his plucky, laughter-loving Xiuxiu, who loved him yet bore him a grudge.... Tian Faqing, you're dreaming! Your whole life is a dream, a dream not yet ended.

Tian sprawled out in his stone cottage in Gong Flat, snoring. Neither thunder nor shell-fire could have woken him.

10

Yes, everyone on earth dreams, new-born babies and old men on their death-beds. Dreams of every kind, fantastic, beautiful, fearful ... transcend time and space, going back to ancient times or leaping ahead into the wonderful future. Past, present and future can be concentrated in just one fleeting moment. Many fables and scenes from operas deal with dreams. Life is said to be an evanescent dream. But emperors have different dreams from their subjects, townsfolk from countryfolk, and young men from girls. Rulers dream of territory and beautiful women, their subjects of growing rich, townsfolk of modern gadgets, countryfolk of grain and cattle, young men of winning a name, girls of their marriage. Some also dream of promotion, a pay rise, banquets, fame or foreign travel to see whether the moon in America, the sun in Britain, are bigger or rounder than China's. What you think of by day you dream about at night. To each his different dreams.

In his cottage in Gong Flat Tian dreamed a mountaineer's simple dream, dreaming for someone else too.

Dreams record a man's thoughts and life, are a store of memories. . . .

At the end of Tian's first year as team leader, a year after his marriage to Xiuxiu, Pagoda Ridge's fine harvest was the talk of the whole commune, the whole county. An iron tree can flower, a feather fly up to heaven, a horse grow horns. Bull-headed Tian Faqing was responsible. Birds have to eat and men to prove their worth. If you skulk like a mole underground, afraid of wind, rain or light, life isn't worth living.

That day the commune convened a meeting of all its eighty-eight team leaders. Each in turn reported the amount of his team's total output, yield per *mu*, the rice delivered or sold to the state, the reserves on hand, food grain and fodder. In those days their slogans were "In agriculture take grain as the key link" and "Raise output to aid the world revolution". So they simply reported on their grain production and distribution, comparing their achievements. Liang Youru, chairman of the revolutionary committee, questioned them one by one, starting with the most advanced models and gradually working down to the eightieth team. But still no mention of Pagoda Ridge. Tian Faqing sat there fuming. In the eyes of the higher-ups Pagoda Ridge was the most backward, lowest team of all, a burden to the commune. . . . By the time Liang had heard the report of the eighty-seventh team leader, he looked tired and had closed his notebook and put his ball-point pen back into his pocket. He asked lackadaisically:

"Well? Is there still a Pagoda Ridge? Want to report on your output?"

Tian's neck swelled as, red in the face, the veins on his temples throbbing, he retorted:

"You top people have no use for Pagoda Ridge! If you want my report, OK. If not I'll go back to the mountains."

"Ha, you talk big." Chairman Liang was too broadminded to take offence at Tian's pugnacity. He reopened his notebook and took out his pen. "Let's have your report, to avoid another poster criticizing me for my *a priori* approach. I hear production's picked up on Pagoda Ridge. Sometimes a dark horse wins the race."

Simple-minded Tian had gritted his teeth and been ready to risk his neck to set Pagoda Ridge on its feet again. Now he announced:

"I'm not afraid to report! This year the average yield per *mu* of Pagoda Ridge Team was 1,101.5 catties! We've delivered our quota of grain to the state. As we weren't asked to sell any of our surplus, sorry, it's still in our barns!"

Tian, glaring like a tiger, was sitting opposite Liang Youru. Head raised, chest thrown out, he seemed in a towering temper. His hefty hands on the table looked as strong as sledge-hammers.

"What's that? Comrade Tian Faqing, please say that again." Liang was gaping, unable to believe his ears. "Comrades, comrades! Listen carefully, all of you.

What's brought about this change in Pagoda Ridge? Wonders never cease!"

All the team leaders there were staggered. The dark horse had really come first. Their eyes, nearly popping out of their heads, showed amazement, scepticism, admiration or delight.

"Brother Faqing, let's get this straight. Has Pagoda Ridge really made such a leap forward?"

"This thousand catties per *mu*, did you grow it, or have you made that figure up?"

"Faqing! I knew you were bull-headed, but I didn't know you could make production shoot up like that."

"Holy smoke from your ancestors' graves must have changed your luck!"

"Why, not to mention anything else, they made a killing last spring buying buffaloes from Jiangxi. By the time we heard it was too late, the folk there had stopped selling."

"Comrades! Brother team leaders! Quiet!" Liang Youru had to stand up to call the meeting to order. "We've only heard the start of Comrade Faqing's report, just the entrée, the main dishes are still to come!" His face was shining, his voice trembling with excitement. "Go on, Comrade Faqing. Go on."

Tian repeated the amount of their yield per *mu* with great pride and satisfaction. Pagoda Ridge, thought fated to be poor, had aroused attention at last and forced people to revise their opinion of it.

"How much food grain have your team members per head?" asked Liang.

"Six hundred and fifty catties," Tian replied.

"What reserves have you kept for the team?"

"We had a poor start. For over ten years we had to

borrow grain, so the team has kept only five thousand catties."

"Seeds, fodder?"

"Don't worry, we farmers have enough gumption to keep seeds."

"Comrade Tian Faqing, tell us briefly how you managed to catch up so quickly after being backward all these years. What valuable experience do you have?" Liang followed the mass line, using the experience of outstanding teams to improve the work of the whole commune.

"Experience . . . we haven't any experience. . . ." Tian was tongue-tied, at a loss. Beads of sweat sprang out on his forehead. He could not breathe a word about the methods Pagoda Ridge had used.

"The leadership wants you to summarize your experience. No need to get het up," Liang encouraged him.

The other team leaders were casting admiring, envious glances at Tian. If he had held forth at length and his answers had come pat, that would have put their backs up. As it was, they liked his show of modesty and the way he was stammering so sheepishly. Brother Faqing was good at organizing farming but he hadn't the gift of the gab.

"Comrade Tian Faqing, you must make a good summary of your experience. This is the political task given you by our commune committee and Party group. This doesn't just affect Pagoda Ridge. It's a great victory for our policy of learning from Dazhai, grasping class struggle and forging ahead with the cultural revolution!" Liang was raising the question to the higher plane of principle and two-line struggle.

"We really have no experience on Pagoda Ridge. If we have. . . ." Tian mopped his perspiring face, "It's the way you said, chairman. Like all the other teams we've stuck to learning from Dazhai and firmly grasped class struggle, stuck to the line. . . ."

"Good! That's the fundamental thing!" Although Tian had only parroted him, Liang pounded the table and sprang to his feet. "Everything depends on our line! Take the right line and the masses go all out to boost production, the revolution forges ahead and everyone's life improves!"

In those abnormal years political propagandists believed in striking while the iron was hot and getting instant results. That evening Liang kept Tian to stay with him, an unprecedented honour. They sat up all night, Liang presiding, and the commune secretary and propagandist making notes, to help Tian sum up Pagoda Ridge Team's experience, this "new victory of the cultural revolution". Tian, a rustic mountaineer, had served a few years in the army but his level was fairly low and he was inarticulate, talking in a disjointed way, unable to marshal his ideas logically. He fidgeted in his seat, on tenterhooks. . . . Finally experienced Chairman Liang told the secretary and propagandist to read out two "supreme instructions" to compare them with this material on how Pagoda Ridge had learned from Dazhai. It was so difficult extracting any information from Tian that sometimes the quick-witted propagandist suggested answers to which Tian limply nodded agreement. Though they all ended up exhausted, Chairman Liang was jubilant at having discovered this model. He felt like a general who, to his surprise, has stormed a strategic stronghold.

A political movement is bound to result in economic success. Very soon an account appeared in the "Work Report" of the county revolutionary committee of how Pagoda Ridge, a backward mountain team, had transformed itself in one year. This was reprinted in the prefecture and then in the provincial capital. As the "proletarian headquarters" had just called for criticism of "emphasis on production" and the counter-revolutionary allegation that the economy was at a standstill, Pagoda Ridge's experience of boosting production through criticism and struggle met the political requirements of that time. Who said that constant movements and struggles disrupted production? Pagoda Ridge had proved just the reverse.

And so before long the provincial newspaper carried an article on Pagoda Ridge, on the front page with a banner headline. This was based on the earlier reports, polished up, and in an editorial note Pagoda Ridge's experience was summarized as: 1. raising high the red banner, 2. flexible application of politics, 3. mass movements, 4. learning from Dazhai, 5. studying philosophy, 6. political night schools, 7. persistent struggle and remoulding, 8. revolutionization of the leading body, 9. comparing the bitter past with the sweet present, 10. scientific farming.

This article printed a thousand *li* away in Changsha reached Pagodə Ridge deep in the Wuling Mountains. The affair was mushrooming and being publicized throughout the province! Tian could only curse inwardly, his heart in his mouth. He should have kept quiet instead of blowing his own trumpet. But it was too late to retract now. He had made an irrevocable mistake. The team members were equally dismayed. Knock-out

Wang, Jiang Shigong, Old Crow Liu and Sister Mushroom came to Tian's cottage to talk the business over. Xiuxiu, who was still in the dark, made tea and prepared a meal.

"Nephew Faqing! Why did you brag to the commune heads? This is no joking matter. We can't hide or cover it up!" growled Knock-out Wang.

Although he sounded so grim, he was wearing a sweater Liangmei had knitted him, smart pants and pigskin boots in place of his old straw sandals. Not until his fifties had he dressed so well.

"Faqing, Uncle Knock-out speaks bluntly because he's so worried for you. He won't praise you to your face, but behind your back he says all of us on Pagoda Ridge are eating off our team leader."

Sister Mushroom hurriedly gave this explanation, for fear Faqing might take offence. She needn't have troubled; he knew Uncle Knock-out's temper. By intervening she had shown her relationship to Old Wang — she was hen to his rooster.

"Seems to me, dammit, we'd better switch back fast and make a clean breast of things to the higher-ups...." Old Crow Liu screwed up his beady eyes, his fat face beaming. Before he could finish Knock-out glared at him to shut him up.

"We can't go back on our word. We may have done wrong and pulled the wool over their eyes, but we'll have to stick it out — there's no turning back...." Jiang Shigong shook his head at Old Crow.

"Uncle Old Crow, you didn't finish...." Now that he had landed them in all this trouble Tian wanted to hear the opinion of everyone.

"We must try to stop this from escalating.... A

tall tree catches the wind. Fame is dangerous for men, fattening for pigs. If the higher-ups find out that Pagoda Ridge is a fake model, a fake red banner . . . we'll be done for." Old Crow was obviously vacillating.

"No! When false is taken for true, what's true is false. It's always been like that. Now that the authorities have held our Pagoda Ridge's red banner so high, they can't hack it down without first considering the political repercussions, the pros and cons. Thousands of people all over the country are more bogus than our team. And some of those swindlers get high posts and power. . . ." Jiang showed himself a true strategist in the way he approached the problem.

"Suppose they send Faqing to meetings of advanced workers to make a report and pass on our experience, what then?" growled Knock-out Wang, knitting his shaggy brows.

"That's easy, dammit, no problem. . . ." Seeing that all the others sided against him, Old Crow had changed his tune. "Isn't there a ready-made article in the provincial paper? I'll rearrange it and write out different versions for Nephew Faqing to deliver at different meetings. That way he can't go wrong. And, to save trouble, we'll add a few more quotations."

"Can't make the same speech at each meeting, or people would grow sick of it." Sister Mushroom frowned at Old Crow, adding anxiously, "This is going to put an even heavier load on our team leader's shoulders."

"Of course Old Crow can see to any writing. Our team had better subscribe to the provincial paper and buy a radio, the kind that runs on batteries . . . so that he can learn some of the new jargon and slogans, and be in the picture." These practical suggestions came from Old Jiang.

"Right! If a revolutionary feared death he wouldn't join the revolution. In any case, whatever happens, I'll claim sole responsibility! Like it or not we have to go through with this." Tian would not go back on his word.

"Tomorrow let's call a meeting of the whole team, to warn old and young on Pagoda Ridge to keep their mouths shut. If anyone blabs or makes trouble, landing us all back in poverty again, I'll see him to Water Hollow!" Knock-out's voice was like muffled thunder.

"Uncles Knock-out, Shigong and Old Crow, there's something I want to make clear. We've made Pagoda Ridge an independent kingdom. I'm the one who set it up, the one who's ruined it. Tomorrow at the meeting I'm going to kneel to admit my mistake. . . . I'm ready to be the scapegoat. But if anyone lets word out, that will just about finish us."

So the four men, meeting secretly in the stone cottage, worked out ways and means for Pagoda Ridge to scrape through.

Sister Mushroom was in the kitchen helping Xiuxiu light the stove and prepare a meal. Both women's eyes were red.

"Sister Xiuxiu, we pulled through hard times. Now we're not short of food or clothes, but we've broken the law."

"Faqing's ill-fated, sister. He must be paying for some sin in an earlier life. . . . If anything happens to him, what will become of me?"

II

Where was he? In the auditorium of the county revolutionary committee? The cultural palace of the prefecture? The Great Hall of the provincial capital?
Lamps studded the ceiling like a skyful of stars. They
lit up silk banners, paper flowers, prize certificates. A
huge red slogan "In agriculture learn from Dazhai"
covered one whole wall of this ten-storey building. But
behind this marvellous political and cultural phenomenon were stalled engines, rusty machinery, flickering
candlelight in housing estates, angry hoots in cinemas
during power cuts. The crucial thing was to ensure
electricity for the rostrum of the Great Hall and all its
loudspeakers. . . . Tian Faqing, a nobody filled with
forebodings, was like a grain of sand in this flood of
light, a grain of sand swirled by the political current,
a charlatan who had sneaked into the ranks of models
and pace-setters. In that sea of light he was conscious
of a black abyss under his feet. He peered round, dazzled. . . . Seemed to see Xiuxiu's bright eyes, Liangmei's jet-black eyes fixed on him. . . .

Tian had just come back to Gong Flat after attending two meetings in the county and prefecture, when
he received another big red card inviting him to a conference in the provincial capital for collectives with fine
records of learning from Dazhai. That red card with
its gold lettering reduced Xiuxiu to tears. Appalled Tian
Faqing. Those endless exultant meetings with lashings
of food and drink were getting him down. They spelt
danger. This time he would have to shake hands with
the heads of the different revolutionary factions, army

representatives and leading cadres, would have to make a speech denouncing the counter-revolutionary crimes of Lin Biao who, only three months ago, had been their "respected and beloved deputy commander". He would be interviewed and photographed wearing a big red flower, would receive both collective and individual prizes for learning from Dazhai. What an honour, what a grand show! He would be the cynosure of envious eyes. Their lawless ancestors in the nether regions would be dumbstruck, overwhelmed.

But Tian did not want that honour, neither did Xiuxiu or the rest of the team. Still he had to accept it, the higher-ups insisted. Liang Youru, the commune chairman, said this was a political duty. Yang Jun of the county revolutionary committee solemnly pointed out that this was essential to the revolution. Tian couldn't get out of going, much as he dreaded it. For him it was hard labour. His heart sank each time he had to wear a red flower or receive a certificate.

This was mental torture. Life had forced Tian to lie, to deceive the authorities. He would soon have schizophrenia. He should have been one of those revolutionaries who are always right, able to come to the top in each political movement, to adapt themselves to any situation, ingratiate themselves with everyone, and keep four different sets of material for different circumstances. Lin Biao who had risen so high only to come a great cropper had said: You can't reach the top without lying. Tian didn't want to reach the top, and felt so uneasy wearing a Dazhai flower that he kept having nightmares.

Xiuxiu in the kitchen was washing up and preparing

swill for the pigs. Tian, lonely, bored and afraid, called out impatiently:

"Xiuxiu!"

At once she washed her hands and hurried to the
bedroom. "What the devil's come over you, turning in
so early? Feeling poorly?" She sat on the edge of the
bed to feel his forehead. He had no fever. As she bent
down to rest her forehead on his, he caught her face in
his hands.

"Come and talk to me, Xiuxiu. . . . I'm all on edge.
This is no kind of life! Better die and be done with
it."

"What's come over you? You're raving!" she scolded. "If you weren't in this fix, worn to a shadow, I'd
pull your ears!"

"Hurry up and clear up in the kitchen, then bolt the
gate and come and talk to me!" Tian lay there limp and
wretched.

Xiuxiu's heart ached for him. She wasn't such a fool
that she couldn't see that he was going through hell,
running fearful risks. She deftly cleared up in the
kitchen, bolted the gate, blew out the lamp in the bedroom and nestled up to her husband, drawing his arm
around her.

"All right, get it off your chest."

"Are you fed up with me, Xiuxiu?"

"Well, yes and no."

"I haven't helped you with our private plot or to
feed the pigs, mind the buffaloes, raise poultry. Sometimes your firewood's damp. . . . I'm a wash-out as a
husband. . . ."

"The idea! The team leader making a self-criticism

at home! Talking like a visitor about 'helping' me. If I'd been fed up, I'd be over it by now!"

Xiuxiu giggled and gave him a playful punch. What possessed her husband, normally so incisive?

Tian's gnarled fingers were pulling her thick hair, tugging so hard that it hurt. But she made no objection to these rough caresses.

"Xiuxiu, there's something I'd better tell you beforehand."

"Yes?"

"It's best to be forewarned, not to leave it too late."

"What?"

"Suppose I don't come back from this meeting I'm off to?"

"Impossible."

"No, it's true. We're deceiving the higher-ups here, running Pagoda Ridge in the stinking capitalist way. We've put the clock back, waving a red banner to oppose the red banner."

"You must be out of your mind! Why run yourself down like that? For the first time in more than ten years Pagoda Ridge doesn't owe the state any grain, we've sold our surplus too. What's wrong with that? The higher-ups, even if they were blind idiots, would have to approve of the way you've handled things."

"I only wish the higher-ups were blind idiots. But they're not. The reports they make are full of supreme instructions, quotations from Marx and Engels. They can talk for hours at a stretch without losing their voices. They're too smart, their level's too high."

"Make them come to Pagoda Ridge to head this team for a couple of years. To see for themselves what it's like up in the mountains!"

"Make them head the team? You're joking! They're so bloated, they look eight months pregnant, soft, white and pudgy. Shake hands with them and they seem to have no bones. They couldn't even climb up here. Not unless they were brought up by helicopter!"

"You cheeky bugger! It's only at home you talk that way."

"A man lives for his wife, she lives for her husband. But at the last meeting in the prefecture I heard that some secretary's wife had denounced him for opposing the Party heads."

"She can't have been his first wife or she'd have stuck by him. Take my word for it, she's a bad lot, on the make, trying to climb up the ladder."

"The way you talk! As if a girl in the mountains knows all there is to know."

"So you're a know-all, eh? You called the higher-ups bloated. But in that film of Lin Biao reviewing Red Guards, he was wizened as a monkey, his skin hanging in folds, not two ounces of flesh on him. Haranguing them with that outlandish accent, as if he were at his last gasp."

"Hey, you mustn't say that outside! Lin Biao's nose-dive hasn't been announced, it's a top secret. . . . But, Xiuxiu, darling, you don't know how much I love you. I should never have met you, landing you in such trouble. . . ."

"Don't start rambling again, a hulking big fellow like you. Want me to beat you?"

"I should never have carried you in my arms over Guanyin Brook. . . . Then most likely we'd never have married."

"Whose fault was that? The first couple of times you

carried me on your back, then you held me to your heart and told me to put my arms round your neck — to lessen the weight, you said."

"When I had you on my back, why did you tickle the nape of my neck with your hair? And brush my back with your breasts, making me want you. . . ."

"For shame! Don't try to settle old scores. . . . I should have reported you that day to the head of our training class."

"Xiuxiu, I know you've been cracking all these jokes to cheer me up."

Suddenly Tian, too tough for any load to crush or any club to knock down, burst out sobbing, clasping Xiuxiu in his arms.

"What the devil! What's wrong now?"

Xiuxiu took the towel from the pillow to wipe his eyes.

"I've reached a dead end, Xiuxiu. . . ."

"Then what about me? For your sake I ran away from home. I'd never have the face to go back to Rich Flats."

"Xiuxiu, dearest, I've let you down. . . . At this meeting in the province, I shall have one foot in the meeting-hall, one in prison. . . . If anything happens to me, what will you do? What will become of you?"

Xiuxiu's heart ached. She had wanted to comfort her husband, yet he kept harping on disaster. She bit her lips to keep herself from sobbing, and turned away from him to wipe her tears. If both of them broke down that would bring them bad luck.

"That won't happen, Faqing, it can't. . . . Listen to me. You've done nothing really counter-revolutionary . . . just kept everyone here from starving. Haven't embezzled anything, done any profiteering. We've handed in our grain tax, fulfilled state purchase quotas."

"When it comes to the crunch that won't count. According to them, the line decides everything. If you take the wrong line then everything you do is wrong. . . . Let's get divorced while there's still time. Then I won't drag you down with me, to have your name blackened for life."

"If you want a divorce you get one! A grown man, aren't you ashamed to talk like that! If you go to prison, I'll take you your meals there. If they sentence you to death, I'll join you! How about it?" Xiuxiu sat up choking with rage, her eyes flashing. She tugged at Tian's ear so hard that he sat up too. "Do you have to talk in that unlucky way? Prison, drag you down. . . . Are you trying to make me furious, to frighten me? Or has some girl bewitched you, so that you want to ditch me and marry her?"

This was the first scene Xiuxiu had made in the year and more of their marriage. Tian realized that he had gone too far, dammit, had been too carried away. The men of Pagoda Ridge feared neither gods nor devils, would brave any dangers. He held Xiuxiu to him in a grip like iron.

"Xiuxiu, with you to back me up, I'm not afraid even to go to the capital!"

"I'm not the only one. Old and young on Pagoda Ridge all back you up."

Three days later Tian set out to the provincial capital. To bring him luck, Knock-out Wang, Jiang Shigong and the rest let off fire-crackers and gave him a good send-off. And all went well at the conference. He read out the speech Old Crow Liu had written for him studded with "supreme directives" and the instructions of Central Committee members. Not hoarse or sweating this time, he spoke distinctly and felt no cramp in his legs. At heart, though, he was still frantic. As he stood on the rostrum in front of the microphone reading out all the fine phrases Old Crow had culled from different newspapers, for a moment he felt like a genuine model, a red banner-bearer. He threw back his head and made dramatic gestures, cutting a splendid figure, sometimes laughing heartily. Was not intimidated by the audience of several thousand, the flashlights of the photographers, the television crew. He felt like a warrior of old galloping alone into battle, was really in the limelight. But all this time he was tempted to make a quite different speech:

"Friends, what I just said is a load of crap! I'm a swindler.... Pagoda Ridge has only made a pretence of learning from Dazhai, holding up its red banner. We haven't put politics in command or grasped class struggle. We've divided up the land between different households, making each responsible for its own fields. We've restored capitalism.... I've no right to be on this platform wearing a big red flower, no right to accept prizes, banners.... I've been telling you whopping great lies...."

But on him he felt the eyes of Xiuxiu, of the old team leader Liu Jiejie, whose eyes had still been open when they fished him out of the brook. All the hundred-odd people of Pagoda Ridge were watching him to boost his morale. They were also warning him: Tian Faqing, if you own up you can clear your guilty conscience. But you've no right to betray us. For the first time our bowls are filled with good rice. Are you

going to snatch those bowls away and smash them?
If you did that you'd be a real criminal, a despicable
renegade. You'd deserve to go to hell, to be fried in
oil, boiled alive, or have molten copper poured down
your throat. . . .

12

Each time Faqing went off to a conference to live on
the fat of the land, receive prizes, wear red rosettes
and watch model operas, the days dragged for his wife
in their stone cottage. She felt as if she were serving
a prison sentence. Women are sensitive. The last few
years they had often been visited by commune chairman Liang Youru and brigade secretary Wang, who
sometimes brought Secretary Yang Jun of the county
or other heads who felt equal to the climb. Xiuxiu
always welcomed them with a radiant smile. They
smacked their lips over the meals she cooked, the mountain tea she brewed, and fired off all sorts of questions. If Faqing was flustered, red in the face or tongue-
tied, Chairman Liang or Secretary Wang would come
to his rescue.

"Do the higher-ups suspect? Suspect that Pagoda
Ridge is a fake model?"

Xiuxiu couldn't be sure about the county cadres.
They were mostly fat, sweaty chain-smokers, their
fingers stained with nicotine, preoccupied by big problems like grasping revolution and boosting production.
But she could see that Chairman Liang and Secretary
Wang were willing to turn a blind eye to certain things
and help her husband fool the higher-ups. A tall tree

attracts the wind, a fat pig is asking to be slaughtered! An ordinary team was ignored by those big shots, who wouldn't sweat up the mountain to inspect it so carefully. Faqing said this county of theirs was as large as certain small European countries, so of course the county heads were run off their feet. They only came to Pagoda Ridge because it was a model.

Each time one of the higher-ups came, Faqing sent Liangmei, still unmarried, to ask her foster-father Knock-out for some game from Monkey Rock. Sometimes he sent her to Muffin Cliff to fetch mushrooms, for although Jiang Shigong had presided over Sister Mushroom's marriage to Knock-out, the latter still sometimes slept in Monkey Rock. He could make the trip from place to place in no time. As for liquor, of course that came from Old Crow Liu's store and was charged to the team. Once these things had been fetched, Xiuxiu set to work cheerfully, frying, steaming or braising tasty or peppery dishes. She made the visitors tuck in, eating and drinking till they were red in the face, so that they would give a good account of Pagoda Ridge to their superiors. It was like the twenty-fourth of the twelfth month when the mountaineers saw the Kitchen God up to heaven, hoping that he would speak well of them to the Jade Emperor to make him grant them good weather and a fine harvest.

Faqing as team leader could not afford to offend any of these envoys from above. Because the mountaineers were only human, they needed food, clothes and a roof over their heads. They lived by their labour, unlike their fathers before them, those thieves and highwaymen. So, Heaven, make the higher-ups turn a blind eye, leave Pagoda Ridge in peace! Let Xiuxiu's husband come back safe and sound from all his meetings. . . .

Of course Xiuxiu hadn't lived badly these last few years, her laughter often rang out, and she was on good terms again with her parents who had become reconciled to her marriage to Tian. Her old neighbours treated her politely too. The only pity was that the two children born to them had died. . . . So when Faqing was away, she missed him all day long. If only he were back, she wouldn't care if he swore at her or beat her. She fed the pigs early, cooped up the hens and had supper, then stood in the doorway looking out. Sometimes she walked to the brook, hoping to hear his footsteps, to see him bounding up the mountain track. . . . Once she went all the way to the big rock halfway down Pagoda Ridge and stood under the red bayberry tree to imagine Faqing coming through the evening darkness. She would rush to meet him, regardless of passers-by, and throw herself at him to pummel his back. "Always meetings, endless meetings! Ditching me. . . ." Then he'd tease her and open his hold-all to show her the dacron blouse and leather shoes he'd bought her, as well as the perspex hairclips and scented face cream. . . . Get away! Do you think I came for these? I'd much rather you bought me nothing, just stayed with me. Then, his hold-all in one hand, his other arm round her waist, they would climb laughingly to their cottage by the brook.

When Faqing didn't come she passed a sleepless night. Dammit, the pillow stuffed with the fluffy ends of reeds seemed too low, too hard; the quilt was too thick, too heavy. She tossed and turned, unable to find a comfortable position. Closing her eyes she recalled how Faqing had gone off with Chairman Liang to a meeting in the prefecture. Chairman Liang had won credit by discovering Pagoda Ridge and making it a model in learning from Dazhai, so now he was to be the deputy chairman of the county committee and would be staying in the county town. Old Liang was a good sort. Each time Faqing came back from a meeting he described how Chairman Liang had looked after him, corrected the draft of his speech, and introduced him to all the men in charge. Had urged him to be modest and prudent, not to give himself any airs.... Chairman Liang had taken Faqing to spend the night in the county hostel, where all their county's models in learning from Dazhai would assemble. These fine fellows with whom he mixed at all those meetings were trusted and relied on by the higher-ups. How many were there altogether? Not more than twenty or thirty she supposed, not enough to fill a coach, the cream of the county's three hundred thousand people! And Faqing was the pick of the bunch as far as his achievements and influence went....

Xiuxiu giggled, her thoughts wandering. In the county hostel Faqing shared Chairman Liang's room, since they came from the same commune, as if on an equal footing. Chairman Liang might joke, "Faqing, this meeting and having a look round will take at least a fortnight. Will you miss your wife?" Trust men, as soon as they left home, to crack jokes about women. Faqing, his head on a snow-white pillow, his brawny arms outside the scarlet quilt, the way he slept at home, would promptly retort, "Tell me first, Chairman Liang, if you miss your wife?" Yes, that was the style. Chairman Liang might say, "We're an old couple, our son's already married, we'll soon be getting our daughter off our hands. But your Xiuxiu is as pretty as a picture, even the monkeys in the hills drool when they see her...." The old devil, still talking so shamelessly at his age. Hurry up and tell him, Faqing, "Now that you have a daughter-in-law, better not have it off with her!" No, Faqing would never say such a thing. That would annoy Chairman Liang. Next time he came to Pagoda Ridge she'd make him a peppery soup to blister his mouth.

Old Liang took Faqing to the prefecture, travelling by a special coach from the county town. On both sides of the coach was red bunting with gold inscriptions to welcome these delegates to the meeting on Dazhai. The road, lined with shady trees, had telegraph wires and high-voltage cables above and red streamers hung across it at intervals. Motor traffic, bicycles and ant-like pedestrians were milling about below this green and red.... But Xiuxiu could only visualize this from what Faqing had told her. She had never once been to such a lively place, never ventured farther than the county town. If she really went to the prefecture, she would probably lose her way in that maze of streets and have to ask directions from the policeman in white at the crossroad.

... The meeting opened. All the lights were switched on, brighter than the midsummer sun. Music was played, and all rose to their feet to sing, *Sailing the Seas We Depend on Our Helmsman.* ... Look, wasn't that Faqing sitting up there on the rostrum, while Chairman Liang sat down below watching him intently? Faqing had a porcelain mug in front of him. He was making a speech, in his hands the draft Old Crow Liu had concocted for him and Chairman Liang polished. Talking into the microphone, he was addressing all those thousands of people on "The Philosophy of Guanyin Brook" . . . .

Before the Spring Festival in 1968, Faqing was saying, their team was too poor to raise a fat pig to share out, so no one would have any pork for the festival. The old team leader Liu Jiejie talked it over with a few others and they decided to get the fish in Guanyin Brook drunk. They hadn't fished there for years, and there were said to be carp over a foot long among the water-weeds between the rocks. Eating fish at the festival would bring good luck.* Of course this would have to be done secretly, or old and young would all rush to catch fish and scare them away. So on the twenty-seventh of the twelfth month, first thing in the morning, Liu Jiejie had a dam built upstream and poured poisonous oil-tea water into the brook below. Where the channel narrowed three *li* lower down, some fish crates were so tightly wedged that not even a shrimp could have slipped through. What Old Liu had forgotten, however, was that the women had a holiday that day to launder their bedding for the festival. They were hard at work washing their ragged quilts when suddenly the water subsided, and white bubbles came floating down. Heavens, that made the women standing barefoot on the bank frantic! When they found out what was happening they were furious. They stamped, slapped their thighs and swore:

"Vicious louts! Drop dead!"

"Buddha will choke you on fishbones. . . ."

---

* "Fish" and "abundance" are homonyms in Chinese.

"May you die without sons, can't even buy a pig! Treating yourselves to fish you'll spill out your guts!"

Though the women worked their fingers to the bone, they never had a good square meal, so now their resentment poured out in a flood of abuse. Liu Jiejie had to swallow this in silence. Still, that Spring Festival each family had two carp as a treat. But for several days the brook remained muddy and smelt fishy. . . .

Not long before this meeting Yang Jun, the number one man in the county, had asked for an account of how Pagoda Ridge Team's poor and lower-middle peasants had set up a political night school to study philosophy. Chairman Liang passed on this glorious political task to Tian. Truly: One word from the élite runs those below off their feet! Tian went to consult Old Crow, who racked his brains all night then came up with a proposal. He explained to Tian:

"Taking the capitalist road muddied our brook and made it stink of fish. It's only since we've taken the socialist road, bashed capitalism and revisionism, that our water's clear and sparkling. So call this report 'The Philosophy of Guanyin Brook!' " As the old team leader was dead and Tian didn't want to cast a slur on his name, instead he spoke of "certain fat-headed capitalist fish".

. . . Look, Faqing's talking so well about philosophy. The big shots keep nodding their heads, the delegates keep clapping thunderously. The reporters are all taking pictures of him, the leading cadres lining up to shake his hand. He's standing erect and smiling, just like a VIP, really cutting a fine figure. More firecrackers, music and a final song. Now Faqing's given a big red rosette to wear, a big framed prize certificate, a set of Chairman Mao's works tied with red ribbon. . . . Seven sets he had received these last few years, some still in their wrapping paper.

Suddenly from both sides of the rostrum emerged two security officers in white uniforms with peaked caps. One stationed himself behind Tian, the other bent forward to say a few words to the chairman of the meeting, then reached for the microphone and made a public announcement: It has been discovered that Pagoda Ridge Team, headed by its team leader Tian Faqing, has for years run an independent kingdom, dividing up the land between different households, each responsible for its own output. They are dead set on capitalism. These double-faced counter-revolutionaries have all along deceived the leadership, the Party and the people. Their pretence of learning from Dazhai has had a most pernicious effect on the whole agricultural front in our province. Now this counter-revolutionary and political charlatan Tian Faqing is being brought to justice! The officer standing behind Tian drew his pistol and aimed it at him, the one who had announced his arrest tore the rosette from his chest, snatched the framed prize certificate from his hands and clicked gleaming black handcuffs round his wrists!

"Let him go! Let him go! He's no counter-revolutionary, no swindler! *You* made us a fake red banner, a fake model! Pagoda Ridge Team didn't want that, but you insisted. All we wanted was something to eat. . . . Let him go! Please, we beg of you. . . . Chairman Liang Youru can bear witness that Tian Faqing is a simple, honest mountaineer, not a counter-revolutionary. . . ."

Xiuxiu woke up from this nightmare bathed in cold

sweat. She opened her eyes and discovered it was
broad daylight. What a mercy it was only a dream. . . .
Faqing, hurry up and come back! It's not safe going
to those show-places outside, so rowdy and chaotic with
dogs fighting over bones. Don't attend any more meetings! Stop being a pace-setter and accepting prizes!
There are too many Buddhas about these days for you
to get away with playing Monkey.

13

". . . Who sold out? Heavens! What black-hearted dog
sold us out? Just let me get my hands on him and I'll
flay him!"

It's in the heart of a cabbage that rot sets in. A fort
is most easily captured from within. They must un-
mask this traitor, lance this ulcer. . . . Tian's worst
forebodings had finally come true.

In the stormy spring of 1976 slogans rent the air again.
"Repulse the Right-deviationists' reversal of verdicts!"
"When the bourgeoisie runs amok, the proletariat must
fight back!" Liang Youru, deputy secretary of the
county, had sent word secretly to Tian Faqing, "Someone reported that Pagoda Ridge is counter-revolutionary, a fake model! You're in for big trouble. The
heads of certain factions in the county revolutionary
committee are trying to blow this up, so as to settle old
scores and reshuffle the committee." The messenger
warned Tian that so much was at stake, he must not
breathe a word about this to anyone. In order to retain
the initiative, Secretary Liang had decided not to let
the faction heads handle this case, but to bring a work

team to Pagoda Ridge to make investigations and settle the business himself.

Tian was staggered by this blow, at a loss what to do. Furious, too, at having been framed and disgraced, his hair bristled, his eyes flashed fire. He numbered off on his fingers the nineteen households of Pagoda Ridge, but could think of no one who would dare betray them.

On Liang's advice he kept this strictly secret, not even telling Xiuxiu or Knock-out Wang, much less Jiang Shigong or Old Crow Liu. He would keep it to himself for the time being to avoid general panic. Let old and young live a few more days in peace. He hoped against hope that when Secretary Liang came up with his work team he would let them off lightly. Because when all was said and done, it was he who had boosted them up as a red banner. And after he discovered so much amiss, he had turned a blind eye and covered up for them. . . . When it came to the crunch, would he turn against them? Surely not! It wasn't as if Old Liang had no conscience, and all these years he'd been in charge they'd given him plenty of their mountain products.

Sure enough, a few days later Secretary Liang came to Pagoda Ridge with a work team composed of five members, including himself, of the county revolutionary committee. They all had pistols dangling from their belts. Their first act on arrival was to impound all the weapons of the team's militia, after which they set to work systematically. They did not call a meeting of the team committee to ask for a report on the situation, as Liang knew perfectly well that Pagoda Ridge had no committee, only a few small heads. Nor did they call a meeting of the whole team to explain why they had come, as there was no collective here, only individual peasants. All along they had hung up a sheep's head and sold dog meat.

The Pagoda Ridge mountaineers reacted quickly to changes in the weather, but slowly to changes in political climate — in this respect they were sadly yet ludicrously obtuse. For the first couple of days after the work team's arrival the villagers said nothing, just eyed each other, wondering if some "reactionary clique" had appeared or spies had been parachuted into the mountains, and Secretary Liang had been sent to ferret them out. Gradually, however, they noticed with surprise that the work team was not relying on Tian Faqing, Knock-out Wang or Old Crow Liu to handle the business.

The first two days the work team behaved like other higher-ups who had come in the past, inspecting the forests and fields on both sides of the brook, the village roads, the villagers' living conditions and their sidelines. They discovered to their amazement that practically every family had a bright, roomy new stone house, young and old were well dressed, their pigs were fat, their cattle in fine fettle, they had flocks of hens and ducks, and among the banyan trees round their cottages they had planted medicinal herbs. They were well off! Diabolical capitalism, of course, was responsible for this illicit affluence. They had reverted completely to capitalism, throwing away the fruits of the revolution. The work team, washing themselves in Guanyin Brook, marvelled at its clear, blue water, so soft to the skin. No wonder the girls up here had such fair, rosy complexions.

After inspecting the complex lie of the land and

sizing up the general situation, the work team began to question a few individuals. The first was Jiang Shigong of Oxhorn Hollow. They had ascertained that everyone else was a genuine poor or lower-middle peasant, he was the only one with a blot on his record, as before and after Liberation he had practised sorcery to swindle money out of the local people. Moreover, the last few years, he had been very active as Tian Faqing's strategist, in cahoots with him.

Old Jiang, now in his sixties, had a hoary head yet youthful face and a clear, ringing voice. When these five higher-ups came in, he at once made his wife brew tea and hurried to offer them cigarettes and light them. Now that their life had improved, most of the mountaineers kept several packets of cigarettes to entertain any visitors from outside.

The higher-ups sat down round the square table covered with bowls of tea, but Jiang did not notice that they had formed a cordon. Liang Youru sat opposite him, and the secretary beside him opened his notebook.

"Jiang Shigong, we've come from the county revolutionary committee, to ascertain certain facts about Pagoda Ridge past and present," said Liang quietly. "So we want you to answer some questions. Just tell us all you know, we won't hold it against you, right?"

"Sure, sure! You heads work so hard, go to so much trouble!" Jiang was smiling all over his face, but on his guard. With the higher-ups here why had Tian kept out of sight? Why had no commune or brigade cadres come with them? And why had Secretary Liang, who already knew him, started off in such a formal way? Since Liang's promotion to the county committee, though his attitude was still genial, he seemed to look down on people and his smile appeared rather forced.

"What's your native place, Jiang Shigong?" Liang began.

"Kejia in Guangdong." Jiang's heart sank when he saw the secretary taking notes.

"When did your family move to Pagoda Ridge?"

"My family? . . . my great-grandparents came here. . . . After all these generations I don't know why. We're ignorant people up here in the mountains, don't keep genealogical trees, and there's no inscription on my great-grandfather's tomb, so I can't report why to the authorities."

"You've a ready tongue, Jiang Shigong, a ready tongue. . . . Before Liberation you practised sorcery. How did you learn that? Who taught you?"

"Before Liberation I learned from my father to blow a horn and perform rites for the dead . . . just as an easy way of earning a meal, and so that people wouldn't bully me. In those days folk really thought I had magic powers. . . ."

"So you've an explanation for everything, eh? But you kept up your sorcery after Liberation! What's your present view of that?" Liang eyed him sternly.

Jiang closed his eyes as if to meditate. He was beginning to panic. They weren't investigating the situation but cross-examining him! Still he managed to answer:

"I fooled superstitious people out of money, and fooled myself in the first place. Later, after the higher-ups criticized me and our team cadres taught me better, I left off. I haven't dabbled in magic for more than ten years. . . ."

This answer made Liang smile in spite of himself,

and some of the work team laughed. Now that the tension in the air had lessened Liang asked, as if casually:

"You're on close terms, aren't you, with your team leader Tian Faqing?"

"Faqing? I don't see much of him.... He doesn't come here to inspect the work unless there's a team meeting in Oxhorn Hollow, so we hardly ever meet." Jiang was too shrewd to lower his guard.

"Jiang Shigong! In the spring of 1971, how many cedars did you fell in the state forest? How much did you sell them for?" Although springing such a crucial question on him, Liang refrained from describing this as "robbery".

Sure enough, this staggered wily Old Jiang. He stuttered, "Those c-cedars.... Let me think.... In the spring of 1971 I was short of cash, so I cut down some trees and sold them.... That was wrong of me, I admit it. I'll pay back...."

"Don't beat about the bush! How many did you fell? How much did you sell them for?" demanded Liang imperiously, as if he knew the answers.

"Let me try to remember.... Most likely twenty, which I sold for about three hundred." Jiang had to give a truthful answer.

"Who organized this felling of trees? Eh?"

"I don't know. Anyway nobody organized me."

"No? Jiang Shigong, you're lying. Every household in your team went to fell cedars in the state forest at the same time. Sheer robbery! Can you deny it?"

"But we.... But later I planted forty cedar saplings in the state forest. I had a look at them just a few days ago. Over twenty of them are as thick as bowls, growing fine."

"So you atoned for your crime? Is that what you mean? What a ready tongue, how smart! And you say you mountaineers are ignorant people. . . ."

Jiang hung his head in silence, expecting a more devastating question.

"Jiang Shigong, you robbed the state forest and sold the trees for three hundred. What did you spend that on?" Liang continued implacably.

"Let me see. . . . That m-money. . . ." Jiang stammered. "Let me try to remember. . . . At my age, my memory's no good. . . ." He tapped his head.

"Don't make us drag it out of you, Jiang Shigong! Do you think our work team came all the way from the county for no rhyme or reason, just to chat with you? Eh? You'd better come clean!"

"Oh, now I remember, yes. . . . Damn my poor memory. . . . I took that three hundred to Jiangxi to buy three water-buffalo calves. Jiangxi was going all out to mechanize agriculture, selling draught animals to buy iron oxen. Buffaloes and oxen were going dirt cheap. . . ."

"How many of your three buffaloes did you sell the next year, and for how much?"

"Two of them . . . for one thousand six hundred. . . . Sold them to a fellow from Baoqing. That was the market price, fair enough." But now great beads of cold sweat were standing out on Jiang's forehead.

Liang was quick to note this and delight in his discomfiture.

"So that year every household on Pagoda Ridge robbed the state forest and bought cheap draught animals from Jiangxi. A year later you sold them at an exorbitant profit. Who put you up to doing these things? Whose idea was it?"

"I really couldn't say.... I did it off my own bat, felling trees, buying buffaloes, then selling two of them.... Nobody put me up to it. I swear it." The veins on Jiang's forehead stood out, but he stuck to his guns.

"You swear it? Still trying to fool people, fool yourself, with superstition, eh? Don't give me that talk! It cuts no ice with thorough-going materialists like us. What we want to make clear is this: Your robbery of the state forest and your profiteering were planned in advance and done collectively. Right?"

In silence Jiang hung his head so low that it nearly touched his knees. The silence was painful, deathly. The secretary next to Liang rapped his ball-point pen impatiently, with a sound like pulling the trigger of a pistol.

"Out with it, Jiang Shigong! Own up, we won't hold you to blame! The Party policy is to make an example of the chief offender but treat his accomplices leniently. We can count you as an accomplice under duress. We can let you off punishment, may not even hold a meeting to criticize you. But only on condition that you come clean...." Liang used psychological tactics, intimidating a culprit yet holding out hope.

"I'm.... I'm not an accomplice under duress...." Jiang suddenly raised his head and straightened up, looking boldly at Liang Youru and the rest of the work team.

"If you're not an accomplice, what are you? One of the deluded masses? How long have you been deluded?

All right, just give us the facts." Liang nodded benevolently and tapped rhythmically with his fingers on the table, as if sure of victory.

"I was the ringleader," Jiang asserted defiantly, loyal to his team mates.

"What? You?" The work team eyed each other incredulously, as if unable to believe their ears.

"I was the ringleader," Jiang repeated calmly.

"The ringleader? You —?" Liang drawled the last word with contempt.

"I'll come clean to save you asking more questions. I was the one who thought up and worked out all the bad things we've done these years on Pagoda Ridge. Selling trees, profiteering, I put the rest up to it. I'm a bad character with a dirty past. I was against the new society, a counter-revolutionary.... Tian Faqing and the rest were just puppets, I pulled the strings.... Now you've found out you can sentence me, but leave the others out. I broke the law, let me pay for it alone.... My kids have grown up and married, go ahead and punish me. At worst you can cut off my head!" He bellowed with laughter.

This frenzied provocation was thoroughly counter-revolutionary. But Liang was not taken in by the old fellow's act. He pounded the table indignantly and stood up.

"Jiang Shigong! A stout fellow, aren't you! You believe in honour among thieves, eh? But this counter-revolutionary trick won't work. You want to sacrifice yourself to shield the chief offender. Comrades, this is the reactionary essence of loyalty among bandits. It provides moral support for a counter-revolutionary! Revolutionary cadres mustn't take it lightly. All right,

Jiang Shigong, let's talk plainly. Were you the ring-leader too in running Pagoda Ridge like an independent kingdom, dividing up the land, with each household responsible for its own output? Not afraid to stand trial, eh? Under the dictatorship of the proletariat, we can find room for you in our prisons, don't worry!"

Liang left one of the work team there to guard Jiang, to prevent his going to Gong Flat to send word to Tian Faqing and form a defensive alliance with him. He knew the art of struggle and leadership, how to avoid the trouble of even signing a detention slip.

14

The news that Jiang Shigong of Oxhorn Hollow was under house arrest spread quickly to all parts of Pagoda Ridge. The uneasy mountaineers on both sides of the brook passed on whatever news they heard, not know-ing what this portended. Only Tian Faqing realized how serious the business was, and that a gulf was yawn-ing at his feet. But having been mentally prepared for this ever since he became team leader, he kept fairly calm. Besides he still had hopes of Liang Youru, who had avoided him this time so that they had not once met. He never suspected that Old Liang could have a change of heart and show himself ruthless. That to prove the firmness of his stand he meant to make a clean break with these criminals on Pagoda Ridge, to crack down on them hard.

This had not occurred to Tian. The one thing that tormented him was the black outlook for his wife. Headstrong, laughter-loving Xiuxiu had been disowned by her parents and ostracized by their neighbours in Rich Flats, for insisting on marrying a Pagoda Ridge man. Only after life improved so much on Pagoda Ridge had they forgiven her, enabling her to visit them again. But these good times were over. Once Pagoda Ridge was shown up, that would put an end to Xiuxiu's laughter, and what would become of her? She would never have the face to go back to Rich Flats. All because of her luckless husband! He had done his best for the team, in front of the villagers he could hold up his head; but in his wife's presence he felt ashamed and guilty. He had let her down, ruined her life.

At night the moon was hazy, the stars dim. The dogs in Gong Flat kept barking at the dark hills, as if there were someone up there keeping watch over all the mountaineers' movements. Sometimes moonlight pierced the clouds to fall like silver gauze on the lattice windows, the ground, the bed, the sweet face of Xiuxiu already peacefully sleeping. She always pillowed her head on his arm, as if leaning against a stout tree. Her lips were curved in a smile and she was dimpling. Sometimes her eyebrows arched when she was dreaming, as if happiness pervaded even her dreams.

Lying on one side without moving, Tian stared blankly at Xiuxiu's face. What was to be done? The next morning, for all he knew, he might be handcuffed and dragged off to prison, yet his wife had no inkling of this.... Poor, unhappy creature.... Normally Tian would not cry out even if cut with a knife, but now his nose tingled, his eyes smarted, he felt a lump in his throat. He held back his tears, however, and forced himself to calm down, then tried to draw away his arm from under Xiuxiu's head. No use. She nestled closer.

He had to go on lying motionless on one side. With his other hand he stroked her hair, the nape of her neck.... When later she turned over, freeing his arm, he sat up keeping his eyes fixed on his wife sound asleep in the moonlight. Her life was too tiring, working in the fields and their vegetable plot, feeding pigs, herding buffaloes, and cooking three good meals a day for him.

"Shall I wake her and warn her?" Tian reached out for her plump shoulder, then drew back his hand. Let her have one more night's good sleep. The thought of that might comfort him in prison.

Tapping on the door startled him. He listened intently.

Tap, tap, tap!

At this time of the night, he reflected Liang Youru would hardly bring his work team there. Before they had collected all the evidence needed and completed their preparations, they would hardly come to disturb him. The soft tapping went on. Tian got quietly out of bed, draped a sweater over his shoulders and tiptoed to the outer room to unbolt the door and open it a crack.

"Who is it?"

"It's me, Faqing, Old Crow...."

"Hush!"

Instead of letting Old Crow in, Tian went out, closing the door softly behind him. He led Old Crow about fifty paces away to sit on a stone at the foot of the cliff.

"What brings you here so late at night, uncle?"

"Bad news, Faqing.... Hell, I must tell you, or a devil will strangle me in my sleep. I'm an old fool...."

His quavering voice startled Tian.

"Out with it, uncle. We're not strangers."

"Faqing.... I've done a terrible thing! Let you down, nephew.... Dammit, I deserve ten years' hard labour, old fool that I am...."

"What are you talking about, Uncle Old Crow?"

"Don't you know what that work team from the county's here for?"

"These last few days I've been thinking someone may have split.... Nobody on Pagoda Ridge would sell us out. But someone else may have blabbed. Here at least we all see eye to eye. And so far we've come through safely."

"You've guessed right, Faqing.... I've come to own up.... Couple of weeks ago, didn't you send me to the county to get Secretary Liang to assign us some fertilizer.... He dragged me home for some drinks ... and how could an old lout refuse one of the higher-ups. I'd had a long journey. I was parched. On empty stomachs we drank two bottles of liquor. And being tipsy I didn't watch my tongue ... especially as he was our old chief."

Tian saw stars. He clutched his knees, trembling convulsively. But he took a grip on himself. Why flare up when the fat was already in the fire? And Old Crow had come at midnight to own up. You couldn't hit a man begging for mercy, that was the Pagoda Ridge rule. He remembered too what a help Old Crow had been to him all these years.

Old Crow Liu had started off as a pedlar in Rich Flats, but had moved to Gong Flat just before Liberation because furs and mountain products were cheap up there. He had set up a little store, trading back and forth in mountain products and groceries. "No rabbit eats the grass near its own burrow." So he gave his local customers good value. And as he had some schooling whereas most Pagoda Ridge folk were illiterate, he was the one who wrote letters and couplets for them. What impressed them most, though, was his ready tongue. He knew how to talk to men or devils, rich or poor, even small children. Because of his gift of the gab, the crude expressions he used and the racket he kept up year in year out, the mountaineers had given him the unflattering nickname Old Crow. By now they'd even forgotten his real name.

The last few years Old Crow had been the team's accountant, one of Tian's able lieutenants. Each time Tian went to a meeting, whether in the provincial capital or the commune, to report on Pagoda Ridge's advanced experience, he would explain what was needed and Old Crow would write it up and pad it out. Moreover he contrived to present their negative experience as positive. The provincial paper to which the team subscribed was kept in his store for him to refer to and learn from. After he had read various long reports and grasped the gist of them, he learned how to plagiarize them. But he often broke out in a cold sweat after falsifying so much material, afraid that if they were found out and a search was made for the chief culprits and evidence of their crimes, he would be the number two man to be grilled. That was why Knock-out Wang called him a "wobbler".

Thinking this over, Tian gritted his teeth in silence. As they were sitting in the dark, Old Crow could not see his grim expression.

"Nephew.... I did wrong," he faltered. "Dammit, if the authorities don't punish me, Old Man Heaven surely will.... I let you down, let down one and all of our team. I can never wash myself clean, not even by jumping into Guanyin Brook. Let me kowtow to you."

With that he fell on his knees. Tian hastily hauled him up. He had got over most of his fury now.

"Sit down, uncle, sit down! I can't handle this, they may drag me off to stand trial first thing tomorrow. So ... unless the folk here settle scores, or Heaven pays you back.... Still, tell me exactly what passed between Secretary Liang and you that day."

"That day — Heaven help me — I'd drunk myself silly.... It was Old Liang who brought it up. Said someone from Rich Flats had reported to the county that Pagoda Ridge was a fake. Had built itself up not by learning from Dazhai but by stealing state trees, profiteering, farming individually and taking the capitalist road.... Because *he*'d made Pagoda Ridge a model, this put him on the spot; but he'd try to play it down and smooth things over. He asked me to give him the low-down and, dammit, I did just that.... Next day when I sobered up, I could have kicked myself. Still, I thought Old Liang would shield us. When I came back, I didn't dare tell you...."

Old Crow wept silently, clawing at the buttons of his jacket, as if to tear out his remorseful, guilty heart.

"Someone from Rich Flats? Are you sure?"

Tian felt a fearful foreboding. Heavens, how had the secrets of Pagoda Ridge leaked out to Rich Flats?

"That's what Old Liang said. The information was sent to a man gunning for him; so soon the whole county committee knew about it."

"Old Crow! I can tell you, you're not the only one.... After eating good white rice for a few years, plenty of people up here have forgotten what's at stake, forgotten that we've made a show of learning from Dazhai while running things our own way. We're still fooling the higher-ups, posing as a red-banner unit. Now that we've been shown up, fine! Some of us will go to prison, some will be lambasted, everybody will have to be re-educated, then go back to political work-points, to messing together. The kids may go hungry again like wizened monkeys, the girls may end up in rags. . . ."

"Nephew, tomorrow I'll go and tell the work team that I was the one behind the scenes responsible for everything. They may believe me, I'm such an old scoundrel." He said this resolutely, grasping Tian's hands.

Tian was staggered. Ever since they had gone it alone, Old Crow had been afraid things might go wrong. But for years he had helped write speeches and do the accounts.

"Uncle Old Crow! Don't go anywhere near the work team. I'm the one they're gunning for, the one who attended all those meetings, delivered all those talks and fooled all those people. Collected all those prizes and red banners. . . . I'm their number one target. But, uncle, there's one thing I want of you."

"What's that?"

"Don't go telling anyone else about your crime! If you go around owning up right and left, you'll make a hash of it! That won't lighten my sentence, not in the least, it'll only make the other team members see red and they'll treat you as a traitor. Then how will your family live?"

This warning silenced Old Crow.

"Got it, uncle?"

By way of answer Old Crow sobbed bitterly.

After he had left, Tian went on sitting there in the dark. He felt nothing but pity and sympathy for Old Crow, and glad that he had warned him. Uncle Shigong was already under house arrest, but the more men who could get by the better! They all had wives and children. Why involve so many people?

Tian clasped his hands round his knees. He felt a surge of strength, nearly burst out laughing. "Come on, work team! I stand by my word!"

He sat there coolly figuring things out. Firstly, he mustn't involve the rest, must shoulder all the blame. It was he who had duped Jiang Shigong and Old Crow into joining in. What about Uncle Knock-out and Sister Mushroom? Their level of understanding was low and they were too narrow-minded, living up in the mountains, too keen on making money. Secondly, this made the position of the brigade and commune cadres precarious. That went for Secretary Liang as well. They'd wanted to set up a genuine model. Tian had tricked them and won their trust. . . . They were also his victims.

He decided to assume the sole responsibility before the work team discovered a "reactionary clique" on Pagoda Ridge and extended their area of attack. But he could not but think of his wife. At once his strength drained away and his heart ached. . . . What would become of Xiuxiu? He could stick it out ten years in prison or in a labour camp . . . but how would Xiuxiu manage? Heavens, Xiuxiu, you make me feel so guilty. How can you stand being kicked around for ten years as the "stinking wife of a counter-revolutionary". . . ?

But how did our secrets leak out to Rich Flats? Had Xiuxiu anything to do with this? The thought was too appalling to contemplate.

Tian sat on the rock till a faint light appeared above the eastern hills. Milky mist wreathed the tree tops. Cocks started crowing. Day would soon be breaking.

Suddenly a familiar figure came up the track. Was that Xiuxiu? When had she got up and gone out? And where had she been so early? Tian's eyes were blurred.

"Brother Faqing! Why are you sitting outside, have you had words with Sister Xiuxiu?"

It was Liu Liangmei. Tian smiled over his mistake, but the two women were amazingly alike. Nearly a year ago, Liangmei had married a purchasing agent in the forestry station, but recently she had returned to Muffin Cliff and refused to go back to her husband. According to Xiuxiu, he had abused her and sworn that she was a slut. . . . And then Liangmei discovered that he was one of the three hooligans who had wanted to rape her that year by Our Lady's Temple.

"Hush! She's still asleep!" Tian's heart sank but he forced a smile. "If you wake her you'll have to make up to her for her lost sleep."

"Oh, everyone knows how you dote on your wife," teased Liangmei.

"What brings you down so early? Off to see a patient?" Tian stood up.

"Dad sent me down here to fetch you. He didn't sleep a wink last night. . . ." Liangmei glanced at the stone cottage, as if reluctant to speak.

"Well, what's up?"

"Yesterday his big buffalo's belly swelled up like a ball; it collapsed and can't stand up. Dad wants you to help him slaughter it, then take the beef down to sell it, if you've time...."

"All right, I'll be coming. There's nothing much needs doing in the fields."

"Go and tell Sister Xiuxiu then, to stop her from worrying."

Tian went straight into the cottage, his heart filled with grief and affection. As he stood by the bed, about to lay an icy finger on Xiuxiu's ear, she sat up.

"Who were you talking to outside just now?" she asked.

Tian explained that Knock-out Wang had sent Liangmei to ask for his help.

"Off you go then," said Xiuxiu. "Who am I to stop you? But why couldn't that wretch Liangmei come in to tell you?" She added, "How is it the work team from the county hasn't been here to find you?"

15

Knock-out Wang had tricked Tian into going to Monkey Rock. There was nothing wrong with his buffalo, and he had no intention of selling beef. But, disturbed by the work team's arrival, he wanted to discuss how best to cope.

"Faqing, till we know where we are, stay here with me! If the work team come for you, I'll talk to them!"

These were Knock-out's first words when Liangmei led Tian in.

"Thanks a lot, uncle! And I really believed you wanted to treat me to beef!" Tian chuckled as if he had nothing on his mind.

"What an old fox that fellow Liang is! First he boosted Pagoda Ridge to the skies, sending you to the province to make reports; now he's brought his work team here to make arrests, and he'll be investigating our case! Have they been to see you? What line did they take?" Knock-out was too forthright to waste time on polite formalities.

"They've not got round to me yet. They're probably 'mopping up the perimeter' first before zooming in on me. Old Liang can't help it, he's in a fix himself." Tian took a basin from Liangmei and washed his face.

"The way you talk! As if nothing was wrong. The fire's singeing our eyebrows, yet you don't turn a hair!" growled Uncle Knock-out.

"Hell, I couldn't sleep all night for worrying!" was on the tip of Tian's tongue, but instead he asked, "What's the use of getting worked up? I've made up my mind, if they don't come looking for me, I won't look them up! Let them choke on this bone!"

"Good! That's more like it!" Knock-out patted Tian's shoulder. "But don't bash your head against a stone wall. Have you thought up a way to cope?"

Tian emptied out the basin, then sat down in the doorway and shook his head.

"Look at you! Are you waiting for them to handcuff you and haul you off to gaol?" Knock-out glared at him.

"What can't be cured must be endured." Tian rubbed his hands with a rueful smile, looking as foolish as an ingenuous youngster.

"Why not go to the county to ask Secretary Yang for the low-down on this work team?"

"I thought of that, uncle. But there's this nationwide

movement to 'repulse the Right-deviationists' reversal of verdicts'. Some rebels in the county have occupied the revolutionary committee. Most likely Secretary Yang is a clay Buddha crossing a stream — he may come a cropper. I figure Secretary Liang has brought this work team here so as to retain the initiative and not give the rival faction a handle against him."

"Ha, nephew, who'd have thought that attending all those meetings outside would make you so shrewd, able to size things up."

"In any case, if other heads brought a work team here to investigate, and found how we've been deceiving the higher-ups these last years, who'd dare to cover it up? They'd probably crack down on us still more heavily."

"Seems you've thought everything out these last two days." Knock-out sighed, his eyes fixed on Tian.

"I shall be jailed, it's only a question of time. . . . But that's all right with me, uncle. It's been worth it. Pagoda Ridge has cleared its debts, each family has food, has built a new house. People no longer look down on us as paupers or spit at us as if we were mangy curs. . . . In exchange, of course, we've run into political debt . . . and I'm the one who'll be called to account for that. If I stand trial alone, that's well worth it. I won't involve our Pagoda Ridge folk, or the brigade and commune cadres either."

Tian announced this calmly, coolly. Knock-out Wang, sitting watching him, could not hold back his tears.

"Dad! Dad! We must think up a way to help Brother Faqing, we can't let him take the whole blame. And there's poor Sister Xiuxiu. . . ." Liangmei, who had been eavesdropping in the kitchen, came out now crying as if her heart would break.

Knock-out Wang kept silent for a time. Then raising his eyebrows he told her, "Hurry up and get us some food, then go to Muffin Cliff and ask Sister Mushroom to come — I want her advice."

Liangmei prepared each of them a bowl of noodles with eggs. The bowl she gave Tian had two poached eggs on top and two more underneath. Her concern warmed his heart, and he ate all four eggs without comment. By the time he finished the bowl he was perspiring.

Liangmei washed up, then went down to Muffin Cliff.

"Faqing, will you listen to me?" Knock-out growled, a spill in his hand as he sat by the table.

"I always like to listen to you, uncle." Tian winked.

"We must think up a way. . . . What I say is, never mind if it's breaking the law, let's first pounce on the work team! We won't beat them, curse them or starve them, just make them work every day on Pagoda Ridge. Let them see how you have to farm these scattered pockets of land! They eat state grain, draw their pay from the state, don't have to worry about food or clothing, so they like to bash other people. But unless we farm we starve. They understand all those big principles, yet can't understand a little thing like this!"

Knock-out's eyes were flashing fire.

"We can't do that, Uncle Knock-out." Tian shook his head, not knowing whether to laugh or sigh. "They'd only say we haven't changed our ways, that Pagoda Ridge is still a den of bandits. And, whatever you say, that work team was sent by the higher-ups. We can reason with them, but we can't defy them.... Can't treat them like the old government troops in the past. If I go to prison, at least it'll be a communist prison, a prison of our own...."

"A prison of our own!" Knock-out snorted. "Is there any prison that isn't dark, dirty and stinking? And now another 'way out' is labour reform. But, dammit, some of our higher-ups are set on making trouble.... What laws has Pagoda Ridge broken? We've delivered our grain tax, fulfilled our state purchase quotas, haven't posted up reactionary slogans or called for anyone's overthrow. Besides, how could those big shots in the capital, with all their bodyguards, be toppled by a few of us in the mountains? We've stuck to our farming, not robbing anyone. But that won't do, they must swoop down on us...."

"Uncle, to us it looks simple. But the higher-ups harp on the line. How we farm isn't up to us. The line decides who's to eat well, who's to go hungry. The line decides everything. And it's way over our heads, so we bumpkins can't understand it."

Tian had meant to calm Uncle Knock-out, but ended up by letting off steam himself.

"Tomorrow I'll take a sack of dried sweet potatoes, and march through the streets of those cities cursing that empress!"

Knock-out Wang pounded the table and jumped up, his neck muscles bulging.

But Tian had cooled off.

"Sit down, uncle, sit down!" he urged. "You said you had something to tell me. Surely it wasn't just this."

Knock-out grunted in disgust and resumed his seat.

"Nephew, this is burning me up.... What I wanted

to say was: Don't go to the work team to let them nab you and handcuff you. Stay up here with me. There are plenty of caves and hide-outs on Monkey Rock. Will they send up a division to search the mountains? Drag this out, play hide-and-seek with them. Suppose they arrest everyone on Pagoda Ridge and lock us all up — then what?"

"They won't leave us alone till they've arrested me, uncle!" said Tian with a grim smile.

"Never mind, first stay here for ten days or so. I'm going to talk it over with Sister Mushroom, and get her to comfort Xiuxiu. Then this afternoon I'll go to beard the work team."

Knock-out pressed Tian down so firmly that he made the bamboo chair creak.

Knock-out Wang was as good as his word. That afternoon, his bedding-roll on his back, he went down to Gong Flat to find the work team.

"Are you Knock-out Wang? Well, well, we were just going up to Muffin Cliff to see you. Now you've saved us the trouble, so much the better."

Liang Youru could not understand Knock-out's sudden appearance, or why he should have brought his bedding-roll.

"Are you Secretary Liang? We mountaineers seldom go to town or have a chance of meeting you higher-ups. Today I've come to ask: What law have we broken on Pagoda Ridge just by farming to make a living? As soon as you arrived your work team nabbed Jiang Shigong. How many more of us are you going to nab?"

Knock-out Wang had rattled this off defiantly.

Liang Youru was used to yes-men, not to such tough

mountaineers. For a moment he was stunned. But he pulled a stern face as befitted his status, although at heart embarrassed, as he tried to make up his mind how to handle Wang. Luckily at this point one of the work team put in:

"Watch your tongue, Old Wang! You can't talk in that wild way to the leadership."

"Who's wild? Me or you? I've never learned to suck up to the leadership!" Wang was still glaring at Liang. "It's Secretary Liang I came to see."

"Let's talk things over quietly, Old Wang...." Liang knew that it would be undignified to dispute or squabble with a crude mountaineer. "Our work team has been sent by the county revolutionary committee to investigate trends in the countryside. What rumours have you been hearing to make you so angry? Eh?"

"Jiang Shigong of Oxhorn Hollow's been arrested — why?"

"Who says he's been arrested? Where? And how?" Liang asked with a show of surprise. "Pagoda Ridge may be small, but it seems to be buzzing with rumours. I can tell you, Old Wang, Jiang Shigong of Oxhorn Hollow owned up to something, something extremely serious; so to ensure his safety we've left one of the work team to look after him. He's still in his cottage with his family, isn't he?"

This silenced Knock-out, to Liang's secret amusement. How simple-minded these mountaineers were — all they could do was bellow! They were easy to handle.

"Jiang Shigong — what serious thing did the ... old fellow tell you?" Knock-out nearly said the "old dog".

"Ha, I can't tell you that, it's confidential." Liang

glanced mockingly at him, thinking: It would never do to let you mountaineers into all our Party and state secrets! You really ought to know your place.

"Well, even if you don't tell me, I know!" growled Knock-out.

"What do you know? Eh? What do you know?" Liang, feeling rather provoked, demanded sternly, "What are you? What class origin? What's your class status?"

"Hired hand!" Knock-out sat up straight and threw out his chest. "And I'd have you know, Secretary Liang, you won't find a single middle peasant here. We're all poor and lower-middle peasants on Pagoda Ridge!"

"But most of your forbears were bandits! Eh? Poor and lower-middle peasants, indeed!" Liang's eyes were glinting. "You're all descended from bandits!"

"All right, Secretary Liang, that's what you, one of the top people, say. . . . My family came from Taoshui in Jiangxi, and farmed there for generations!" Knock-out, instead of backing down, was taking Liang to task.

"Watch your tongue!" Though Liang regretted his slip, he pounded the table angrily and stood up. "If you won't listen to reason, we shall have to teach you a lesson. I warn you, if you don't break with Tian Faqing, it'll be all the worse for you!"

"Good, let's have some plain speaking. So you're putting your cards on the table at last." Now that Liang had flared up, Wang had cooled down. "Just let me ask you higher-ups, what rule has Tian Faqing broken? In the six or seven years he's headed our team, Pagoda Ridge has stopped asking for relief. Relying on our own labour, we've had enough to eat, warm clothes to wear."

"That will be announced all in good time," put in another member of the work team. "It's still too early to reach a conclusion."

"Go on back now! We're busy here." Liang waved Wang away. "We'll come and find you when we're ready to question you."

"No, Secretary Liang. I'm not leaving until you give me a straight answer." Knock-out plumped himself down on the doorstep to sit motionless as a stone lion.

"Ha, another Jiang Shigong! Have you come to give yourself up? Tian Faqing certainly has loyal lieutenants!" Liang shook his head with annoyance, smiling grimly. "Tell me, how did Tian Faqing get you to come and put on this act? Eh?"

"I came off my own bat. Can't you see I've brought my bedding? My wife and daughters will bring me food every day."

"Just look! Isn't it splendid — honour among thieves!" Smiling all over his face, Liang patted Wang on the shoulder. "Go on back Old Wang. You want to be locked up to make a self-examination, but we can't keep you. We have to carry out Party policy. If Tian Faqing comes clean, we shall do our best to save him and treat his case leniently."

From his rich experience of struggle, Liang decided that the time was not yet ripe to lock up men like Knock-out Wang to extract confessions from them. That might upset their plans and cause confusion, might even goad the mountaineers to revolt!

Knock-out Wang went back with his bedding-roll to

Monkey Rock. He was thinking: All right, you don't dare hold me. Well, I'm going to keep you here. You won't leave Pagoda Ridge till you've given me a straight answer!

16

How did Tian and Xiuxiu part? There is an old saying, "Husband and wife, birds in the same wood, fly apart in time of danger." Till his dying day Tian would never forgive himself.... After two days with Knockout Wang in Monkey Rock, the lack of news from Gong Flat made him increasingly worried. It was like being in prison. What the devil could have happened? He felt a fearful foreboding. Ten to one Xiuxiu was responsible in some way for this disaster. It was a man from Rich Flats who had informed against them to the county committee; and, according to Old Crow, his information was accurate and specific. No one else on Pagoda Ridge had relatives or friends down there, only Xiuxiu. In the past the Rich Flats villagers had regarded all on Pagoda Ridge as bandits and would spit if they passed one of them on the road, whereupon the Pagoda Ridge man would see red and lash out at these swindlers. After Liberation, though they ended their feud, the two teams kept to themselves. These years old and young on Pagoda Ridge had stuck together, carefully guarding their secret. So how had it leaked out to Rich Flats? Could Xiuxiu have been sent to them as a spy? No, impossible. Ridiculous! Yet this preyed on Tian's mind.

If Xiuxiu was the informer, that would be the end of

them both. He would be arrested as a counter-revolutionary, and the mountaineers would punish her for her treachery. Would drive her out. Heavens, he would never be able to hold his head up again. Even if he survived his labour reform, he would have no home to go back to.

How could you be such a fool, Xiuxiu? I defied the law, put my head in the noose. But how could a weak woman who'd married a mountaineer not be loyal to us? How could you sell us out, bringing disgrace and ruin on yourself?

The third evening Tian climbed to the top of Monkey Rock at sunset. Blue sky, white clouds, far-stretching peaks, nearby trees and cliffs, all were bathed in the crimson afterglow. As far as the eye could see, a red radiance suffused earth and sky. Tian's body too was blood-red. Suddenly he felt dizzy, filled with dread. He closed his eyes tightly until the sun sank behind the mountains. Then his heart stopped beating so wildly. He decided to go to Gong Flat under cover of darkness to see Xiuxiu and question her; to take a last look, too, at his cottage, pigsty, hen-coop, cowshed and vegetable plot. Then, in some labour camp thousands of *li* away, he could take comfort from the memory, pluck up the courage to stick it out until he could return home.

Just then he heard footsteps. Light, hurried, familiar footsteps. Had Xiuxiu come? He looked down. Yes, it was Xiuxiu panting up in the dark, carrying a canvas hold-all. She hadn't spotted him.

"Xiuxiu!" he called.

"Faqing! Faqing!" She fell, sobbing, into his arms. "How cruel you are, hiding away up here and not even trusting your wife enough to tell her. I thought you were selling beef with Uncle Knock-out... but I saw him in the distance at Gong Flat two days ago, and that set me wondering. . . ."

"Never mind, I'm here safe and sound, aren't I? Don't cry!" His arms around her he asked, "Who told you I was here?"

"Liangmei. . . . My husband treats me like a stranger, tells her things he won't tell me. How hateful of you." Xiuxiu rested her head on his chest, her tears wetting his clothes.

"I didn't want to frighten you, didn't want the work team to pester you." Tian's love for his wife was clouded now by doubt. He gently pushed her away and sat down on a nearby rock.

Not knowing what was on his mind, Xiuxiu wept as she squatted down and reached for the hold-all. "Here's a change of clothes for you, two pairs of cloth shoes, your toothbrush and tooth-paste.... I know you won't be back for awhile. I boiled a few dozen eggs too...."

"Come on, sit down, let's have a talk." Tian pulled her to his side, his heart very heavy.

Xiuxiu sat close to her husband, forcing a smile as if to comfort him.

"What's the news from Gong Flat these days? Have the work team been looking for me?"

"No. Seems they've been saying: A monk can run away but not with his monastery. And Monkey King, for all his magic power, can't somersault out of the palm of Buddha's hand...."

"Nonsense! Have I run away? Where would I run to?"

"Faqing, I heard something worse. Liangmei told me yesterday, she's worried too. . . . Uncle Knock-out called together some young firebrands at Muffin Cliff yesterday. They mean to guard the pass to Pagoda Ridge . . . swear they're going to split the work team up in Oxhorn Hollow, Muffin Cliff and Water Hollow, to set them quarrying and planting trees. . . . Won't let them go until they've made it clear what they're here for."

Tian pushed Xiuxiu away and pounded his knees, cursing and breaking out in a cold sweat. "Dammit! If they do that, we'll get it in the neck. We'll be a real 'independent kingdom' — real counter-revolutionaries!"

"Is Pagoda Ridge done for then?" Xiuxiu tugged at his arm, trembling. "Another thing, Faqing, I'm afraid to tell you. . . ."

"What is it?" He rounded on her fiercely.

"Liangmei says Jiang Shigong is ill, in a bad way in Oxhorn Hollow. . . . Several times the old fellow tried to slip out, but that man from the work team stopped him. . . . Liangmei said he wanted to talk things over with you. . . ."

"Why be afraid to tell me?" Tian's eyes filled with tears at the thought of Jiang Shigong.

"And Liangmei said Uncle Knock-out and the rest have sworn, once they've driven out the work team, to punish Old Crow Liu. He was the one who sold out, went to the county and informed against us. . . . For his treachery they're going to truss him up and make him kneel below the old camphor tree in Gong Flat, for old and young, men and women to spit at him and beat him. Then his family will be banished to Water Hollow, not allowed to show their faces in the daytime. . . ."

Xiuxiu had sobbed this out, shuddering.

For a while Tian said nothing. In the deathly silence

between them they could hear the wind soughing below.

"Xiuxiu, tell me!" Tian seemed suddenly transformed: even his voice had changed. He was grinding his teeth. "Aren't you pleased to have Old Crow as a scapegoat for you? You have a nerve, smiling! It's crying you should be! Own up, wasn't it you who told Rich Flats our secrets? Out with it! Don't try to fool me. . . . If you do, I shall kill you, you bitch. . . ."

"Faqing! Faqing — are you crazy? Let go of me! You'll break my arm. . . . I'll tell you the honest truth. . . . Last winter my parents made it up with you so that they'd let me go home. You know how pleased you were, and back I went. Mum and I had a good cry together. . . . Dad bought liquor and invited over the brigade secretary, whose son I'd refused to marry. . . . I'd not been a good daughter, but my parents had forgiven me. I was laughing and crying by turns, overexcied. . . . They insisted on my explaining how a poor team like Pagoda Ridge had grown so rich these last years. I didn't watch my tongue, talked carelessly. . . ."

"Stinking slut! So I guessed right! I ought to kill you!"

In a fury, the blood rushing to his head, Tian knocked his wife to the ground. Before he could kick her, she pleaded, "Brother Faqing, Brother Faqing. . . ." His heart softened, he bent down and hauled her to her feet.

"Listen! Go straight home to Gong Flat, take a few hundred dollars, a hundred grain coupons and clear out! Back to your old home in Rich Flats. I'm through with you. There's no place for you here on Pagoda Ridge."

Xiuxiu suddenly vomited blood, then asked faintly, "Brother Faqing, what about you?"

"Me? I'll give myself up to the work team! Ask them to take me away tonight. If I wait till those others make trouble, every soul on Pagoda Ridge will be arrested as active counter-revolutionaries."

"Faqing, Faqing! Don't do this to me. . . . I can't go back to Rich Flats. Wherever you go, I'll go too. . . ."

Tian ignored the poor creature kneeling at his feet. Having grabbed the canvas hold-all which had accompanied him by special coaches and trains to so many meetings outside, he pounded down the track from Monkey Rock.

17

Jia-jia-jia! What was that sound jarring on his ears? Crows cawing on the roof? Ducks squabbling outside? Or had something gone wrong with the microphone at the rally to learn from Dazhai? *Jia-jia-jia!* Cryptic and ominous, it was as difficult to identify as it is to differentiate truth from falsehood.* During that unprecedented "revolution", falsification was one of the tactics for self-preservation. True and false intermingled till it was hard to tell one from the other. The result was pseudo-socialism, a show of learning from Dazhai, or raising high the red banner. For years they had trained themselves to be two-faced, trained themselves in double-talk. At rallies during the daytime they swore to

---

* *Jia* means "false".

unite to seize power, to fight; at night they sent out armed contingents to smash their opponents' headquarters. In the daytime they wept, hung their heads, confessed their crimes; at night in the adobe cadre school, they cursed Wu Zetian, the Empress Dowager, and those swine in the Cultural Revolution Group. By day, they attended classes to "struggle against self and combat revisionism", then smuggled home plexiglass and imported stainless steel to make a table-lamp or four-poster double bed. During meetings they contrasted past bitterness with present joys; but once home they griped because the commune's co-op had no kerosene, not even candles. They passed the day drinking tea, smoking, reading the newspaper, and stressing the long-term importance of suppressing revisionism; the evenings, however, were spent jockeying for promotion, finding jobs for their relatives or a place in the army or college for their children. . . .

"You have to lie to get on in life" — that was the current maxim. Lin Biao was its chief exponent, but there were lesser liars in the provincial and prefectural committees. And wasn't there something phoney, too, about Yang Jun, the number one man in the county, and Liang Youru the chairman of the commune? The masses are reasonable. So what about Pagoda Ridge, this tiny fake red banner? It was dwarfed by comparison with those really big frauds. Besides, it wasn't as if Tian Faqing had wanted to be an official, seize power or pull someone down; he'd just wanted to help the mountaineers get by. It was the commune and county heads who had boosted him up as a pace-setter, a model to prove the value of learning from Dazhai. . . . But this argument by analogy was too naive; their case was ten times more complex. Falsification had become an ultra-Left social trend. They couldn't get off by pleading their relative unimportance. . . .

That raucous sound — crows cawing or ducks quacking? — woke Tian from his dreams as soon as it was light.

"Brother Faqing! Brother Faqing!"

Who was calling him? Liangmei? Or Xiuxiu? Tian opened his eyes to stare blankly at his mosquito net, completely confused. Was this 1973, when he was back from a meeting in the provincial capital? Was it the spring of 1971, when he drew a lot making him the team leader, and the old team leader drowned himself in the brook? Was it 1976, when he was arrested? Or 1979, when he was released? Was he in the labour camp surrounded by barbed wire beside Lake Dongting? Or back in his cottage in Gong Flat? Was he still dreaming? Heavens, he had so many nightmares. When he woke he thought he was still dreaming. Where was Xiuxiu now? In the past, he had only to reach out to clasp his wife in his arms. She used to get up at dawn to light the stove and get breakfast, feed the pigs, let out the hens, then go to the vegetable plot to pick pumpkins, beans and peppers — where was she now?

"Brother Faqing! Brother Faqing!"

It was Liangmei calling and tapping on his door.

Tian sat up, rubbed his eyes hard and realized he had not taken off his jacket the night before, not even washed his feet, just flopped down to sleep. He went slowly, listlessly, to open the door, but saw nothing but mist outside, dense white mountain mist. Somewhere hidden in the mist ducks were quacking cheerfully. They must be in Guanyin Brook. Where was Liangmei? Had she left him to go on sleeping? He went back inside and took from his canvas hold-all a khaki satchel, which he slung over one shoulder. Then, having locked the door, he went to the brook. In his satchel was a bottle of liquor from Lake Dongting which he had brought back specially for Uncle Knock-out. Was it appropriate, though, for a man just back from a labour camp to give a present like this?

That early spring morning, mist covered the Wuling Mountains. Someone five steps away was only a shadowy figure. Hillsides, trees and people seemed afloat in a sea of swirling white clouds.

"Brother Faqing!"

All of a sudden Liangmei was standing before him, a bamboo pole in her hands. Mist had pearled her hair, her big bright eyes were flashing; she had a plastic cape over her shoulders, had rolled up her trouser legs and was wearing rubber sandals. The calves of her legs were crimson with cold. Once again Tian was staggered by her likeness to Xiuxiu.... From the tip of her pole hung some tattered cattail-leaf fans. What could she be up to? He stared at this young daughter of the mountains who had already tasted the full bitterness of life.

"Why are you staring, Brother Faqing? I'm commander-in-chief!"

As if to greet this announcement the ducks set up a lively quacking.

"In charge of ducks? Whose ducks? Aren't you the team's barefoot doctor?" asked Tian curiously, as if new to the place.

"Can't a barefoot doctor have a sideline too? Each

household raises poultry nowadays," she answered rather archly, planting her pole in the ground.

Now Tian could make out white plumage, red webbed feet in the clear green water, as the ducks flapped their wings and chased each other. There seemed to be about three dozen of them.

"Where do you keep them at night, so many ducks?"

"Not in our cottage, obviously. I've built a bamboo enclosure by the brook."

"Not afraid of having them stolen?"

"What an idea! Who steals poultry up here now? And no one from outside's going to climb all this way up the mountain to steal a few ducks."

Liangmei laughed so softly and sweetly that Tian joined in, his face flushing. Yes, the mountaineers seemed to be living well. And their forbears had not been thieves but highwaymen. As for thieves outside, why should they steal ducks? They had TV sets, refrigerators, watches and tape-recorders. After three years away he'd asked questions no child in the mountains would need to ask.

"With all of you raising so many hens and ducks, the brook can't have enough tiddlers and shrimps to feed them. Where do you get the grain?" he couldn't help asking.

"Brother Faqing, you don't understand, but it's not your fault. The policy has changed, relaxing restrictions. Grain can be bought or sold at the fairs. And anyone willing to work can open up wasteland and grow crops on the hillsides."

Here was Liangmei explaining the policy to the man who had been team leader for seven years! Why not just say the policy had changed? "Relaxing restrictions" sounded ominous, as if this policy could be altered any time by the higher-ups. In the hard years, restrictions had been relaxed; when the economy picked up, they had been tightened up again, regardless of the promises that no changes would be made for five or eight years.... Everything else had been fine after Liberation, except for the way the policy chopped and changed. That was why so many villagers had taken advantage of relaxed restrictions to fell trees, open up wasteland and go in for profiteering. Why not make hay while the sun shines?

Liangmei walked along on the bank wielding her pole to drive the ducks upstream. Tian followed, on his way up to Muffin Cliff to see her foster-parents. She kept one eye on the ducks, the other on him. As it was so early and most of the mountaineers were still abed, they did not meet anyone.

They made their way upstream in a silence broken only by the quacking of the ducks dabbling in the brook and the chirping of birds in the trees. Soon they reached the graveyard where the bones of generations of their forbears lay, and where in 1962 Tian, a student in the agricultural school, had disguised himself as a "heavenly general" to frighten Jiang Shigong. He wondered if the old man was still well after all these years. Halting abruptly he asked:

"Liangmei, is Uncle Shigong still in Oxhorn Hollow?"

"He died some years ago." Liangmei stopped too, turning to look at Tian.

"When did he die? How?"

"Three years ago, the night the work team took you away. . . . One story was that he jumped out of his window; another was that he fell over the cliff, spilling out his brains. . . . He wasn't found till the next morning. When we laid him out, we couldn't close his eyes — they were still staring. Everyone said he wanted to go and catch up with the work team, to have a last word with you. . . ."

Liangmei dropped her pole, covered her face with her hands and wept.

Tian's eyes brimmed with blinding tears. . . . He had a mental picture of Jiang Shigong going up with him to Muffin Cliff to find Knock-out Wang that year . . . leading the mountaineers to take an oath by the old team leader's grave . . . sitting in his cottage in Gong Flat, booming out that he was going to splice Knock-out and Sister Mushroom . . . finally falling over the cliff, unwilling to close his eyes even in death.

"Know where he's buried, Liangmei?" With an effort Tian held back his tears.

"In the graveyard. . . . Dad had an inscription carved for him."

Liangmei picked up a stick to beat the dew off the grass, and led Tian over the uneven ground to a low mound under the cliff. It was covered with weeds, long neglected. On the tablet before it was inscribed: Grave of the poor peasant commune member Jiang Shigong. Tian bowed to the tablet in silence. Then, wanting to show more respect, with a glance at Liangmei he went down on both knees. Head lowered he murmured, "Uncle Shigong! Uncle Shigong! Faqing is back . . . cleared of all the charges against him. Faqing isn't a counter-revolutionary. We farmed to suit local conditions, making each household responsible for its own

land, so that our people could live. That wasn't
wrong.... Rest in peace, uncle, close your eyes...."

Liangmei stood stupefied. Before she could reach out
to him, Tian brushed the dew off his knees and stood
up, then strode out of the graveyard without one backward look. The well-disciplined ducks in the brook had
gathered in the shallows to wait for instructions. When
Liangmei flourished her pole again there was a fresh
outburst of jubilant quacking as her charges sent foam
flying.

"Liangmei, I've a question to ask you."

"What is it, Brother Faqing?"

By now, perhaps influenced by the carefree, rollicking
ducks, the two of them felt able to talk more freely.

"How was Old Crow Liu's family driven to Water
Hollow?"

"Oh, how did you know about that?"

"I met him yesterday evening under the red bayberry
half way up the mountain. He looked like a ghost. I
nearly went for him."

"Well . . . serves him right! After your arrest that
spring, word got out that Old Crow Liu had spilled the
beans, the old wretch, when he went to the county
town for fertilizer! Everybody saw red, wanted to slice
him to pieces! His whole family stank, everyone spat
at them. Old Crow Liu was scared stiff. He kept kneeling to dad, protesting that it was someone from Rich
Flats who had blabbed, he'd only spoken carelessly in
his cups to Secretary Liang. Dad couldn't make up his
mind whether to brand him as a traitor or not. . . ."

"Old Crow told me he's a leper now."

"Retribution for his crimes, the old sod. . . . Before
we'd decided what to do to him, his hair and eye-

brows fell out. In two weeks he was completely bald
... so much the better! Everyone said: Serves him
right! Old Man Heaven has eyes. He was afraid to go
to hospital, for fear of being shut up in a lepers' colony.
So we drove his whole family to Water Hollow.
They're not allowed back, not allowed to show their
faces. . . ."

"We were wrong, Liangmei. Wrong!"

"What do you mean?"

"You've been unjust to Old Crow. He wasn't the
one who reported Pagoda Ridge's counter-revolutionary
coup, setting up independent. . . ."

"We wronged Old Crow? I can't believe it. Who
was the informer then? Who sold us out?"

Tian thought of Xiuxiu. But he knew she had not
betrayed them deliberately. They were all victims.

"Tell me, Brother Faqing! Who sold us out?"

"It was a political movement. Understand?"

Liangmei's eyes flashed with surprise, and there was
a speculating look in them. She and Tian both had Xiuxiu in mind. Their hearts were beating fast. They wanted to speak of her, yet both were afraid to name her.

18

Liangmei and Tian drove the ducks past many folds in
the hills till they came to a broad flat strewn with
stones and pebbles. As the mountains all around shut
out the sunlight, the stones were overgrown with moss
and lichen, making the place seem dark and sinister.
And here the brook splayed out through the stones,
scattering to form a network of flowing water. Where
the flat bordered on the mountain, Liangmei had built a

bamboo enclosure in which to feed her ducks and pen them up.

Having driven her flock in here, from a nearby thatched lean-to she fetched half a crate of grain and, holding this with her left hand on one hip she scattered the grain evenly on the ground with the right. The ducks waddled to and fro, craning their long white necks greedily to peck it up.

Tian watched her woodenly. How deft, sturdy and able she was! And on the way she had confided to him that since running away from the forestry station that year she had not remarried. Uncle Knock-out had told her to mind Brother Faqing's stone cottage in Gong Flat, and to sleep there at night until he came back. Tian's cheeks burned, his heart beat fast, as if he had done something wrong and let his wife Xiuxiu down. Having had no news from her for three years he did not know whether she was alive or dead, still living with her mother in Rich Flats or with a second husband far away. All he had heard were some unreliable rumours. . . .

After feeding the ducks Liangmei went into the lean-to to tidy up, emerging without her pole and plastic cape. She had rolled her trousers down and changed into a pair of gym-shoes. How tall, slim and graceful she looked! Tian stared at her so unblinkingly that she reddened and asked rather pertly:

"Well, will you know me next time?"

Tian hastily looked away, muttering:

"Sorry, Liangmei, you remind me so much of my poor Xiuxiu. . . ."

He hung his head. Liangmei sighed.

"Come on, Brother Faqing, I'll take you to see my dad and mum at Muffin Cliff."

She jumped from a stone on to a path up the mountain, leaning down and reaching out to help him up. On the slopes beside this path were neat rows of newly planted cedars, plot after plot. Between these saplings, soft shoots of spring maize had already pushed through the soil in the rain, dew and spring sunshine. Tian was amazed. Three years ago, he remembered quite distinctly, this had been a barren hillside, yet here it was planted with saplings and maize!

"Last year, Brother Faqing, it was decided that anyone who cleared and sowed these slopes could keep the crop. We're better off now in the mountains than ever before." Liangmei answered his unspoken question.

"Ah, so that's the policy. . . . But these private coppices right and left are like a patchwork of big-character posters."

Tian smiled rather bitterly. It seemed to him that after heading this team for so many years he should understand it better, not need all these explanations from Liangmei.

Up and up they climbed through small cultivated plots where thriving safflower carpeted the ground. He had seen this growing on the fertile, well-watered banks of Lake Dongting. So now this rich fodder, this first-rate fertilizer had been planted up here deep in the Wuling Mountains. His eyes lit up. This had been unheard of before.

"Brother Faqing, dad says the best safflower on Pagoda Ridge this spring is in Old Crow Liu's fields in Water Hollow! His family's luck must have turned.

With their safflower already two feet high, they're bound to have a good crop."

She waited with a smile to hear his reaction.

"So now it's all open and aboveboard, eh, the fixing of output quotas for each household?" Tian was suddenly furious, his eyes frightfully dilated.

"That's the policy of the higher-ups now, Brother Faqing. We don't have to do it on the sly any more."

"But because I made each household responsible for its own output, I was forced all those years to be a fake red banner, then sent to a labour camp as a counter-revolutionary!"

"I know. Last winter dad started saying: Now that the policy's changed and our responsibility system is legal, why don't they clear Tian Faqing? Why not send him back? He made me write several letters complaining to the county court."

"That was good of Uncle Knock-out. But I haven't been cleared, just let off lightly, released ahead of time. And even if they cleared me, my family's finished. . . ."

Tian stood as if rooted to the ground, less pleased than wretched over this home-coming. His angry eyes filled with tears. He had lost too much, could never get it back.

Liangmei was shocked by his look of despair and resentment. Tears started to her eyes too. To comfort him for the shame he had undergone she impulsively took his hand.

"Brother Faqing. . . . At least you're back. Try to look on the bright side. The present policy amounts to clearing you. . . . Think of all you did for us. . . . And you're still young and strong. You can make up for what's lost. . . ."

Liangmei's touch and her sympathy warmed Tian's heart. He gripped her hand hard, not caring whether he hurt her, because she was giving him the courage and confidence to start a new life.

"Liangmei, what about Xiuxiu? You should have told me before. What's become of her?"

"I wanted to tell you yesterday evening, but I was afraid to. . . . For three whole years we had no word from you. . . . Brother Faqing, promise me . . . not to take it too much to heart."

"Go on, tell me! Come to the point!"

"All right. Look at you flaring up before I even start. . . . The evening you were arrested, in the spring of '76, didn't Sister Xiuxiu go to Monkey Rock to find you? The next morning after breakfast, without a word to anyone she just stuck a note on your door asking me to mind the place for her, then went down the mountain carrying a bundle. . . . As soon as I read her note the next day, I hurried to Rich Flats. Her parents had no idea what had happened. They said Xiuxiu spent one night at home, looking upset, then went back to Pagoda Ridge. I had to rush back to Gong Flat. But there wasn't a sign of her. I waited and waited. . . . Fed the hens and ducks for her every day, and grazed the buffaloes. . . . But she never came back. . . ."

By now Tian's face was fearfully white, as white as paper. He staggered as if he would fall. Liangmei caught his arm and made him lean on her shoulder.

"But what became of Xiuxiu? Where did she go?"

"Take it easy, Brother Faqing, I'll tell you. . . . Half a year or more I waited, wearing out my eyes watching for her, thinking maybe she was dead, till a letter came. . . ."

"A letter? From where?"

"From Lake Dongting. She'd managed to find out in the county town that you'd been sentenced to labour reform there.... She hadn't the face to go back to Rich Flats, and dared not go back to Pagoda Ridge. So she went by train, bus and steamer to Lake Dongting to look for you. She wanted to join you in your labour camp. But the lake is too big, more than eight hundred *li* around, with over a dozen counties. She asked everywhere, but couldn't find out where you were. And someone told her your sentence was for life. . . . She lost hope, saw no way out, threw herself into the lake. . . . But Heaven had pity on her, a fisherman rescued her. A decent fellow he was, on the old side but a bachelor. . . . Sister Xiuxiu said in her letter, after her narrow escape she was going to be true to you all her life."

Liangmei broke off here and fell sobbing into Tian's arms. Unable to control himself any longer, he pushed her aside and gave way to a storm of weeping. . . . Both sat on the path shedding tears over Xiuxiu's cruel fate. At the same time they found consolation in the fact that she was alive, had not drowned herself in Lake Dongting but found a place of shelter.

They lost track of time, till they realized that the mist was scattering slowly, revealing the outlines of mountains, rocks and trees.... Tian rose to his feet, regretting the rough way he had pushed Liangmei. Tears in his eyes, he bent down and reached out both hands to help her up. She looked at him tearfully but with no sign of resentment.

"Liangmei."

"Yes?"

"The world's turned upside-down, just the two of us left. . . ."

"No, you're forgetting my foster-parents and all the folk on Pagoda Ridge. Dad's team leader in name now. Everyone will welcome you back, we owe so much to you."

"Are Yang Jun and Liang Youru still in charge of the commune?"

"Yang Jun's been promoted. He criticized his mistakes and the masses have made allowances for him. Liang Youru has more problems, his case is still up in the air."

"If Yang Jun has really analysed his mistakes, he may change his mind about Pagoda Ridge, restore my Party membership and make me a cadre again. He may even make us pace-setters in carrying out the line of the Third Plenary Session, farming according to our local conditions and getting on in life by hard work. No one can obstruct the Party policy!"

This incisive statement breathed confidence and strength. Liangmei's face lit up — this was their old Tian Faqing, staunch and unyielding.

"Liangmei."

"Well?"

"I've something to ask you."

"Yes?"

Tian halted and stared at her.

"Do you live on Muffin Cliff too?"

"No, all on my own in Gong Flat. Someone has to stay in the clinic."

"Did you get your share of land? Who's tilling it for you?"

"My land. . . . It's waiting for you to till it, Brother Faqing!"

But as soon as these words left her lips Liangmei cried, "Mother!" Then flushing crimson she turned away to cover her face in her hands.

This exclamation was also a crude swear word. She should never have blurted it out. Tian reeled with the shock. Still, he got a grip on himself and told her with deep feeling:

"Dear Liangmei . . . you were right to say the Party policy's cleared me, but I've let poor Xiuxiu down. This year I'm going to repair the graves of your father and Uncle Shigong. Next year I'll have saved enough cash to make a trip to Lake Dongting to see Xiuxiu."

"Brother Faqing, look, aren't those my foster-parents coming down from Muffin Cliff! They'll be overjoyed to see you. . . ."

The clouds parted, the sun came out, scattering the mist. The sky was high, the air clear on this fine early spring day in the Wuling Mountains.

1981

The Log Cabin Overgrown
with Creepers

FOR many years the story of a Yao girl has been told
in the forests of the Wujie Hills, a young woman called
Pan Qingqing, or Azure, who was a tree warden deep
in those ancient and mysterious forests. She was born,
grew up and married in the hills, and in all her life she
only once went to the forestry station, which was itself
remote enough. The young men there had only heard
of this marvellous woman but had never set eyes on her.
Her family had lived in Green Hollow for generations
in a log cabin overgrown with creepers, a cabin built of
fir trunks so strong that no axe would make an impression on them or wild boar shake them. The parts of the
trunks that were sunk into the ground had long since
turned black and grown layer upon layer of wavy
mushrooms in lace-like patterns. Behind the cabin a
mountain stream ran clear throughout the year.

The cabin's links with the outside world were a
narrow track and a telephone line that had been put up
before the "cultural revolution" to carry fire reports but
had been cut by a heavy fall of snow one winter. Since
the beginning of the "cultural revolution" there had
been a never-ending succession of bosses at the forestry
station, and they had all been too busy cooking their
political pies to send anyone to reconnect the line, so

that this symbol of modern civilization no longer reached this ancient forest. But for the occasional sound of a hen, a dog or a baby from the cabin and the column of light blue smoke rising from its stove the thousands of acres of woodland around Green Hollow would have been peacefully sleeping day and night. Not all the songs of the birds in the hills and all the blossoms opening and falling on them would ever have woken it.

Azure had lost both her parents early. Her husband was a Han Chinese called Wang Mutong, a tall, powerfully built man strong enough to kill a tiger. Husband and wife were both forest wardens. Mutong liked a couple of cups of Azure's corn wine before his meals, and except that he got drunk occasionally and beat her black and blue he was not a bad husband. He cared for his wife, never sending her up the hills to fetch firewood, of which he always kept plenty ready cut in stacks. He did not make her cut and clear firebreaks through the trees, and for over ten years there had never been a forest fire in Green Hollow. Nor did he expect her to till the soil and plant the crops. He saw to it that their big plot of land by the stream always had more onions, pumpkins and other fresh vegetables than the four of them could eat. All that Azure had to do was to feed the pigs, suckle the babies, wash, make and mend the clothes, and look after the house. At twenty-six or twenty-seven she was still as lively and fresh as an unmarried girl. Mutong could not read a word but he was bursting with self-confidence and he knew everything. He felt that he was the real master of Green Hollow: the woman was his, the children were his, and the cabin and the hills were his, though of course he did come under the forestry station. As the leadership had sent him to look after this part of the forest, that made him like a minor vassal in charge of his own fief. Before she'd had the babies Azure had often asked to visit the forestry station that was some 45 kilometres away but he had never let her go, sometimes hitting her savagely or even forcing her to kneel for long periods as a punishment. He was afraid that if his beautiful wife had her eyes opened by that lively, bustling place she would start getting fancy ideas. She might have been led astray by those smooth and pushy young men at the station. He only stopped worrying after she had given him the babies, first the boy and then the girl, which left her firmly tied to his belt and truly his woman. It was now the turn of the younger generation to be hit and forced to kneel. He ran the whole household by strict rules. The places of husband and wife, as of father and children, were all clearly set out in Green Hollow. Differences of status counted for a lot in this miniature society.

Mutong and Azure lived in virtual isolation from the world. It would be an exaggeration to say that she followed him in everything, but they were both used to each other and they got along without trouble. Mutong would go to the forestry station once a month to collect their wages and bring back the rice, oil and salt for the family. Every time he came back he would tell her what had been happening at the station and the news he had heard there. Azure would listen with her dark and gleaming eyes opened wide and her mind filled with amazement. It was as if her husband were describing some foreign country on the other side of the world. In the last few years her husband had been telling her a lot about young students rebelling and making trouble.

Teachers who wore glasses were being dragged around the hills with placards on them like performing monkeys. The forestry expert who had studied for half a lifetime was supposed to have drowned himself in a little pond so shallow that he had not even got his back wet. "We're better off as we are in Green Hollow. The gleaming black earth here is ever so fertile. You just have to stick a piece of firewood into the ground for it to grow and come into leaf. We're not educated. We bother nobody and nobody bothers us."

Some of what her husband said Azure understood and some she didn't. She was thoroughly confused, and was worried for those learned scholars who lived beyond their hills. Book-learning was a disaster, and she found herself thinking that she and her husband were lucky to have avoided it. She had heard him saying "We're better off as we are in Green Hollow" so often that she came to believe it herself. She did not ask much of her husband, but simply wished that he would not hit her too hard when he lost his temper and started laying about him. Every evening at nightfall they shut the door of their cabin and went to bed. Half a pint of paraffin that he brought back from the station was enough to keep that lamp burning six months. Only when the moon and the stars happened to shine in through the wooden-framed windows set high in the walls could they spy on how the couple spent their nights.

"Azure, I want you to give me more babies."

"We've got Little Tong and Little Qing. You told me the forestry station won't let people have big families any more. Don't women have to be sterilized?"

"Never mind that. Five more wouldn't be too many."

"Don't you care about how I'll have to suffer?"

"Suffer? Women don't mind a bit of suffering at child-birth."

"I'm scared of the people at the station telling us off."

"To hell with that. The worst they can do is refuse to give us extra grain rations. We've got soil and water here in Green Hollow. Just look at my hands: they're as big as rice-measures. Do you think I couldn't raise a few more kids? I'll clear a cotton field next winter, and you can fetch the spinning wheel and handloom your mum left you and clean them up."

"Get on with you. You think I'm a pheasant that you can keep in these hills."

"You're mine."

Azure said no more as her husband held her tucked under his armpit that smelled so sharply of sweat. She was very docile. She belonged to him. If he wanted to beat or swear at her that was only as it should be. She was in the bloom of youth, and could bear children as painlessly as a tree bearing fruit. When she fed the babies the milk flowed endlessly like sap from her white breasts. Her husband was young and strong. He could kill a tiger or catch a wild boar. When he embraced her, his arms were like a ring of iron; they did what husbands and wives probably do in other places, and he had so much strength it was as if he did not know what to do with it.

In the summer of 1975 the One-hander came to Green Hollow. Let there be no confusion: he was not a man in authority but a city youngster who had come to settle on the forestry station in 1964. His real name was Li Xingfu and they said he had been born in the year of

Liberation, 1949. He was tall, slender and rather elegant, and quick at selecting seeds and looking after saplings. He knew how to get on with any of the forestry workers or officials he met. But he had been carried away by his enthusiasm for travelling around the country exchanging revolutionary experience as a Red Guard in 1966, and had left a perfectly good hand lying by the railway track when hitching a ride on a train. From then on one of his sleeves had hung empty. After a few years hanging around in the city he had come back to the forestry station and this was when the workers there had nicknamed him the One-hander. From then on the station's leadership had been down on him. They had telephoned each of the felling districts and forest management teams but they had all refused to take him. Apart from the fact that the One-hander could no longer do heavy manual work he had been one of the "young revolutionary warriors". If he started exchanging revolutionary experience in some mountain hollow he would be as useless as a piece of wet beancurd dropped in a pile of ash that you couldn't either blow or wipe clean. One day, while Wang Mutong, the warden of Green Hollow, came to the station to fetch the grain for his family the station's political director bumped into him. Smiting himself on the back of the neck the political director thought: Yes! Why not send Li Xingfu off to Green Hollow to be a forest warden with Wang Mutong and his wife? The work was not too light or too heavy but just right, and on top of that there was nobody else for dozens of miles around apart from the very reliable and straightforward Wang Mutong and his wife. There was no one Li Xingfu could exchange revolutionary experiences with but

monkeys and pheasants. Wang Mutong's first reaction
to being given someone to work under his leadership
was delight, which turned to disgust when he realized
that this subordinate Li Xingfu was the One-hander.
"Wang, my friend, you've been wanting to join the
Party for years, haven't you? This is a test that our
organization is setting you," said the political director,
slapping him on the shoulder. "You'll have no problem
keeping him in order — he's only got one hand. I'll
have a word with him myself in a moment and make
him agree to three conditions: in Green Hollow he'll
have to obey your instructions in everything, he'll have
to report everything to you, and he'll have to get your
permission if he wants to leave the hollow. Show a bit
of spirit. Try to reform this educated youngster who's
gone wrong." Only then had Wang nodded his assent
and decided to take the test that the organization was
setting him by shouldering the burden of "education
and reform".

Thus the One-hander had come to Green Hollow and
become an important new member of the little society
headed by Wang Mutong. Some twenty or thirty paces
from their own ancient log cabin Wang Mutong and his
wife built him a little, low cabin with walls of upright
logs and a roof of fir bark on the bank of the jade-clear
mountain stream. The new cabin and the old, the little
one and the big one, became neighbours. At first Wang
Mutong had felt no hostility towards the One-hander
and liked being called Elder Brother Wang by him.

The One-hander was captivated from the very first
by the beauty and peace of Green Hollow. Every day
Wang Mutong would send him to sit in the watchtower
on the ridge, so that each morning he would climb the

narrow path that snaked through the mists of the great forest. It was like walking in a very hazy dream. The milky-white mist that covered the mountain and filled the valley was so thick it seemed to be a liquid on which you could float. When the sun showed through and the mists began to disperse at nine or ten in the morning he felt he was in another, enchanted world as he sat in the watchtower on the ridge with the brilliant greens of the foliage above him and below his feet clumps of tall Guangdong pines and Chinese hemlock trees rising through the rolling mist. But the One-hander knew the woods and the valley were no fairyland. He was aware that Wang Mutong and his wife were both young, and that she was tender and beautiful, with big, dark eyes that could talk and sing, although she tactfully kept a proper distance between them. But young people cannot bear loneliness. Was he destined to exchange experiences and make friends only with the golden monkeys, the thrushes and the grouse in this green valley?

Wang Mutong's boy Little Tong was seven and his daughter, Little Qing, five. At first the children had been rather afraid of "one-arm", but the situation had changed after the One-hander caught Little Tong some birds, brought Little Qing back some blossoms from the mountains to wear in her hair, and let her look at herself in a little mirror. The children started to call him "Uncle Li" or "Elder brother". A few days later Little Tong insisted on going to sleep in the One-hander's cabin and refused to go back when his mother called for him. Mountain children are lovable in their own special way. When a snake slithered into the little cabin, making the One-hander shake with terror, Little Tong told him that snakes never bit people unless they were trodden on. Little Tong went on to tell him with graphic imitations about the three kinds of snake in Green Hollow. "Green bamboo snakes are very lazy. They usually lie coiled up in the bamboo without moving." He put his head back, closed his eyes, and pursed his lips as he went on, "They spit their poison out like this" — he blew through his lips — "to lure birds, and as soon as the bird comes close they pounce and get a good bite on it. Then they coil round the bamboo again and take their time eating it up. The shouting snake is different. Its skin's the same colour as mud. It looks terrific going through the grass. It rears up about waist high, pushing the grass aside, like this." He made his eyes bulge, opened his mouth wide, and kept stretching his head forward. "It goes 'Hoo, hoo', and it's really scary. There's another sort that's thick as a chopper handle and as long as a carrying-pole. Dad calls it a forty-eighter, and when it goes along it shakes its head all over the place. You'd think it was crazy." The One-hander, afraid that Little Tong was going to do another imitation, put his hand on the boy's head and asked, "How do you know all that?" "I've seen green bamboo snakes myself and Dad told me about the shouting snakes and the forty-eighters. Dad catches snakes and sells them outside the mountains." The One-hander looked at the boy, of an age to be going to school, imitating the snakes, thought of that long, cold thing slithering out of the cabin, and felt miserably sad.

Adults observe children and children observe adults. The One-hander brushed his teeth and rinsed his mouth out every morning. Little Qing always poked half of her face out of the door of their cabin to gaze wide-eyed at this amazing sight. One morning she came timidly over and asked, "Uncle, does your mouth smell bad?" The One-hander, whose mouth was full of toothpaste, did not understand what she meant.

"If your mouth doesn't smell bad why do you rub it with that brush every day?"

The One-hander had to laugh. When he had finished washing his face he said to Little Qing, "Ask your mum to buy you and Little Tong a toothbrush one day and brush your teeth every morning. Then they'll be lovely and white."

Little Qing was not convinced. "Mum never uses a brush, and her teeth are lovely and white."

"Does your mum's mouth ever have a nasty smell?" the One-hander asked, trying to press home his argument.

"She loves kissing me, and her mouth smells ever so nice. If you don't believe me kiss her yourself and see."

"Stop talking such nonsense, you little devil. Come back at once," Little Qing's mother called from inside their cabin.

The One-hander's face felt hot and his heart pounded as if he had just done something wicked. He shot back into his own little cabin.

It was a trivial incident, but Wang Mutong had heard. He dragged Little Qing to the doorway of their cabin and made her kneel there as a punishment. It was obvious that he wanted the One-hander to see. Although nothing suspicious had happened he now had eyes in the back of his head and was on his guard.

The life of the two households in Green Hollow flowed as calmly as the jade-green mountain brook behind the cabins. Although the deep places only came up to your calves and the shallow parts just covered your heel it could reflect the dancing trees, the clear blue sky and the leisurely floating clouds. It now reflected something new, a tall fir pole that the One-hander had put up outside his wooden cabin: a radio aerial.

This was to stir up trouble. The little black box in the One-hander's cabin could talk and sing. It broke the immemorial silence of the night among the ancient mountain forests. At first only the children took their courage in their hands to go to listen to it in the little cabin after nightfall, but after a while Azure herself began to drop in for a while on the pretext of fetching them home to bed. Of course, the next thing every evening was for Wang Mutong to appear to take his wife and children back to bed. Once his tone of voice was a little rough and "It's too early," Azure answered back with something like petulance. "If we go to bed the moment it gets dark I hate having to wait so long for daybreak." When Wang Mutong heard his wife say that she hated the long wait in bed till dawn a dark cloud fell over his heart. The tall and strongly built forester never went to listen to the devilish voices singing in the black box. He was going to preserve his inviolable dignity as a man and watch closely to stop things from developing any further.

Soon afterwards the One-hander organized Azure and the children to tidy up the piece of ground between the two cabins and make neat stacks of firewood and other things by the doors. The muddy and uneven ground that used to be filthy with dogshit and pig's urine was now level and clean. The One-hander said that he wanted to plant flowers there and teach Azure and the children to read and do the radio exercises. The thought made Azure's face all smiles. The children followed the One-hander round all day, and it was always "Uncle says this" or "Uncle says that's wrong". Anyone would think he was closer to them than their own father. This upset Wang Mutong, who did not like what he saw. Although the One-hander had only one arm he was gradually changing life in Green Hollow, like a worm silently turning the earth over. "Bloody show-off. He wants to impress us all in Green Hollow with his education. Anyone would think he's better than me."

He was not surprised when the One-hander made four suggestions about the work. The first was that the forestry station should be asked to repair the telephone line that had been out of action for years and to install a loudspeaker for cable radio between the two cabins. The second was that they should put up painted wooden notices on all the mountain paths into Green Hollow with the Forestry Code on them. The third was that he and Wang Mutong should have a system for patrolling the mountains and fire-watching with two eight-hour shifts a day; when on duty they should not make traps with bent saplings, dig up edible roots, or do any other work on their own account. The fourth was that there should be a politics and literacy class that the children could join in. When Azure heard this suggestion she smiled and gave her husband a wordless look with her big, bright eyes that obviously said, "Look how educated he is. He has such clever ideas — they sound wonderful."

Wang Mutong saw all this at once. It was very painful. His face went hard, he tightened his lips, and his eyes spat fury. "You smell good, don't you, just like a brand-new latrine," they seemed to say. "You can keep your fancy nonsense." He glared savagely at his wife then said to the One-hander very bluntly, "City boy! They always used to say that a stranger should follow the local customs, and the guest do what suits the host. You may not be a guest, but you're certainly not the host. There hasn't been a forest fire here in fifteen or twenty years. All the leaders we've had in the forests of the Wujie Hills have always said my work's good. I've been a model worker every year. I don't need any wires or boards or shifts or classes. You'd better sharpen your billhook and get yourself fit. The forestry station made me the boss here. The three conditions the political director told you about weren't just hot air."

Wang Mutong was an intimidating sight as he stood there, his arms akimbo and his eyes flaming with anger. The One-hander gazed wide-eyed with horror, his mouth hanging open and his face pale from shock. Azure could not bear to see it, but she dared not provoke her husband's savage and violent fury by showing her own anger or speaking out of turn, so she could only try to ease the tension by saying to the One-hander, "Li, he's not very educated. He talks a bit rough. . . ." But when she saw that her husband was on the point of exploding she shut up. "Rough I may be," Wang Mutong said with a mocking laugh, "I suppose you're very smooth. The roughs control the smoothies these days. The roughs are in charge, Li Xingfu. Don't you forget that the leadership sent you here to be educated and remoulded." With that he turned his massive body away and stormed off, putting his feet down so hard that they left deep footprints.

The One-hander's four suggestions had run up against

the rock of Wang Mutong and disappeared without trace. He felt deflated. Yes, he had been sent to Green Hollow to be educated and reformed, but he could not help feeling afraid of Wang Mutong. He knew that there was very little he could do to improve his present state, but he was full of energy and could not let himself stay idle, because idleness made him depressed, lonely, fed up with life, and thinking he would do better to jump off a precipice and be done with it. He had two books that he had kept from before the "cultural revolution": *Trees* and *A Forest Fire Prevention Manual*. He took *Trees* with him on his daily patrols of the mountains and taught himself to recognize the hundreds of different kinds of broadleafed evergreens that grew there with the help of the illustrations in the book. To prevent his time here from being completely wasted he decided to do a survey of the forestry resources of Green Hollow that would be of use when felling began in the future. Thinking that Azure would understand him he told her of his plan, and she was as warm and friendly with him as if he'd been her own brother. "Silly thing. Go ahead and do it, but don't talk about it to anyone else." "Won't Wang mind?" "You won't be doing anything wrong. You...." When she said "You...." she drew the word out. Her dark eyes shone so bright he could see himself reflected in them; they shone straight into his heart. He was afraid to look into them, though he did not know why. Azure's "You...." echoed over and over again in his heart.

It was autumn. The One-hander collected the seeds of some rare and valuable trees, including a rare fir, golden-leaf magnolias and south China camphor trees that he intended to raise in a little nursery. He planned to carry them into the forestry station later as seedlings for the technicians to raise. Some land had to be burnt and cleared for his nursery, and as he knew that Wang Mutong would not be at all interested he had to ask Azure to help him.

That day Wang Mutong was in the mountains setting traps. The One-hander and Azure had chosen the slope where wild aubergines grew next to the vegetable patch, a piece of land that Wang Mutong was intending to clear for cotton. They set it alight and soon thick smoke was billowing out above the roaring wind and flames. The two of them were relaxed and happy, laughing and shouting like brother and sister. They never expected Wang Mutong to come rushing down the mountainside in a high temper. He glared coldly at them, took the billhook from his belt and cut down a little pine tree that he wielded with both hands to put the fire out. The One-hander tried to explain, but Wang Mutong gave him a terrible glare and roared, "Cut out this new-fangled nonsense! I've got other plans for this land. Li Xingfu, write a self-criticism tonight for burning land without my permission." "Who am I to hand it to?" "Who to? Do you think that just because I don't read I can't be your leader? I'm telling you, you'd better behave yourself when you're under me." Hearing these awful things said Azure gave her husband a tearful look. "Go back and feed the pigs — the swill must be cooked by now," he said as harshly as if he were some malevolent deity.

The One-hander stole a lingering look filled with pity at Azure and watched her turn and go back without saying a word, wiping her tears away with the back of her hand.

Everyone needs to feel self-confidence and self-respect. Fail to mend a little crack and a yawning gap will open up: even the earth itself will split open. Wang Mutong felt that the One-hander had flung down a challenge. His own wife was getting out of hand: she wasn't as docile and tender as she used to be.

One day Wang Mutong had to go to the forestry station to fetch the family's grain. Normally he would spend the night there, but this time for some peculiar reason he had felt very uneasy as soon as he set out that morning. There was a worry nagging at him that he could not get out of his mind. He was a powerfully built man and his blood was up, so he did the journey of some ninety kilometres there and back the same day, with a load of sixty kilogrammes of rice on the return leg. When he got back that night he stank of sweat. The door of his cabin was half open and the lamp was still on. His wife must still be up. That was odd. He went inside to find nobody there. Then he heard laughter and singing coming from the One-hander's hut. He felt the stove: It was cold. He was now ablaze with an anger that nothing was going to calm down. He rushed out and stood outside the One-hander's window. He could see it all clearly: his own wife sitting with her chin in her hands, Little Tong leaning against her knees, and both of them listening with rapt attention to a woman singing devilish songs in that accursed box. And the One-hander had Little Qing on his knee with his face touching hers. He could hear that the song coming from the black box was a Yao love song.

"It's lovely. My mum loved singing it when she was alive. . . ." Wang Mutong could see his wife's eyes shining devilishly as she gazed at the One-hander so sweetly. "You Yaos have always been wonderful singers and dancers. . . ." The One-hander was looking at her in that shameless way too. Wang Mutong could bear to see no more. He had to control the flames of his anger to stop himself from shouting obscenities when he said, "Little Tong, Little Qing, like going to the music hall, do you? Is this your way of shortening the wait till daybreak?" Only then did Azure realize that her husband was back. Pulling Little Tong with one hand and Little Qing with the other she rushed to the door. "Just look at you, you're so worn out you're soaked in sweat," she said. "Why didn't you spend the night at the station?" He ignored her, and by keeping his teeth clenched he prevented himself from saying something that he did not want to say: "If I'd stayed the night at the station I dare say you'd have spent it at his place."

Back in their own cabin Azure quickly lit the stove and heated his water while cooking him a meal. She did not warm him up any wine because she was afraid he might beat her up if he got drunk. That night Wang Mutong showed exceptional restraint. His silence was terrifying, freezing the atmosphere in the hut. He gave himself a rub down and washed his feet with the warm water then went to bed and to sleep without a word, paying no attention to the food his wife had set on the table. She seemed to understand what was upsetting him: several times she tried to make up with him by pushing hard at his naked back with both her hands, but he lay there as heavy and immobile as a gunpowder barrel. It was terrifying.

Wang Mutong was not only physically strong: he could work things out and think for himself. He felt that his position in Green Hollow was under threat, and the spark of mutiny was spreading from Azure to Little Tong and Little Qing. Was he going to sit there calmly watching the One-hander gradually luring away his wife and his children? Was an upright, tough and hard-working model forest warden going to be beaten by a weedy little one-armed city boy sent to the countryside? He decided to start by consolidating his position in his own cabin. The next morning his face was set and his eyes glaring as he announced in a voice like thunder, "Little Tong, Little Qing, kneel to your father! Kneel! Now, listen. From today onwards if either of you or your mum sets one foot inside the little cabin I'll gouge your eyes out and break your legs." Azure's face went pale as she heard this ban being proclaimed. Little Tong's and Little Qing's teeth were chattering as they knelt behind her. They were trembling like a pair of saplings in a cold wind.

Before the One-hander set out to work Wang Mutong went to his cabin to ask for the self-criticism he had demanded several days before. When the One-hander said he had not yet written it he said, "Do you think that what I say is just hot air that counts for nothing? I tell you frankly, Li Xingfu, that the leadership at the station put you completely in my power. From now onwards you won't be allowed to talk or act out of turn. All you'll be allowed to do is behave yourself. I'm giving you another day's grace. I want your written self-criticism first thing tomorrow morning."

Wang Mutong glared at him with his leopard eyes and shook two fists that were like sledge-hammers as he went on to lay down three new rules. "Listen! As from today you will report to me every evening here in your cabin on what you've done each day. If you're busy you can ask me for leave, and when you're not busy don't come into my cabin whenever you feel like it. And, thirdly, if you try to lead anyone in my family astray with that devilish box of yours you'll catch it from my fists. With just one finger I could pull out your fir pole with that wire on it and throw them over the hill."

He worked along two lines: internal pacification and resistance to outsiders. He also took some practical steps to enforce his prohibitions. Previously they had always gone past the One-hander's cabin whenever they left their own hut to take the dirt track that led east to the forestry station or to cross the stream westwards to sit in the fire watchtower on the mountain or to patrol. Wang Mutong now wielded his pick and shovel to cut a new path for his family. Of course, this meant making a detour of a good hundred paces when going to the mountain or the station.

This was the situation that the One-hander had no choice but to accept. Wang Mutong's status and position in Green Hollow was as strong and stable as that of a ruler of an ancient forest kingdom and it brooked no questioning. He had never gone to the One-hander's cabin very often before, but now that his wife and children dared not come any more he would go and sit there every evening to hear the One-hander's report on what he had done that day. He evidently enjoyed this taste of being a powerful leader and kept the One-hander as docile and well controlled as a so-called class enemy.

Thus it was that the One-hander withdrew into his little cabin like a snail pulling back into its shell. Even the songs from the little black box were quieter now. In the face of harsh reality, which had once again given him a black eye, the One-hander had to admit that he was beaten. Life in Green Hollow went back to its usual sleepy pace.

The weather was very odd that winter: it thundered constantly but there was no snow. Older people took it as an omen of a winter and spring drought. Every morning Green Hollow's vast ancient forest was hung with hoar frost shaped like dog's teeth, and the evergreens seemed to be wearing suits of jade sewn together with silver thread. It was a gleaming white world that did not disappear before noon. The two cabins at the bottom of the valley were crowned every morning with white jade, and the gurgling flow of the mountain stream behind them was now silenced by the hard shell that lay on it.

On these freezing frosty days Azure had no work to do outside apart from feeding the pigs twice and cooking a couple of meals, so she would turn out her basket of rags to sew soles for the children's shoes. When her husband took Little Tong and Little Qing out to play in the hills Azure would sit by the stove with a piece of cloth in her hands. Sometimes she would sit there lost in thought for half a morning. Every day Wang Mutong would bring back hares and badgers that he had caught on the mountains and take off their skins to be nailed up on the wall. The fat meat being stewed in the earthenware pot could be smelt for miles around. The strange thing was that the smell of the meat now made Azure feel sick, just as if she were expecting again. A great stone was crushing her heart, and underneath it there was still something alive. Her husband had been beating her a lot recently and she was covered in bruises. She could scarcely breathe in peace from morning till night as she watched his expression and his eyes. When he started hitting her she could only hope that his fists would land on her back or her legs or other places that did not matter. She wept till her tears ran dry and then till they flowed again; her fate was so bitter, and her husband so cruel. She felt that it was only the One-hander who respected her and treated her as a human being. That tyrant of a husband treated her like a criminal. She felt as sorry for the lad as she did for herself. But she was angry with him too. Of all the places he could have gone to why did it have to be Green Hollow? He'd ruined their lives.

The worst thing of all now for Azure was smelling her husband's acrid sweat in bed at night. Many nights of silent weeping gradually developed a spirit of resistance in her. Every evening when she went to bed she would obstinately turn her face to the wall. She might have been nailed there: she would not turn over however much he tugged and pushed. "I'll kill you," he muttered through teeth clenched in fury. "Go ahead!" "Whore! You just want your fancy man." "Are you going to beat me again? He'll hear, and the story will get out." "Bitch!" "Help! Mum! Hit me again I'll scream." Azure now had the courage to stand up to her husband. She did not know why, but he was afraid of the One-hander hearing their secrets, and she was worried too about him knowing how she was mistreated and beaten every night.

Life can be very abnormal, and so too can emotions. Azure felt herself changing, though she did not know whether it was for the better or the worse. This freezing cold winter she wanted to dress herself up a little, which she had not before. She now liked wearing the silver gray woollen headscarf that she normally kept at the bottom of her trunk and her rose-red corduroy outer jacket. She kept herself as clean and tidy all day as if she were just about to go visiting, and even filled the copper basin her mother had left her with clear water from the stream to look at her own reflection. Some years ago she had asked her husband to buy her a looking-glass to hang on the wall from the forestry station, but every time he came back he said that he had forgotten. Now she realized that he had been doing it deliberately. He had been afraid that she'd see how pretty she was: a face like the moon, bright eyes, a mouth like a petal of red magnolia wet with dew, and two dimples. She looked lovely when she smiled and lovely when she didn't. Anyone would fancy her. The One-hander? No! How shameful. Her heart started to beat wildly. Her mind was in a whirl. She covered her burning cheeks with her hands and would not look up. It was as if she had done something wicked. Recently she hadn't been able to stop herself stealing looks at the One-hander's little hut. The strange thing was that the more her husband refused to let her go there the more attractive it seemed to her. The One-hander's radio, soap, face-cream, and all those other amazing things from the four corners of the globe were as alluring as a new world. Li Xingfu's name Xingfu meant "happiness", but was that skinny, pale-faced lad happy? Every day he had to chop the firewood, wash his clothes and cook his meals, all single-handed, and he did not so much as glance at her. When he saw Wang Mutong the poor thing looked as if he'd seen a tiger. She felt sympathy, tenderness for him often with the bewitching shyness of a Yao girl.

Once the One-hander came back from the forestry station with some sweets wrapped in silver and gold paper that he slipped unobtrusively into the children's hands. Little Qing was clever enough to unwrap one of them and pop it into her mother's mouth. Azure at once hugged her daughter tight and kissed her over and over again on the lips. "Little Qing," she asked as if in dream, "does your mum's mouth have a nasty taste?" "No, no." "Does it taste sweet?" "Yes, very sweet." Heavens! What a thing to be saying to her own daughter! She blushed deeply, and as the sweet in her mouth slowly dissolved the delicious juice seemed to flow straight down into her heart. She covered her daughter's soft pink cheeks with her own sweet kisses. Her strict husband saw none of this, and it was none of his business. If he had seen her he might have killed her there and then.

One day when Wang Mutong had gone into the mountains to set tree traps Azure went to the stream to fetch a bucket of water. She saw the One-hander rinsing his clothes in the water so icy it cut to the marrow of the bone. His only hand was red with cold. Putting the bucket down she went over to him, took the clothes, and started rinsing them out for him. He stood up at once and took a couple of paces back. "You shouldn't, Azure," he said. "If Wang sees you he'll. . . ."

She carried on rinsing without looking up. "Why shouldn't I? I'm not doing anything wrong."

"I know. . . . But he'll hit you again."

She stopped for a moment, not moving.

"Look. Your arm's all purple."

"Shut up, you fool. One of the pigs charged me in the sty."

It took all her self-control to hold back the tears that welled up. She longed to run somewhere where she could howl aloud. She rubbed and shook out his clothes several more times, then picked them out of the water, wrung them till they were a huge twisted knot, and dropped them without a word in his galvanized pail. She did not look back at him as she picked up her bucket and went, forgetting all about the water she had come to fetch. Once back in her cabin she leant against the door, weak in the limbs and completely drained of strength. Her heart was pounding so hard it seemed to be about to leap out of her chest. She did not cry. Indeed, she wanted to laugh. This was the first time in her life she had done something for another man behind her husband's back. This terrifying first time comes sooner or later in everyone's life. After the pounding of her heart had subsided Azure felt happy for a very long time. Her husband noticed nothing when he came back from the hills that night. She had won a victory.

The winter drought and the freeze went on till the end of the year. The branches of many of the broad-leaved evergreens around Green Hollow were stripped bare, and they stretched their withered bony arms out to heaven like so many starving and thirsty old men. The hillsides were thickly covered in fallen leaves of every shape and colour that rustled as they blew around in the frosty wind, making the mountains resplendent with their rich colours of gold and jade.

The long drought made it impossible for the One-hander to go on lying low in his little cabin. He was up before dawn every morning to patrol the mountains with his billhook at his belt and his fire prevention manual under his arm. Several times he plucked up his courage to suggest to Wang Mutong that they ought to clear all the firebreaks and sweep the dead leaves from the paths. Because of his hostility to the One-hander Wang Mutong paid no attention to him and ignored nearly all of his suggestions. Wang Mutong was in charge of Green Hollow, and other people had better keep their mouths shut and stop being so bloody keen. But this time the One-hander had some kind of premonition and he did not give in. He decided to take some precautions himself. He persuaded Azure to clear all the undergrowth, firewood, dead leaves and fallen branches away from the two log cabins. He also used every spare moment he had to read aloud from his fire prevention manual to the children, which really amounted to reading it to their parents too. One morning Wang Mutong heard a conversation between the One-hander and Little Tong.

"Uncle Li, what does 'running into the wind' mean?"

"If there's a forest fire you can get away by running towards where it's coming from."

"Uncle, what do we do if our cabin catches fire?"

"Go and crouch down in the stream. Stay on this side where there aren't any big trees."

"Rubbish!" Wang Mutong was going to hear no more. "You're trying to bring us bad luck, talking like that." Having scared the boy off with his angry words he turned to the One-hander and demanded, "Li Xingfu, are you planning on starting a forest fire in Green Hollow?"

The question left the One-hander dumbfounded.

"Why else do you spend all day thinking about how to escape from one?"

"Brother Wang, fires and floods are cruel things."

"In that case do you think that there's bound to be a bush fire in Green Hollow this winter?" Wang Mutong contemptuously snatched the fire prevention manual from Li Xingfu's hand, flicked through it a couple of times without being able to read a word and threw it back to him. "I suppose this teaches you how to tell fortunes. You know what's going to happen, do you?"

"Brother Wang, the drought's gone on for so long and the hills are covered with fallen leaves. Every night the radio says...." The One-hander always looked sordid, guilty, pale and weak in Wang Mutong's presence. The word "radio" made Wang Mutong laugh derisively. "Has that black box of yours been singing any of those disgusting love songs recently?"

The One-hander did not know whether he wanted to laugh or to cry. Keeping a straight face, he replied, "Wang, I've got a suggestion to make. Shouldn't we put in a request to the forestry station asking them to get the telephone line repaired? Otherwise if there were an emergency here by any remote chance we'd have no way of contacting the outside world."

"If you want to make your request, go to the station and make it. I'll give you two days' leave. Why don't you see if they'll send a firefighting team to Green Hollow while you're about it?" Wang Mutong gave the One-hander a mocking glance, yawned unconcernedly, and added, "I can tell you without boasting that in the twenty or thirty years I've lived here I've never seen a forest fire."

After the evening meal Wang Mutong went to the

One-hander's little cabin as usual. What the One-hander found different this evening was that instead of his usual hectoring manner as if he were dealing with a public enemy Wang Mutong spoke very pleasantly. "Young Li, you're planning to go to the station, aren't you? I wonder if you could do me a favour." He produced a sheet of paper that he had brought with him and asked the One-hander to write out his application to join the Party. This was surprising enough, but the next thing was that Wang Mutong put his finger in his mouth and bit it open with a loud crunch. He waved the bleeding finger in front of the One-hander's face as if it were a tiny flag. "Soak your brush in this and write it quick for me. 'Dear forestry station leadership, I'm writing this letter in blood to apply for Party membership. I'm not educated, I'm a rough person, but I have a red heart and I do what the Party tells me....'" The horrified One-hander quickly found a battered old writing brush, soaked it in the fresh blood from Wang Mutong's finger, and wrote the application in blood as quickly as he could. The very sight of the blood made him tremble. He was covered in cold sweat.

When the blood letter was written Wang Mutong folded it up carefully and put into an inner pocket next to his skin. When it came down to it he could not trust the One-hander and allow a political unreliable to hand his sacred application in to the station.

The next morning Wang Mutong was out burning the undergrowth by his vegetable garden, which he was planning to extend. He had not ever bandaged up the wound on his finger. He was a good worker and already had about a quarter of a hectare of land cleared for vegetables. The station required him and his wife to raise three pigs a year. These had to be smoked and handed over as cured meat at the end of the year; the rest they could slaughter and eat themselves. He cared nothing about ideology and isms, but he trusted the Party just as he trusted himself. He liked the Party and the Party liked him, and he reckoned that the Party ought to consist of people like himself. He collected huge piles of fallen branches and leaves, rotten stalks and dead plants from the hillside that he carried to his plot to burn. He collected ashes for fertilizer like this every year, and winter drought or no winter drought this year was going to be no different. The One-hander was very worried about him doing it in so dry a winter, but he did not dare say anything to Wang Mutong's face. He slept badly at night, troubled by nightmares of monstrous and terrible fires as beautiful as sunsets, fires flowing like great rivers. On two nights he got up quietly, went to cut himself a fir sapling from the hillside, and stood on guard by the bonfire that Wang Mutong had burned the previous day. He stayed there for most of the night, the icy wind cutting into his hand, feet and face as painfully as a knife. Why was he watching over the bonfire? He hadn't written a letter in his own blood, and even if he had nobody would have believed him. The flames were shooting up from the fire and the sparks were flying. It only needed a few of them to set the dry twigs and grass on the hillside alight for a forest fire to spread with the speed of the wind. He wondered whether he should go to the station and put in two requests, one for them to get the telephone line repaired straight away, and the other for someone to be sent to inspect the fire precautions in Green Hollow and persuade Wang Mutong to see sense.

He secretly told Azure of what he wanted to do. The last few days her eyes had been swollen like peach stones and she wept as she nodded in reply. Her expression showed that there was much that she wanted to say to him, for whom she felt pity, love, resentment and anger.

That afternoon the One-hander was crouched over his stove cooking some rice to eat on his journey when Azure suddenly rushed into his cabin, openly defying the strict ban her husband had imposed on her. The One-hander stood up in confusion, not knowing what to do. She looked as if she had just come back from working on the vegetable patch. She was wearing only a thin shirt on her top half. It was rather tight and the top button had come open, showing the most alluring glimpses of her full breasts.

"Azure, you. . . ." The One-hander had not even the courage to finish asking his question. He was so flustered that he did not even look up.

"Idiot. Sometimes you're ever so clever, but sometimes you're such a fool. I'm not an evil spirit come to bewitch you." The sight of the One-hander's embarrassment and confusion made her feel more tender towards him than ever. It was a maternal tenderness.

"Azure ... you. . . ."

"I've come to ask if you'll do something for me when you go to the station."

Only then did the One-hander calm himself enough to look her in the face.

"Here's a hundred yuan. I want you to buy us a radio like yours, and a round mirror, and some soap, and some of that cream with a nice smell you put on your face on frosty days, and a brush each for me and

Little Tong and Little Qing to brush our teeth with every morning, and we want to put up a pine pole with a wire on it. . . ."

He stared at her with wide-eyed and utter astonishment. This woman from the forests was a goddess of beauty. Her breasts were full, her limbs were exquisitely proportioned and she was brimming with health. She was also tender and gentle, and her body was full of youth and life.

"What are you staring at me like that for? I'm a victim too, just like you." She turned aside with a touch of winning anger as her cheeks flushed and tears began to roll down them.

"All right, all right. Azure, you are good. I, I. . . ." The One-hander was as if spellbound by something about Azure that glistened and shone. A moment later he came to and blushed. "Azure, if you spend all that money at once, won't you be afraid of what Wang. . . ?"

Azure had been gazing at him with happiness and pleasure until ". . . won't you be afraid of what Wang. . . ?" ruined everything. It was a handful of salt thrown into a heart full of sugar.

"Afraid? I've been afraid of him for ten years and more. . . . He's been catching animals every winter and selling their skins every spring. Besides, we both earn wages and don't spend much of them. There are piles of ten yuan notes at the bottom of our trunk. . . . He's too mean to spend them. . . . I'm not afraid. . . . Living with him here. . . . The worst he can do is kill me."

As she spoke the tears welled up in her eyes, as they did in his too. "Azure, I'll take the money and buy the things for you. Don't cry, don't cry. You're a victim too. I'm very sorry for you. I hate myself, hate myself.... Stop crying, Azure. There, there. If Wang sees you when he comes down the mountain he'll beat you again and swear at me...."

"You're no man," said Azure. "You're even less than one of the creepers on our cabin." She shot him a glare filled with all the anger in her heart, turned and went out of his cabin.

"Azure! Azure!" The One-hander followed her to the door and made an involuntary gesture, stretching out both his hands as if to embrace something beautiful. But all there was instead of his left arm was an empty sleeve.

The One-hander went to the forestry station. Big new slogans were being painted all over the place, such as "Down with the Rightist Reversal of Verdicts", "Criticize the Bourgeoisie Within the Party".* Cadres and workers were arguing vociferously and going in and out of the spacious office of the station's political department. The One-hander felt that the right person to report to was the director of the political department, as he had sent him to Green Hollow in the first place. He had waited outside the office nearly all morning and only managed to squeeze in just before the lunch break.

"Oh, it's you, Li Xingfu," said the political director. "Why are you back here?" He was standing in front of his desk and just about to go out; Li Xingfu's arrival made him stay. He patted his aching head, then put his hands on his hips and fidgeted with the lower half of his body. But his manner was reasonably friendly.

The One-hander grabbed the chance to tell the direc-

---

* These were slogans raised in the political movement started by the "gang of four" to attack Comrade Deng Xiaoping in 1975. (Ed.)

tor as briefly as he could about the need to restore the telephone line to Green Hollow.

"Restore a line that's been out of action for ten years or more?" The political director put on an expression of amazement. "Is that Wang Mutong's idea? Oh, it's yours. You'd better understand, Li Xingfu, that Wang Mutong's our man in Green Hollow. He may not have much education but he's politically reliable. He's been a model forester for a dozen years or more.... A telephone would need investment capital and material. It couldn't be repaired just by shouting an order. Besides, a big movement's just beginning. The whole county from top to bottom is going to be attacking the rightist tendency to overturn verdicts. That will be the main thing and much more important than everything else. Do you understand?"

The One-hander then made his request for the station to send people to inspect the forest protection and fire prevention in Green Hollow and reported how Wang Mutong was making bonfires in the dry season. He was terrified that the political director would be too impatient to knock off work to hear him through to the end.

"Oh dear, and it looked as though you'd been making a lot of progress recently, Li Xingfu." The political director put on another show of great astonishment, then looked very solemn as he continued, "Let me tell you once again. The station leadership has complete confidence in Wang Mutong. You should follow his leadership in Green Hollow and let him educate and reform you. Don't try to run your own show. And they say.... Well, his wife's young and very good-looking. Don't start getting any funny ideas. What would you do if someone cut off the arm you've got left? Eh? You're an educated youngster. You've got a future. . . ."

Thus it was that so far from being able to report the state of affairs to the station the One-hander was given a very cold dressing-down. It was perfectly obvious that the leadership did not trust him at all. He felt that there was no point in going on living like this as if he were a mangy, scabies-ridden dog who got kicked and driven away wherever he went. He spent a couple of days hanging around the co-op and the tree nursery on the little street at the forestry station. He wished his parents had never sent him to school and longed to be an illiterate, stupid boor like Wang Mutong. The way the world was now ignorance was something to be proud of. It had been decided that the more you knew, the more reactionary you were, and that only the likes of Wang Mutong could make revolution. Finally he started to miss Green Hollow, Azure, Little Tong and Little Qing. At least there were three people in that remote and isolated corner who didn't look down on him and regard him as evil. The thought made the One-hander feel a little easier in his mind. He went to the station's grain store to buy two months' supplies of oil, salt and rice and then to the co-op to buy a transistor radio, soap, face-cream, toothpaste, toothbrushes, and a mirror the size of a small basin for Azure. Finally he went to the food store for steamed buns equivalent to a kilogram of flour. Early the next morning he set out back to Green Hollow with his purchases suspended from a carrying pole.

He carried on till the sun was starting to set, by when he had reached Black Cwm. There was only one more ridge to cross before Green Hollow, and he would be back before dark in the little log cabin where he was to settle down and find his destiny. He had already noticed the black smoke rising above Green Hollow. Was Wang Mutong still making bonfires for ash? But why was there so much smoke? It didn't look like the smoke from bonfires.

Although he was exhausted he did not stop to rest but hurried up towards the pass. He could smell the fire on the other side of the mountain and hear the crackling of the flames. Had a forest fire really started in Green Hollow? Where else could the smell and the noise be coming from? As dusk gradually fell the sky reddened on the other side of the ridge. Was it the glow of sunset or the glare of a blazing forest?

He rushed up the path, his body soaked in sweat, and beads of it the size of fingertips on his forehead. Some kind of supernatural power seemed to be driving him towards the pass. All of a sudden the valley was filled with a sheet of red, flowing fire that shimmered beneath his eyes. Green Hollow! He almost passed out. Green Hollow was a sea of flame. The mountain wind whipped up tongues of fire, line after line of them, thousands of giant red centipedes writhing all over the hillsides around the hollow. Thick smoke poured up from the galloping flames in the valley. Ancient trees that had stood for a thousand years were now pillars of fire lighting up the heavens. Rocks were exploding in the heat like landmines. Rolling fireballs, red arrows and dancing crimson snakes merged into a burning torrent, the strange and terrifying beauty of a forest fire.

"Azure! Little Tong! Little Qing!"

Leaving his carrying pole at the top of the pass the One-hander ran shouting down towards the blazing valley. In this crisis he could not abandon Azure, Little Tong and Little Qing. They were the only three people who meant anything to him in this valley. He ran flat out and only luck saved him from tripping over. He did not know how far he had run through clouds of choking smoke when he saw a woman crawling towards him, her hair matted, her face covered in soot, and her clothes in tatters.

"Azure, dear Azure! What's happened? What's happened to you all?"

The One-hander shouted aloud for joy when he realized that this was Azure. But when she saw him she could only stretch her arms towards him imploringly and collapse on the ground. He rushed over to her and half squatted as he put his arm round her. "Dear, dear Azure. It's me, Li Xingfu, Li Xingfu. Dear Azure...."

The One-hander's throat went dry and his voice hoarse as he called to her and wept for ten full minutes until she came round. She opened her eyes and could only murmur, "It's you, it's you, I've found you...." before lying back in his arms, sobbing.

"Don't cry, dear, don't cry. Tell me how the fire started. Where are Little Tong, Little Qing and Wang?" The One-hander shook Azure's shoulder as he asked.

"Let's go. Help me up." As she spoke she struggled to her feet and staggered up the mountainside. The One-hander helped her as he listened to her story. "That evil man ... the cruel bastard.... At about noon on the day you went to the station he found out that there was a hundred yuan missing from the wooden box. He kept saying I'd stolen it to give my fancy man. He wouldn't believe a word I said. He just beat me up, and went on till every inch of me was bruised and aching.... May Hell take him. Then he locked me into your little cabin and left me there for three days and nights. He didn't even give me a drop of water. It was only very late last night that I finally scratched and pulled a plank loose and crawled to the stream for a drink. Then I saw that the mountain was on fire. It started from his bonfires. Let it burn. Let it kill all the animals in the mountains."

"What about Little Tong and Little Qing?"

"The hellhound! Once the fire started he put the box with the money in it on his back and took Little Qing and Little Tong down the stream ... the way you taught them." Her body went weak and she leaned against the One-hander's shoulder. She was not weeping any more. There was even a kind of exultation in the way she ran her fingers through her own hair than stretched her hand out to run them through the hair plastered to the One-hander's forehead by his sweat.

The catastrophe numbed him with horror. They climbed till they reached the top of the pass and found the carrying pole he had left there. Only then did he remember his steamed buns and his bottle of cold water. He got them out at once for her to eat. She was so hungry that she downed a steamed bun in three or four mouthfuls. After she had eaten four he would not give her any more, he only let her drink. She went on leaning against his chest, resting with her eyes shut.

He hugged her tight as he gazed in fascinated horror at the galloping flames twisting wildly in the wind. Suddenly he remembered that behind the mountain opposite was Love Hollow, where there was a stand full of rare firs and golden-leaf magnolias that the specialists in the station said were precious survivals from the last minor glaciation, living fossils on the verge of global extinction. At the thought of this he said to her, "Azure dearest, let's make our way round to the back of the mountain opposite while the fire's still only half-way up the mountainsides. We can go by the firebreak that runs along the top of the ridge. If we can save the trees in Love Hollow we'll at least have something to say for ourselves should we ever go back to the station."

As he spoke the One-hander looked back at the narrow track that led to the forestry station. His expression showed that it was a last farewell.

"Whatever you like. Wherever you go I'll go with you." Food and the short rest had restored the life force in the Yao woman. She was strong.

The forest fire in Green Hollow was spotted by a military radar post over fifty kilometres away, and the forestry station of the Wujie Hills was immediately informed by telephone. Only then did the station's bosses begin to panic and mobilize large forces to go into the mountains to fight the fire. But by then a third of the thousands of hectares of primeval mixed broadleaf forest had been destroyed. All that was left in the valley were bare, charred trunks and branches looking like devil prisoners just released from hell.

A week later Wang Mutong turned up with the two children at the forestry station, his wooden box on his back. Nobody knew where he had gone to escape the disaster. Azure and Li Xingfu had disappeared. Wang Mutong swore with tears streaming down his face that the fire had been started by Azure and her lover, the One-hander. It had been nothing to do with his own bonfires. The station had made him a model forester for a dozen or more years now. To show where his heart lay he respectfully presented his application to join the Party written in his blood to the station Party committee. Naturally the station leadership believed his tearful story and sent militia to search for the culprits. But after combing the blackened mountains for several days all the militia found were the charred bones of wild animals. Nobody knew whether the One-hander and Azure were dead or alive.

As it happened the forestry station, like every other corner of China, was then preoccupied with a great class struggle that was supposedly going to settle the destiny of the country and the Party. Rather than disturb or deflect the main direction of the movement to "counter-attack against the rightist tendency to reverse correct political verdicts" they explained it by their usual class struggle theory and reported to their superiors that "the forest fire started by class enemies has been put out in good time by the revolutionary cadres and masses". There the matter ended.

Wang Mutong refused on his life to go back to Green Hollow. Fortunately the station was then also responsible for a stretch of ancient forest at Heaven's Gate Cave, next to the borders of Guangdong and Guangxi, where the old forest warden had died. So the leadership sent Wang Mutong with his two children to succeed the old warden in that rough, hard, self-sufficient way of life. It was said that Wang Mutong married a widow from Guangxi the same year. As before, he set out each day at dawn and went to bed at nightfall, and he was as full of energy and strength as ever. It happened that the widow had a son and a daughter too.

It would only be natural if when they all grew up they married Wang Mutong's children and lived in the ancient log cabin at Heaven's Gate Cave for generations.

But after the fall of the "gang of four" there was a great deal of talk in the forestry station. Some people said that if the One-hander and Azure were still alive somewhere far away they would be living quite differently. Even more reckoned that with so many wrong and unjust verdicts being put right across the country Azure and Li Xingfu might turn up any day at the station demanding that justice be done to them too. Why not? In the last couple of years the mighty trees in Green Hollow that had survived the fire gaunt and blackened had been putting forth fresh green branches and new leaves.

Translated by W. J. E. Jenner

It Happened in South Bay

SOUTH Bay Town has long been known for its "legged fish". Succulent and nutritious, they are a delicacy in the Wuling Mountains, regarded as a tonic. Some time ago a certain paper claimed that eating these "legged fish" helped to stave off cancer. Whether this was medically sound or not, it resulted in an influx of customers to South Bay, and the price of tortoises went up at each successive market. Who doesn't want to live to be a hundred?

South Bay, a semi-agricultural, small market town in the hills, stood beside Carp River, down which logs could be floated, bamboo rafts poled. Its banks were densely wooded, and in the craggy cliffs on either side were warm, moist caves in which these tortoises lived. Rumour had it that if they bit a fisherman's finger, the pain would make him howl like a stuck pig, and they would only let go if struck by lightning. Worse still they shared their caves with vipers.

Xiao Lianhe of South Bay was skilled in catching "legged fish". Over fifty, he worked as a butcher killing pigs. Catching "legged fish" was simply his hobby. You would have thought all the tortoises in the river were his preserve, for whenever the fancy took him, or if he had special guests to entertain, he would pick up his creel, tell his daughter Handy to boil a pan of water, and be back in less than half an hour with a fine catch.

Xiao had an elder cousin Li Rende, chairman of the town's revolutionary committee. They had been inseparable all their lives, sharing thick and thin together, admired by the townsfolk because they were closer than brothers. Both had started life as fish peddlers, reeking of fish. Before Liberation and just after it, they peddled vats of fish on carrying-poles, working as a team. In spring and summer they sold roe and fingerlings; in autumn and winter, live fish. Li had an engaging manner, was quick-witted and a good planner, able to size up the market and know the right price to charge. Xiao was active and hard-working, rising early and turning in late, able to carry a hundred-pound load for over a hundred *li* without stopping to rest. So they had a division of labour. Li did the talking, planning and accounting; Xiao, the carrying and the hard work. Though only poor peddlers, with Li's brains and Xiao's brawn they made an excellent team. In 1956 they changed their professions. Xiao became a butcher, catching tortoises as a side-line, which suited him down to the ground. Li was appointed head of a neighbourhood committee, after which he slowly climbed up the official ladder.

Towards the end of the fifties, when he was head of the Leap Forward Night School, Li proposed:

"Brother Lianhe, I've put down your name for our school. You ought to study some politics and general knowledge."

"I'm in my thirties, brother. Why should I study? All a butcher needs to know is how to weigh meat and reckon up the cost. My evenings will be better spent going down to the stream in the moonlight to catch the 'legged fish' laying eggs. . . ."

His mind was full of "legged fish".

Early in the sixties Li became the secretary of his street's Party branch. He tried to recruit his cousin.

"Brother Lianhe! Why not apply to join the Party? You can't write? The schoolteacher can write your application for you; all you need do is put your fingerprint on it. . . ."

"I've had no schooling, brother. What use would I be to the Party? I'm not up to the standard of a Party member. . . . Fact is, an ordinary fellow like me, all I want to do each evening is go down to the river to catch 'legged fish'. Clear turtle soup makes a treat for the whole family. . . . I can keep you supplied too. . . ."

Always harping on "legged fish". He thought only of his belly, had no high ideals. Li wanted to speak to him sharply, but then he thought of Spring, the younger sister his bride had brought with her, who was suffering from dropsy. Both devoted to her, they were counting on Xiao's tortoises to build up her strength. So Li refrained from expressing his disapproval.

In the seventies Li became the deputy chairman of the town's revolutionary committee, and he offered to give Xiao a job as a cadre on the state pay-roll, so that he could be Li's right hand. But Xiao failed to appreciate this favour. He had no gift of the gab, felt cut out for rough work, and was more than satisfied with his butcher's job and his tortoise-catching side-line. He had no desire to carry a despatch case or wag his tongue for a living.

"Brother Rende, you're an official, I'm one of the hoi polloi. It's enough for you to shine. I'll stick to my job. Besides, you're putting on weight and haven't the strength to carry a load. If you should come a cropper in some movement, I'd have to support both our families. Catching 'legged fish' I would manage."

"Legged fish", always "legged fish"! There was no boosting up such a dolt. But after the downfall of the "gang of four", when policies were reversed, instead of coming a cropper Li came through with flying colours and was made chairman of the revolutionary committee. No easy feat! Being kind-hearted and keen, seldom giving himself official airs or abusing his power, he had managed to please both the higher-ups and the townsfolk. Young and old alike admired him.

By now he had lost hope of Xiao making political progress or becoming his right hand. However, Xiao was a good sort and Li could always count on using his labour power. For instance, each time superiors came to the town the revolutionary committee would serve them "extra dishes" in their hostel. (As banquets were forbidden, they called these "extra dishes", though in fact they were more sumptuous than most banquets.) And naturally these "extra dishes" included "South Bay legged fish". So each time Li had to ring up Xiao, who would take his creel at once down to the river, strip naked and dive in to catch tortoises. Luckily Xiao always carried an antidote for snakebite. With his reeking hands he never failed to catch enough tortoises for Chairman Li's requirements. Sometimes official guests enthused at such length about "South Bay legged fish" that Li had a few plump ones strung together and put in the back of their jeep.

Once word got out that tortoises could cure cancer, the fame of these "legged fish" spread and Xiao's skill in catching them acquired new importance. He was referred to as "the legged-fish expert", "a dab hand at catching tortoises", and was often commended by the heads of the town. Filled with secret satisfaction he liked to recall all the chairmen, managers, ministers, commissioners, county heads and secretaries who had eaten his "legged fish" and asked Li who had caught them. Now all the top men of the district and county (not to mention commune heads) knew of the skilled tortoise catcher in South Bay.

Li was smart enough to realize how indispensable Xiao was to him in his leading position. What would happen if some big shot were to turn up when Xiao had a fever and couldn't dive into the river? Should he find him an assistant? A successor? Would Xiao be willing to share his antidote for snakebite and his skill in catching "legged fish"? And would any young fellow be willing to learn from him?... Better first encourage his enthusiasm. Several times Li was on the verge of proposing to the revolutionary committee that they should confer a special title on Xiao. But he never got round to this. Commendation called for careful discrimination, so as not to lay yourself open to criticism. A circumspect man, he weighed all the pros and cons. As head of the town he was well aware of being in the public eye, liable to become the focus of all kinds of contradictions. For years he and Xiao had shared thick and thin; all the townsfolk knew how close they were to each other. If he gave Xiao a special title, what would they think? Would they approve? Or accuse him behind his back of favouritism? Something correct, all open and above board, could be distorted and twisted.... And even if that didn't happen, would the honour go to Xiao's head? Would he be too proud to be at Li's beck and call?...

A wise man has many scruples. So Li never made up his mind to confer an honorary title on Xiao in the name of the revolutionary committee. He simply mentioned it twice to him, to encourage him to do still better. Strange to say, Xiao, who hadn't wanted to attend the political night school, join the Party or become a cadre, started longing for a title now that he was fifty-three. Honours are so tempting, enticing. And Xiao had worked gratis for the revolutionary committee spring, summer, autumn and winter, no matter how cold the water. After catching all those "legged fish" for honoured guests, he really deserved a title. When he hinted this, Li showed his artfulness. Patting him on the back he urged him to have patience; the Party wanted to test him, and he should pass this test by keeping up his good record. These delaying tactics irked Xiao. Others, too, felt that Li was exploiting him.

That autumn Xiao bore Li a grudge when his daughter failed to be admitted to college. His Handy was two years younger than Li's sister-in-law Spring. They had gone to school together, grown up together, and both of them finished high school together that summer. When the college entrance results were published, both had just scraped through the entrance exam. But at the end of August, Spring was notified that she had been admitted to the district normal college, whereas Handy had drawn a blank. Xiao resented this. It seemed to him unfair. To his mind Handy was better-looking, more considerate to others and brighter than flashy Spring. Spring, twenty now and still unmarried, thrust out her breasts and wore a short skirt in summer to show off her bare white legs, the shameless baggage.

What rankled most was that Li, with all his connections, had given some friends ten tortoises weighing a good ten pounds, which had taken Xiao two whole blazing noon breaks to catch, to get her through the back door! Do you think "legged fish" are so easy to catch? They hang out with vipers whose bite can be fatal! Just for those ten turtles, chairman, quite apart from everything else, you should have put in a good word for Handy too. Then Spring would have had a friend to keep her company in the normal college.

Of course Xiao kept these grievances to himself, not even telling his own wife and daughter. Handy sulked, complaining tearfully that she was as good as Spring, who had been accepted because her brother-in-law was an official. Though father and daughter thought alike, he urged her to show more sense and not to compare herself with her uncle's family. She should be pleased for Spring and congratulate her. Spring is over twenty, you're only eighteen, let off all the household chores so that you can revise your lessons; and next year or the year after you're bound to pass. You may even get into a first-rate university, not just a normal college. So Xiao suppressed his annoyance and went to Li's house to offer congratulations, praising Spring for being so smart. And Li made time to go and see Handy, to boost her morale. Slapping his chest he promised, "Handy, if there are any job openings, any vacancies for substitute teachers, I'll do what I can for you. If you pass the entrance exam next year, I'll get you into college!..."

The twenty-eighth of August was a Sunday, Spring's last Sunday at home before taking the bus to the district to enroll in the normal college. Being rather spoilt, she asked her sister and brother-in-law to let her have one last meal of "legged fish".

Li beamed. What a good idea! He promptly picked up a creel and set off cheerfully with her to find Xiao. They bumped into him halfway down the flagstone street, his clothes covered in blood, as if on his way home from his butchery.

"Brother Lianhe! Just the man I wanted to find!"

Li and Spring blocked the way, as if afraid Xiao might make off.

"What do you want, Brother Chairman? You could have sent Spring to tell me, why trouble to come yourself?"

"Uncle Lianhe!" cried Spring. "I'm leaving tomorrow to study in the district, I'd like some 'legged fish' for supper. See, my brother-in-law's brought his creel. We'll go with you. . . ."

Being young she had blurted this out without beating about the bush.

Xiao's face clouded. His Handy's failure still preyed on his mind. He said, "I thought you had some important business! What's so special about 'legged fish' . . . . I've caught a cold and I don't want another soaking." He rubbed his forehead. In fact inwardly he was fuming: When the revolutionary committee asked me to catch tortoises for honoured guests, that was public business, only right. You're simply the chairman's sister-in-law, you haven't enrolled yet in the normal college, to say nothing of getting an official post, yet here you are ordering me to catch "legged fish". D'you call that public business?

Li, a faint smile on his face, watched him in silence and sensed what was on his mind. But instead of disclosing this or reproaching him, he stepped forward to say softly, "Brother Lianhe, my wife has spoiled Spring. Do me this favour, will you? I'll go down to the river with you and carry the creel.... It's seldom I have a Sunday free, you know...."

Xiao relented then. He must give Brother Li this face. So he agreed, although reluctantly, and accompanied them to the river. He told them to rest in the shade of a clump of weeping willows and, red in the face, asked Spring to keep well away while he undressed. Blushing she turned her back on him, but said:

"Still so set in your ideas, Uncle! Why, in pictorials and films all those athletes and actresses wear nylon tights or bikinis to show off their figures. And models pose in the nude for art students."

Although Spring had grown up in a small mountain town, she hankered after the modern trends in cities, which she only half understood. Li, being broad-minded, just raised his eyebrows and smiled. But Xiao felt grossly insulted. Stooping to take off his trousers he growled:

"People have to wear clothes to cover their nakedness. Shameless dogs and bitches they are in those films, men and girls kissing and cuddling in broad daylight!"

He said this to work off his last few days' resentment, but at once regretted it. Why storm at Spring? With a plop he dived into the river, to let the clear green water wash away his frustration and fury.

"Legged fish", being amphibians, live in caves in the river bank, hibernating in the winter, coming out again in the spring, and laying their eggs on the shore in midsummer when the heat of the sand will hatch them out. After the eggs are laid the tortoises find themselves a secluded cave and pile one on top of the other to form a kind of pagoda. On the shell of the topmost coils a viper, keeping guard. So it takes a bold, vigilant man who knows their ways to grope in the cave till he finds the tortoise pagoda, and draw out the bottom one, then the next, till all that is left is the top one. He cannot take that for fear of disturbing the viper on its back, because a vipers' bite, nine times out of ten, is fatal.

Chairman Li and Spring sat side by side under the willows, hugging their knees and leaning forward to watch. Xiao dived to the bottom to grope along the banks. And as these were only about five metres high and the water was translucent, they could make out his naked body quite distinctly. But of course Spring did not associate this middle-aged uncle of hers with those graceful figures in pictorials and films. . . . The only sound on the bank now was the shrilling of cicadas, the wind in the willows and the lapping of the water. The inverted reflection of the green hills and trees, interspersed with emerald bamboos, formed a lovely landscape.

For some reason or other, perhaps because his dudgeon had made Xiao less deft than usual he surfaced, then dived down time and again, scattering bubbles like pearls; yet the creel at his waist remained empty. Li and Spring grew tired of waiting. He seemed to be playing hide-and-seek with them. . . . After coming up to take a deep breath he would glance at them both, then submerge again.

"I thought you told me Handy's dad could catch tortoises any time he wanted to. What makes him so slow today?" Spring sounded disgruntled.

"Don't you worry, he'll catch you some." After this

reassurance Li sighed. "You bookworms pay no attention to farming. All the chemical fertilizer used nowadays has begun to pollute the river, and more and more people are eating tortoises, even filching their eggs. Naturally their number's decreasing. Handy's dad has had his work cut out, for over ten years now, supplying us with 'legged fish' for honoured guests. But not once has he let us down."

"It looks as if he'll let us down today though. . . ."

"Come, sister, as a college student you'll live on the fat of the land. Why insist on tortoises. . . ."

"Are tortoises so precious only officials can eat them?"

"Anyone can eat them — for five or six yuan a pound . . . ."

Just then they saw bubbles in the water. Xiao surfaced, holding a couple of plump tortoises, three or four-pounders by the look of them.

Chairman Li and Spring bent down, their hands outstretched, to haul Xiao and his catch ashore. Dripping with water, his underpants clinging to him, he turned away to dump the two tortoises in the creel. Before putting on his trousers he swore, "Brother Chairman, a snake bit my hand!" Holding the middle finger of his left hand to his mouth, he sucked at it then spat, sucked again and spat.

Li turned dizzy with consternation. No wonder Xiao was deathly pale and trembling. The poison was already taking effect!

"Did you bring your antidote, uncle? Your cure for snakebite?" Spring stamped in desperation.

"How could I? You stopped me halfway and dragged me here." Drops of sweat and water were streaming down Xiao's face, contorted with pain.

"Quick, brother! Can you walk? Lean on me. We're not far from the clinic. I'll get hold of some doctors."

Chairman Li went straight into action. Staggering forward supporting Xiao, dripping with sweat they hurried to the clinic, into the emergency ward. And Li had enough self-possession to find the superintendent and urge him to spare no pains to cure Comrade Xiao Lianhe — his life must be saved! Four senior doctors put on their white coats and hurried into the emergency ward. Xiao had collapsed limply on to a bed, his hair tousled, his eyes closed and his lips blue in a face the colour of wax. The doctors gave him injections, administered medicine....

Li, frightened out of his wits, was beside himself. He called Spring aside and roughly slapped her face.

"This is all your fault, you bitch!" he swore. "Got above yourself! Had to eat tortoises! Don't you dare cry. Go and help nurse him. His life must be saved."

Five livid fingerprints on her tender cheeks, Spring was too afraid to protest, knowing she was to blame. She went meekly back to the emergency ward.

Li strode out of the clinic's gate. In spite of all this confusion he remembered the two plump tortoises in the creel dumped there. He now hid this among some banians just inside the courtyard wall, then went back into the clinic and paced the verandah.... What should he do? If Xiao were to die, how could he explain it to the townsfolk? How could he account for this to Xiao's family? With their breadwinner gone, how would they manage? Could the revolutionary committee give them compensation, pay them a subsidy.... And in future when higher-ups came and wanted to taste

"South Bay legged fish", who could catch them? They really should have found Xiao an assistant, a successor. . . .

He was in a terrible predicament. Especially as this was Sunday, and the news that Butcher Xiao had been bitten by a snake while catching tortoises and was at death's door spread like wildfire through the town. People flocked to the clinic to ask for news or see him. Xiao's family was much liked. . . . His wife and Handy were reduced to tears, though not knowing the whole story. They grabbed hold of Li on the verandah and begged him to save his cousin. How could they live without him? Li felt desperate. Luckily the superintendent came to his rescue, explaining that the patient needed quiet. If they made a scene that would endanger his life. So mother and daughter stopped sobbing and were allowed into the emergency ward.

Resting his head on his hands Li slumped into a chair in one corner of the verandah. He was inwardly cursing himself, and his sister-in-law even more for landing him in this trouble. He felt too ashamed to look anyone in the face. He had let down his cousin, so loyal to him all these years. . . . Then he became aware that Xiao's daughter Handy was sitting beside him sobbing.

"Chairman Li, it's up to you . . . my poor dad. . . . Such an honest man who's had a hard life. . . . You promised to give him a title, but never did. . . ."

Had she no sense, this child? Your dad's at death's door, yet you blether about a title. What good would that do him now? Still she went on sobbing and pleading, "Can't you give him a posthumous title?" No wonder this crazy girl hadn't been admitted to college.

Li tried to calm her down.

"Your dad lived a blameless life, never did anything to be ashamed of.... Not like me.... I'm a cheap scoundrel...."

He had blurted this out in a tizzy in his distress.

Suddenly Spring came skipping along, clapping her hands, her bruised face wreathed in smiles. She told Handy:

"Your dad's come to! He's come round, Handy! He told the doctors a snake bit him in the river, but he took that antidote he carries with him...."

"Spring! Spring!" Li cried ingratiatingly.

"Bah! So you remember! If I don't get my sister to slap you five times my name's not Spring!"

She rubbed her tender cheek which was still smarting.

Even so, relief coursed through Li. He stood up and shook himself, as if to shake off bad luck, or as if wondering if he had been made a fool of. There was something rather fishy about this whole business. He had nearly lost his self-confidence, ashamed to look anyone in the face. Now a burden was off his mind, he could relax. His self-confidence restored he walked calmly to the emergency ward and looked through its glass window. Xiao had recovered consciousness. Lying on a snowy white sheet, his face appeared quite ruddy....

Calamity was averted. Without a word to anyone Li left the clinic. But when he went to collect his creel it was lying on the ground and there was not a sign of the two plump tortoises. Had they escaped, or had some naughty boy filched them? Well, even the best-laid schemes may go awry. As chairman of the town's revolutionary committee, he could hardly announce this now or institute a search. He swore half-jokingly to himself:

"Tortoise bastards!"

Ninety-Nine Mounds

IN the Wujie Mountains a valley some twenty *li* around has the strange name Ninety-nine Mounds. On its four sides loom mountains wreathed in mist or rosy clouds, which seen from a height looks like a spray of milky-white coral. This locality is said to be rich in precious stones, gold and silver; for in its hills are ninety-nine Han grave-mounds, over two thousand years old, which give the place its name.

In fact, Ninety-nine Mounds is far from rich. Its slopes, once covered by towering old trees, are today bare boulders with nothing growing there after the years of turmoil except a few shrubs and brambles. Luckily the mountaineers live frugally and work hard, going contentedly about their tasks. And a certain stubborn pride makes them cling to their simple old ways. They stand up for the place's good name and think the world of their local celebrities, whether boxers, brigands, chaste women or virtuous wives. They take a similar pride in their gnarled trees, their mouldering tablets and secret herbal prescriptions. Many is the argument they have had with outsiders over whether their grave-mounds are genuine Han tombs. They have even come to blows over the question of whether their stone lions date from Tang or from Song. No one is allowed to question their convictions. This loyalty of theirs, though rather bigoted, is quite lovable. The story which follows is about one of their local celebrities and a remarkable phenomenon which occurred there.

In Bayberry Gully at the southern foot of Ninety-nine Mounds lived thirty-three-year-old Sister Bayberry. Since her husband's death she had raised her little son there, with no thought of remarrying. Bayberry trees kept that gully green all the year round. And when the berries ripened in May and June the refreshing fruit made your mouth water. Unfortunately bayberries don't keep, and they had no distillery. So each year they ate some, sold some, and left half of them to rot on the ground, attracting swarms of flies and other insects.

Through the gully ran Bayberry Brook, on one bank of which stood Sister Bayberry's cottage. The brook flowed past her door, the trees behind were green in all four seasons. If she opened her door and back windows, emerald leaves thrust in, as if to catch a glimpse of her! She was of medium height, neither thin nor plump but strongly built and high-breasted with thick glossy hair. Her face was neither too round nor a perfect oval. She had two little dimples and long eyelashes. She usually kept her bright eyes demurely lowered, but when she raised them archly most men were bowled over. She seldom smiled and, when she did, would turn away to hide her face in both hands, so as not to be thought a flirt. She always wore dark, loose-fitting clothes to hide her natural curves, not wanting anyone to ogle her.

This morning, after boiling the pigswill and feeding her poultry, Sister Bayberry sat down quietly by her doorstep overlooking the brook to sew. She came from the foothills and had married up here when the "cultural revolution" had turned everything upside down. Her husband, a cadre in the county town, was a stout fellow with some education and they were very much in love. But he threw himself into each movement as if possessed by a devil, and finally became involved in some "counter-revolutionary case", which cost him his life. So she was left stranded up there in the mountains. She wept as if her heart would break, wishing she could have been buried in the same grave. For now, at only twenty-four, she was labelled the "wife of a counter-revolutionary", and left to cope with a month-old baby. But she refused to remarry. Though she had plenty of brothers and uncles outside, she wouldn't move home, determined to bring up her son to avenge her husband. . . . It was hard for a widow in the bloom of her youth. She had to be constantly on her guard against gossip. Yet she couldn't help having dealings with the men in her production team, who attended the same meetings. And now that each household had a production contract she needed help with her ploughing, harrowing, sowing and other field work. A widow had to turn to men for help, and they were a mixed lot. Some considered her fair game, and had no genuine concern for her. She could only swallow her tears. On spring, summer and autumn nights, having bolted her door and closed her shutters securely, she would lie down fully dressed, her baby in her arms, ready to defend herself with the pair of scissors tucked beneath her pillow. Men would come to the cottage then to serenade her. . . .

Now her position had improved. No longer treated as the "wife of a counter-revolutionary", she could hold her head higher, speak up and look people in the eye. As she was still young, kind-hearted wives now and then came to propose matches to her, urging her not to let her youth slip past.

Sister Bayberry was sewing a shoe-sole now, a shoe-sole for a man. Rubber-soled shoes were popular here, but hand-sewn cloth shoes were a betrothal gift. Who were these for? She couldn't say. Sometimes her cheeks started burning, and she felt as if on fire.   For she had recently turned down four suitors. These men had first sent a messenger with a proposal, then presented themselves at her door with a red package. No wonder everyone said her luck had turned.

Two of the four men she hadn't even considered but immediately sent packing. One was Meng, a wicker-weaver from Ox King Temple whom she considered uncouth. One was Wang, the hunter from Willow Bank, whose gift had been five leopard-skins worth three or four hundred dollars. Short and lean, he was in his thirties but looked over fifty with his lined face and gnarled hands and feet. Being soft-hearted, Sister Bayberry felt bad about turning them down, sorry to hurt their feelings. As for her two other suitors, she found it very hard to choose between them.

One was an ex-armyman and a brigade cadre, Liu. The other, Yao, was a well-known herbalist like his father before him. Of course he had merely sent word to her through a go-between. These were two of the ablest local men. A few years ago she wouldn't have presumed to look them in the face, but now she had to choose between them.

Ex-PLA man Liu lived in Ash Hollow in the next gully. All the trees there had been burned down, and now nothing grew there but grass. He was thirty-five this year, an honest cadre and a decent fellow. One of the best hunters, farmers and foresters in these parts, he was liked by all and known as Brother Liu. Since the death of his wife three years previously, Sister Bayberry had had her eye on him. She liked his strength, the way he could hold his drink and keep his end up. But as she was still under a cloud while he was a Party cadre, he naturally steered clear of her. Now that her status had changed, to make up for his previous neglect he kept coming to see her. But she thought: Men are fickle. Why did you ignore me before? Besides, he had two children of his own. If she married him and she took her own little boy with her, it wouldn't be easy being a stepmother! Her only son Paipai was very dear to her; she expected great things of him when he grew up. Brother Liu, a Party member and brigade cadre, had a name and was ambitious — would she be able to keep him? To make him toe the line? Suppose he got into trouble like Paipai's dad and left her with four mouths to feed? Then where would she be?

As for Yao, when a matchmaker first mentioned his name to her she had nearly laughed outright. She had never thought of him as a possible husband. He had a pharmacy in West Mist Flat opposite Bayberry Gully. On the door was pasted the couplet:

Good Fortune Comes to Stay
Evil Is Swept Away.

Yao, getting on for fifty, had never married. He belonged to an older generation. It would be like an uncle marrying his niece. Yet when she thought it over the prospect was tempting. Yao had won a name throughout the Wujie Mountains for his miraculous skill in curing diseases. He had become a legendary figure.

The mountaineers said that he had many secret prescriptions handed down by his forefathers. Some had known him, with one potion, to enable a barren woman to conceive; with two other powders, steeped in rice wine, a woman who bred like a rabbit could be made to miscarry. He was alleged to have wonderful herbs, the names of which he would not divulge, to make men and women sterile without undergoing a painful operation; and he could reconcile husbands and wives who had been at loggerheads. He also had infallible cures for rheumatism, snake bites, stings and other aches and pains, as well as broken bones, sprains, colic, chills, diarrhoea and heat-strokes.

What aroused the greatest admiration, however, was his possession of a rare "magic fungus", a sovereign remedy. As the jingle goes:

A magic fungus in a family
Ensures it riches and nobility,
Brings a village prosperity
And a region fertility.

This goes to show what a priceless treasure it is. Yao knew charms and spells, could swallow fire, grasp knives and walk on swords. He could fell a man to the ground with one blow of his fist, or topple him with two fingers. So no one in their right mind would take him on. To punish an evildoer, it was said, he simply squeezed into the crowd in the market to tap him on the back, or laid knotted reeds on the path to trip him up. Then, on reaching home, the fellow would flop on to his bed aching from head to foot, to lie for two weeks at death's door. Only when Yao was sent for and the sick man confessed his crime would the herbalist cast a spell on a bowl of water and make him drink this — then he would be cured.

Sister Bayberry, coming from another village, had listened rather sceptically at first to these stories of the herbalist's magic powers; but they were so convincingly told that in the end she believed them. On her occasional visits home, when her relatives asked about him, she described his wonderful cures as if she had actually seen them with her own eyes.

The bayberry leaves outside her cottage rustled in the spring breeze. Sunlight dappled the shade beneath them. The leaves seemed to be watching, wondering what she was thinking. She had stopped sewing to stare vacantly at the thousands of berries slowly changing colour. Was she longing for them to ripen? Disappointed by their tardiness? Her feelings were mixed.

In June a warm south wind ripened the berries, which fell like purple agate or red jade. Some were deliciously sweet, others set your teeth on edge. The girls and young women who loved sweet-sour fruit were overjoyed.

Sister Bayberry picked a basketful of red fruit to sell at Plantain Village down on the plain. Having combed her hair and changed her clothes, she set off with a smile, tripping lightly beside the brook, her path running along the bottom of the gully. Mountaineers carrying crates hurried past, as if Plantain Village were paved with gold and silver. But she was in no special hurry.

She made way for Meng of Ox King Temple, as he swung along with a load of brushes, sieves, baskets and crates. He was a skilled craftsman, a good wicker-weaver. She made way too for Wang the hunter, who had slung on his back the skins of wild cats and hares. He was said to be a crack marksman, who shot his quarry through the eye so as not to damage the hide. Was she to sell her fruit to buy oil, salt or cloth for shoes? Or just to mingle with the crowd to have a closer look at Brother Liu and the old herbalist, the better to compare them? A woman of thirty-two has her own criteria, and she was inclined to think that thirty-five-year-old Brother Liu wasn't up to fifty-year-old Yao. It was a strange, fateful choice. But the herbalist's prestige and his ability to cure all diseases exerted an irresistible attraction.

In recent years people had flocked from far and wide to ask Yao to take them on as his apprentices. Even Brother Liu often hung around his stall, and the commune secretary Wei tried to pick up tips from him too. As for the eager youngsters, they seemed to think that if they could learn his skills they would be set for life. The trouble was that the herbalist turned them all down, refusing to teach anyone but his own sons. Oddly enough Sister Bayberry thought this a very good thing. What pleased her even more was the news that two silly girls had come, one after the other, to offer to live with him and bear him sons so that his priceless knowledge would not be lost to the world. . . . And what had his answer been? "Thank you, no! My shop is no place for child brides; I mean to marry a widow." Imagine that! Apart from Sister Bayberry what other widows were there in Ninety-nine Mounds?

By now she had reached Plantain Village. Since the restrictions on trade had been relaxed, the market was always crowded with stallholders and pedlars hawking their wares. You could buy goods of every kind there, Sister Bayberry pushed her way through the crowd, her tunic sticking to her perspiring back. As her big red berries were the sweetest in the market, customers crowded round. She soon disposed of the lot for several dollars. After buying oil and salt, cloth for shoes and half a catty of sweets wrapped in cellophane for her small son, she went to the fuel market where woodcutters with bare bronzed backs, a white towel over one shoulder, wearing straw sandals, were squatting by their loads of firewood. She didn't see Brother Liu there. Being a cadre he took all his firewood to the largest state-owned restaurant in the place.

Sister Bayberry squeezed her way next to the medicine market. Her basket wasn't heavy, she could hold it on her head. Sometimes the crush was so great that her feet left the ground. The air was acrid with sweat, oil and smoke. ... She soon spotted Yao's stall, surrounded by customers. From its awning hung coloured pennants presented by grateful patients and praising his skill. His trestle-table, made out of two doorboards, was laden with a variety of bottles and tins, pills and powders, roots and creepers, tiger bones, deer plasters, monkey paws and snake gall. Sister Bayberry stood on tiptoe to peer over the shoulders of those in front. To her surprise Brother Liu was sitting there instead of the herbalist, attending to patients and making out prescriptions like a genuine apprentice. Had Yao really taken him on? Hadn't he sworn to teach only his own sons? Most likely this was a temporary arrangement. Liu had propped up his carrying-pole behind him, its hooks glinting like bright spear-heads in the sun. Sister Bayberry stood as if rooted to the spot, while Brother Liu treated patients and joked with those who had gathered to watch the fun. He was playing his part to the hilt!

"Doctor, they say you're a vet too. Since when have the canons of medicine lumped men and beasts together?"

The speaker had evidently mistaken Brother Liu for Yao.

"There's no great difference between men and beasts, don't you know that, brother? They all have five internal organs, six vital organs, three souls and six animal spirits, seven emotions, six desires, ten orifices. . . . In the Three Kingdoms period the great physician Hua Tuo cured men and cattle, both."

Liu reeled off this patter as if it were second nature.

"So men are cattle, cattle are men? Whose brilliant idea is that?"

"I'm just saying their illnesses can be treated alike. Men are men, cattle are cattle. . . . Take copulation for instance. Your brother and his wife couple behind closed doors, don't they? But not your hens and ducks, they mate in the yard or a pond."

A roar of laughter went up. Sister Bayberry pursed her lips and smiled, thinking that it was a smart answer, though men were really too crude.

"Hey, doctor! I hear you're a prize boxer, that you can floor a man with two fingers. Is that true?"

Another stranger had taken Brother Liu for the herbalist. Customers came to this market from miles around. Most of them had heard of Yao but never met him.

"Want a demonstration? Come on. I promise not to break any bones, but you'll ache for three days."

Liu struck a menacing pose, sticking out three fingers.

"No, I'll take your word for it! Let me off!"

The man tried to back away, but the people behind pushed him forward.

"Come on, have a try. What's there to be afraid of?"

Liu raised threatening fists to bluff him.

"I take your word for it! I've got a family to support, don't beat me up!"

The man slipped through the crowd and slunk off.

Everyone watching roared with laughter. Some yelled, "Stop him!" "Don't run away, you fool! This isn't the herbalist. He doesn't demonstrate his magic powers."

Sister Bayberry, watching the fun, felt that selling herbs was better than selling firewood. But now a young man dressed like a cadre, with a yellow inspector's armband, pushed his way forward shouting:

"Where's Doctor Yao gone? Food and drink are ready in the tax office. They're just waiting for him to start."

"You want my master? He's taken a packet of tonic to Secretary Wei in the commune office."

Liu was passing himself off as the herbalist's apprentice.

"But Secretary Wei's in the tax office waiting for him! When did you become his apprentice, Brother Liu? Do you mind going to find him?"

Good-natured Liu agreed readily. But first he looked

round and asked, "Is there anyone here from Ninety-nine Mounds? I want someone to keep an eye on this stall for me."

Sister Bayberry felt rather flustered. She was tempted to volunteer to sit by the stall attracting admiring glances; but she was afraid that if people who knew her saw her they might gossip behind her back. While she was hesitating, Liu called out:

"Sister Bayberry, do me a favour! I've got to go to the commune to find my master, all his important friends are waiting for him."

.... Soon all those from Ninety-nine Mounds at the market knew that Sister Bayberry was minding the herbalist's stall. Some said that he had made a good choice, some that she was in luck; others that, despite the age gap, a skilled herbalist marrying a pretty widow would be like a lion mating with a unicorn — a thoroughly suitable match. How their tongues wagged! Sister Bayberry only minded the stall for half an hour without even seeing Yao; however, she didn't lose any of his herbs and actually sold two dogskin plasters for him. A few new customers even took her for the herbalist's wife! Dammit, she was only standing in for a bit.

When Liu came back, she picked up her basket and left.

For several days after the market Sister Bayberry felt restless, at a loss. Each noon after tilling her fields, feeding her fish and shutting the pig into its sty, she would sit by her door in the shade sewing a shoe-sole. Every day berries fell from the tree till there were hardly any left. And the sun beat down more fiercely, making her languid. Brother Liu came over every other day to ask if she needed help. She always declined politely and brewed him a bowl of tea, but had little to say to him. Instead of looking through the leaves at neighbouring Ash Hollow, she now looked at West Mist Flat three or four *li* away on the opposite hill, with fields and a brook between. The brook was bridged by a pine plank, and beyond it was a crossroads where five roads met. Under an old camphor tree there stood five menacing old stone lions. West Mist Flat, a good village, was where her small son Paipai went to school, yet she hadn't visited it for a long time.

"Mum! Mum! Grandad Yao called me into his shop today. Gave me a lot of goodies! See, he told me to bring you this. . . ."

Without stopping to put down his satchel, Paipai rushed over triumphantly, a package in his hands.

Rather taken aback she took and opened it. Inside were over a dozen thick stems of angelica, a tonic and cure for irregular menstruation. . . . Yao hadn't examined her, hadn't felt her pulse; how clever of him to know that she had this trouble.

"Aren't you pleased, mum? Grandad Yao. . . ."

"Who says I'm not pleased, Paipai? In future don't call him grandad, call him uncle. Understand?"

"All right. Grandad, uncle, it's all the same to me." Paipai was quick off the mark.

The next morning Sister Bayberry took thirty salted duck eggs out of her vat and put them in a basket for Paipai to take to Uncle Yao as thanks for the angelica.

"Mum! Grandad Yao. . . . I mean Uncle Yao has given me lots of sweets, better than the ones you bring back from the market. . . ."

That afternoon when Paipai came back from school

his pockets were stuffed with sweets wrapped in gold paper, silver paper and cellophane. He ran straight to his mother's arms.

"You shameless little beggar! Was Uncle Yao pleased with the duck eggs?"

"And how! When I called him uncle he asked who had told me to. I said: Mum told me to."

"You silly boy, Paipai...."

"Anyway he was really happy, kissed my cheeks, my nose, my mouth.... That moustache of his tickles...."

Her heart thumping, Sister Bayberry threw her arms round her little boy and kissed him too, on his cheeks, his nose, his mouth.

With the child as their go-between, Sister Bayberry and Yao grew closer together. But the herbalist had a strong sense of propriety and stood on his dignity. Apart from his gifts to the little boy he took no other initiative and never came to her cottage. This made her respect him still more. How could he with his fine reputation and all his admirers take her and her son seriously? At the same time she couldn't help resenting this. She thought of finding some pretext to go to his shop ... but was afraid of making herself conspicuous, of giving rise to talk which would make him despise her.... She was still young and not bad-looking, not clumsy or stupid, but how could she draw him out?

The weather was now so sweltering that the leaves of the bayberry trees were shrivelled and drooping. Dogs and cats lay in the shade, their pink tongues lolling out. After hoeing her sweet potatoes one day under the blazing sun, Sister Bayberry was prostrated by the heat. Aching from head to foot, she ran a fever, lost her appetite and had a hacking cough. Paipai, without being prompted, went to fetch Uncle Yao.

Sister Bayberry was lying in a coma, unable to open her eyes. She dreamed that a great fire was burning the bayberry trees, her cottage was ablaze, the acrid smoke was choking.... She was awakened by a call from Paipai and saw a shadowy purple figure approaching.

"I've been too busy to come. Are you ill, sister? Oh, a high fever!"

Paipai must have raised one corner of the mosquito-net. Yao stopped her from struggling to sit up. He sat on a stool by the bed to examine her, made her put out her tongue, felt her forehead, then her pulse.

"Let me tell you your symptoms, sister," he said. "If I'm right, I'll prescribe you medicine. If I'm wrong, I won't charge you a cent; you can find a better doctor .... You've had a heat-stroke, feel on fire, and the fever won't go down. Your mouth is dry, you're feeling dizzy, your nose is all blocked up. There's a buzzing in your ears, you have a dry cough and you're limp, ache all over, and have no appetite.... Am I right, sister?"

"Thank goodness you've come, brother.... I feel so awful...."

"Well, now I know what medicine to prescribe.... Which do you prefer, decoctions, pills or powders?"

"Whatever you say, brother...."

"Suppose I give you some acupressure to clear your nose and relieve your headache and pain."

For a second she hesitated. Her forehead seemed slightly clearer. But Yao had gone to the kitchen for a bowl, and was filling it with water.... She needn't be afraid, with Paipai there.

The mosquito-net was raised again. Sister Bayberry's bare back was like white jade. Lying face down she couldn't see how he was casting a spell, could hear a muttered incantation. . . . Splash! The magic water cooled her back, relieving some of her pain. Then two big hands with long nails pinched, massaged and kneaded her back, now soft, now hard, now fast, now slow. Her back smarted as if burning, but her limbs felt deliciously relaxed.

"That'll do. What fine skin you have, sister. You can get dressed now."

The net was lowered again. Although still limp, she was no longer seeing stars. Her dizziness had passed, and with it the bitter taste in her mouth. . . . But dammit, her heart was thumping, her cheeks were burning again. This was different from her previous symptoms though.

"You really do have a magic touch, brother. . . ."

"You're flattering me, sister. I don't mind telling you, I charge five dollars for this treatment in the market. . . . Secretary Li and County Head Zhang have both had it, and both of them call me 'teacher'. As for Secretary Wei of the commune, he gets me to massage him each market-day, although he's as strong as an ox!"

Peering through the thick mosquito-net, she saw Yao's dim figure preparing pills and powders.

"Thank you, brother. How much will that medicine cost. . . ."

"I'm fond of little Paipai, he's a smart lad. . . . Smarter than a grown-up, sister."

Sister Bayberry felt she had been a fool to ask the price like that as if they were strangers. . . . She had to bite her lips to keep from crying. Luckily he couldn't see her properly through the net.

"I've got a favour to ask you, brother."

"Ask away."

"If you're so fond of Paipai, will you take him as your son and teach him to be a herbalist when he grows up. . . ."

"Very well. Here, Paipai. . . ."

"Paipai, say dad! Say you'll learn his skill when you're bigger. . . ."

"Don't embarrass the boy, sister. . . . He can't count as my own flesh and blood. . . ."

When they heard that Sister Bayberry was ill, Meng the wicker-weaver and Wang the hunter called to see her. Both were still attracted by her. As for Liu from Ash Hollow, he came every day. Actually she was much better although still weak and shaky. One evening, tired after picking a basketful of bright red peppers, she rested against one of the stone lions under the camphor trees at the crossroads. The spreading trees cast a cool shade, and the many passers-by resting against their roots had rubbed them smooth and shiny. These hoary trees were said to be immortal. Three flagstone roads and two dirt tracks converged there, the roads from West Mist Flat, Ash Hollow and Bayberry Gully; the tracks from Willow Bank and Ox King Temple. So this crossroads was the hub of Ninety-nine Mounds. The rampant lions with their gaping jaws were regarded as ancient relics guarding the way. By day people liked to cool off there; but at night they found the place sinister with red and green will-o'-the-wisps darting around it. Some claimed to have seen the Han general Han Xin inspecting his troops here, drilling them with flashing weapons beneath these trees. . . . Men from the province and county town had come to inspect these fine statues, and had wanted to take them away to exhibit them; but the mountaineers would not hear of this. And as communications were so bad, without their help the lions could not be moved. So they had taken root here to protect the place, a most imposing sight.

The sun, still fairly high, hung like a big red disc from the westernmost branch of one camphor tree, flooding the earth with a crimson light. The lions seemed to be frolicking tipsily. The evening breeze rustling the leaves was casting flickering shadows on the ground. Sister Bayberry too was bathed in crimson light. She was just about to leave when she heard footsteps behind her and saw Brother Liu bounding down the steps from West Mist Flat.

"So it's you, Sister Bayberry! Wait, I've got something to tell you!" She enjoyed seeing Brother Liu — he always had so much to say to her and told her all kinds of news.

"What a fright you gave me, brother!" She leaned back against a stone lion to hear what he had to say. She had some news for him too.

"Have you heard? Secretary Wei of the commune is in trouble!" One foot on a lion's paw, he first retailed this gossip from outside.

"Secretary Wei? What has he done?" She was curious to know how this might affect her.

"Ha! . . . Apparently he drank the wrong medicine, then started charging about like a sow in heat. . . ." Liu broke off, flushing, and gave a sheepish laugh.

"There's nothing wrong with him, why dose himself

with medicine? What did he take? . . ." Sister Bayberry could guess. She had to purse her lips to suppress a smile.

"Old Wei and Yao of West Mist Flat are thick as thieves."

"Aren't you Yao's apprentice!"

"He's never taken me on. I'd be hard to handle."

"Brother Liu, does this mean Wei will have to step down?"

Liu stared at her, his eyes gleaming. He had edged round the lion towards her . . . but she slipped away to sit on the other side.

Ignoring this he went on:

"Dismissed for a self-examination. Shit! Just going through the motions. Half a month ago he was dismissed from the commune. Now he's been made superintendent of the district hospital, in charge of all the medical work of five communes. He's still a section chief in the county committee — just under a new signboard. Officials like him and that charlatan of West Mist Flat are birds of a feather!"

Liu wrenched at the lion as if suddenly furious.

"What are you so mad about, Brother Liu?" she asked. "Why attack your own master like that?"

Sister Bayberry smiled affectionately at him. Though rather afraid of Liu's temper, she enjoyed seeing him fly off the handle. Over thirty, he still carried on like a boy, making her feel like an elder sister towards him.

"Sister Bayberry! In this world you must learn to tell true from false. I know what you're up to. I'm no fool. Some men are devils, make no mistake about it!"

She was stung by this implication.

"You mean all the other people here are fools, that they're mad to look up to him the way they do?"

"Sister Bayberry, do you know why I hang around his stall at each market? Why I call him master?"

"Why?"

"To find out what he's all about. You know all those pennants hanging over his stall — where did he get them? He forked up the money himself and asked patients to send them to him! To make a show.... And he has no 'magic fungus', no sovereign remedy; that's a made-up story. His forefathers weren't famous physicians either; they were grave-robbers down in the plains who didn't move up here till his father's time. He himself started out as a travelling vet castrating poultry and pigs and mating cattle. Started as a cattle matchmaker!"

"A cattle matchmaker.... Where did you hear that?"

"Don't you believe me? One year when he was drunk he spilt the beans!"

"Don't be cross, Brother Liu.... I know it's me you're thinking of, or you wouldn't make up these stories about someone looked up to by everybody here. People would be furious if they heard you."

"Let them be! He says he can swallow fire and walk on swords, I bet that's phoney too! He can't knock a man to the ground with one blow. If you want me to prove it I'll challenge him one day in public. If he really has magic powers I'll let him smash me!"

"Don't try, Brother Liu, you'd get hurt.... Please, please don't.... Do promise not to...."

"Sister Bayberry, who'd have thought a woman like you would be bewitched like everybody else and lose your head completely!"

"I'm an ordinary person, like everyone else...."

"You'll live to regret this, Sister Bayberry, when you find you've fallen into a bottomless pit!"

"Thank you. I know why you've got your knife into him.... It's all very well to talk that way to me, but if you repeat this outside the whole of Ninety-nine Mounds will think you're mad, will hate you!"

"Me mad, is it?... Me mad? You're the one who's mad. All of you.... Take it from me, the day will come when those quack remedies of his will be shown up!"

"You can't get the better of him, Brother Liu...."

"Hell! Mountaineers are a superstitious lot. It's *you* I'm worried about."

"I can do my own worrying, brother. I'm thirty-two, my son's already at school."

"Then give me an honest answer!"

Liu roared this out like a lion.

"There are questions you mustn't ask.... And you should understand without being told.... I can only love you like a sister ... you must forgive me. I haven't got room for two men in my heart."

Sister Bayberry, tears in her eyes, leaned back against the stone lion. Then she held out her hand, meaning him to clasp and kiss it. This was the way young women in Ninety-nine Mounds dismissed suitors whom they liked and respected. If the man had no guts he would clasp her hand and kiss it — for the first and only time.

Liu, however, with both hefty hands warded her soft one away and sprang to his feet, his eyes bulging and stiff-necked as a stone lion.

"I'm not a beggar who wants your charity, nor your hand to send me away!"

With that he pounded along the road to Ash Hollow

without a backward glance, kicking up clouds of dust.

Tears poured down Sister Bayberry's face — she wanted to run after the bull-headed fellow to call him back. Instead she sat motionless. The last rays of the setting sun were gilding the nests on the old camphor trees. On her way home she felt sad, as if she had lost what she prized most on earth.

A storm snapped trees, black clouds pressed down, thunder and lightning crashed, and it poured with rain .... The sky seemed a black cauldron turned upside down. What a fearful roar — what was it? Had Brother Liu been knocked out by Yao, unable to eat a thing for three whole days? Heavens, that had been her fault. Why didn't you listen to me, Brother Liu? There are plenty of other good women for you to marry. And Yao, you shouldn't have been so jealous. You had no quarrel with Brother Liu. Living on the same mountain you should have had pity on him.

Whoever started the trouble should help end it. She must go to West Mist Flat to ask the herbalist to relent and go to Ash Hollow to cure Liu. Otherwise this would be on her conscience for the rest of her life.

A summer storm ends as swiftly as it starts. The rain-washed bayberry trees were a brilliant green; the muddy brook, with its swirling white bubbles, was sweeping along leaves, twigs and tufts of grass.... Why, who was that tall fellow splashing through the brook, his trousers rolled up to his thighs!

"Is that you, Brother Liu? You weren't knocked out then? How can you laugh? You had me worried stiff!"

"I'm made of steel, sister. How could I be knocked out?"

"You didn't fight it out then?"

"We fought — he hasn't any magic powers."

"Oh . . . he must have let you off lightly. Didn't want to hurt a neighbour." She heaved a sigh of relief.

"Trust you to think the best of everyone. You're too good-natured by far. But you can't tell true from false. What to cut open my chest and look at my heart? Eh?" Liu tore open his shirt.

"No, no! Brother Liu, don't scare me. Go away. Don't say such dreadful things!"

He splashed off through the water again, spattering foam. It was cruel to drive him away, but what could she do? At least he was still strong as an ox, alive and kicking. She wouldn't have to have him on her conscience.

Sister Bayberry's eyelids drooped. This fright had made her sleepy. After listlessly walking home she curled up on a couch. She needed a good rest, not having recovered completely from her last illness. . . .

"Sleeping in the daytime, for shame!" she scolded herself. In a dream she seemed to have fed the pig and poultry and swept the yard. She sat down with her sewing, her thoughts wandering. Dammit, she'd not been to West Mist Flat for ages. He was too well-known, too respected to call on her. Couldn't be helped. Feeling relaxed, she cheerfully fetched a basket, put in the cloth shoes she had just finished making, then covered them with freshly picked plump red peppers, and topped these off with a dozen white new-laid eggs. Next she changed her clothes and did her hair in front of the mirror before locking the door and bolting the garden gate. Having crossed Bayberry Brook, she took the flagstone road to West Mist Flat. Dammit, by now she was feeling nervous again. She stopped from time to time to look around, to see if anyone was lurking in the woods. Though nowadays the world was at peace, and no one treated her as the "wife of a counter-revolutionary". No one would inspect her basket to see what "capitalist wares" she had hidden there.

The flagstones, washed clean by the storm, showed her reflection. By their side grew small flowers and grasses. The neat crops in the fields looked manicured. This was owing to the responsibility system. Over twenty years of shouting slogans, of eating from one big pot, were not as effective as this contract system. . . . It had proved a cure-all, like Yao's herbal prescriptions.

Sister Bayberry smiled to herself as she passed the fields, crossed the pine bridge and reached the crossroads. Standing by the old lions she realized that her feet were rather swollen, she was tired. She glanced at the road to Ash Hollow, then at the two dirt tracks, as if afraid Liu, Meng and Wang might come into sight. But all was quiet, there was no one there. She liked silence, didn't like people prying into her affairs. Should she go first to the school? Then to the shop? But she could hear shrill voices: the children were still having a singing lesson. So she went to the shop with her basket. Had she come to see relatives or express her thanks? Neither. She paused, nervously smoothing her hair, then braced herself. This was nothing to be ashamed of, coming to see the doctor. All the local people came here, as well as other patients from miles around. She lightly mounted the steps to the level ground at the top, half way up the hill. It was quiet except for the clucking of hens, the quacking of ducks. The neighbours had gone to the fields. The shop with its single front had a black tile roof. Its signboard was flanked by the couplet:

Good fortune comes to stay,
Evil is swept away.

The door stood open. Unaccountably it struck her as strangely high, the room as strangely large. Her legs nearly gave way and she saw stars. The same thing had happened when her mum had taken her to burn incense in the Jade Emperor's Temple; but then she had been only a slip of a girl. Yao was an old acquaintance, and he had adopted her son! She straightened up, shifted her basket to the other hand and stepped over the threshold. A big rack of medicine stood by the wall. And all round the shop hung root, creepers, monkey paws, snake gall and the like....

There was no one there, but she suddenly heard a woman giggling in the back yard, then what sounded like cats miaowing. She could hardly believe her ears.

"Is Brother Yao in?" she got up the nerve to call.

"Is that you, sister? Are you better now?"

This answer came only after some delay. It was odd that she always visualized Yao as an image with a halo.

After what seemed a long wait the staircase creaked, and he came down. So he had been upstairs. Yet she'd heard the back gate close softly.

"Just passing by, sister, or have you come for some medicine?"

He sounded rather offhand. In his presence she felt constrained, not at ease as she did with Brother Liu. She stared at him, unable to say a thing. She couldn't see his face distinctly. Dammit, why were his features always so blurred.

"Sit down, you look rather off colour. Is anything wrong?"

He indicated a seat. A couch, actually. She perched cautiously on one end, smiling sheepishly. It was a comfortable couch. Probably most of his patients sat there or lay there. She took a breath and said hoarsely:

"Last time you cured me ... but I never.... I've brought you some red peppers and new-laid eggs...."

"Now there's no call for that ... we're relatives."

He had sat down opposite her, and seemed to be staring at her. The strange thing was that, although they were so close, she still couldn't make out his features. Each time their eyes met she felt hypnotized.

"Paipai hasn't been home for lunch these last few days, always coming to see his dad...." She felt less awkward talking about her son.

"We're good friends, Paipai and I."

"He's still small, you mustn't spoil him."

"Don't you?"

"I don't want him to turn out badly."

"He won't. It's still early days."

"The biggest tree grows from a seedling!"

"But not every seedling grows to be a big tree. It may be snapped by the wind, blighted by frost or struck by lightning...."

"Don't talk in that unlucky way — not about our son."

"Our son, aha, our son!"

"That was a slip of the tongue, don't laugh at me."

"Don't worry, you couldn't say anything wrong."

"Dad ... you...."

"Me? I'm doing all right. Lack for nothing.... I've enough put by, I can tell you, to last my lifetime. . . . But I need a helpmate to mind the shop when I go out on my rounds."

"So that's what you were angling for when you made friends with Paipai."

That morning Sister Bayberry helped chop up herbs. She swept the floor, dusted the place and washed Yao's clothes, then cooked the midday meal.

. . . . When school was dismissed the children came dashing out, Paipai among them, his satchel on his back. Heading for the medicine shop or for her cottage? Paipai, laddie, come here quick. . . .

"Mum, mum! Why are you curled up asleep on the couch? Your rug's dropped on the floor!"

Sister Bayberry woke with a start.

"What, wasn't there a storm? No thunder and rain? Haven't I been anywhere?"

"What storm? The road's covered in dust!"

So it had been a nightmare — how eerie. Sister Bayberry flushed crimson. She sat up, afraid to look her small son in the eyes. Half to herself and half to him she said:

"Mum just dozed off, I haven't been anywhere. . . ."

Sister Bayberry's impending marriage to Yao was the talk of Ninety-nine Mounds, a subject discussed by all.

"That young widow of Bayberry Gully is in luck; she'll be managing Yao's medicine shop!" "Isn't fifty too old for thirty?" "What does it matter? Men of eighty have sometimes married brides of eighteen!" "This will be the making of Paipai. He'll step into Yao's shoes, learn his prescriptions and skills." "What will Brother Liu do, now that his bird has flown!" "Yao's wedding's a big event for Ninety-nine Mounds. Everyone should chip in with money or help out to make it a really grand do. We'll drink ourselves under the table!"

As all the different views were aired, Sister Bayberry marvelled at how her status had changed. In the past, apart from a few men who ogled her everyone else had ignored her. But now, wherever she went she was met by friendly smiles, respectful nods. Men called out greetings as they approached, inviting her to drop in or asking if she needed help with her fields. They urged her to send out plenty of invitations and prepare a tip-top wedding feast, with the best cigarettes and sweets. Women gushed, "Why, sister, is that a new tunic you're wearing? It looks good on you!" "You look radiant with joy, just like a girl in her twenties, not like the mother of a strapping boy." "You're the only one in our parts fit to marry Master Yao." "My dad has heart trouble, sister. I hope you'll find a good cure for him later on."

Most embarrassing of all, Meng the wicker-weaver and Wang the hunter came as if by mutual accord to Bayberry Gully to offer their heartfelt congratulations. This was a fine thing, they declared, for Ninety-nine Mounds! There would be an heir to all those secret prescriptions. They hinted that if she had chosen some-body else, they wouldn't have stood for it — would have kicked up a row!

Happiness seemed to be shimmering all around her. At first this took some getting used to. It dazzled her, made her dizzy. She felt like someone climbing a bar-ren mountain who suddenly reaches green trees, beds of flowers and a fountain running through a pasture. Enchanting! By degrees she became accustomed to be-ing treated with respect, shown concern by all around her. Felt intoxicated, as if walking on air. Glorying in her new reputation, she began to look down a little on other people; yet the thought of him, the sight of him dazzled her and filled her with awe. She would never refuse him anything again. . . .

Although Brother Liu had been angry at her, he still came every other day to help her. A good strong worker, he easily managed to farm her fields and Paipai's as well as his own. But he had his principles, and after the date of her wedding to Yao was announced he never went to her cottage. He avoided her too on the road or by the brook. And she was still anxious, having heard that he had several times challenged Yao to fight it out with him, wanting to prove him a fraud. Yao, however, always refused, on the grounds that they were neighbours with no long-standing feud between them. Still Liu remained adamant. He had announced his intention of using his demobilization pay — 700 yuan — to open another pharmacy in Ninety-nine Mounds stocking Chinese and western medicine, as a rival to Yao's shop.

While Sister Bayberry was making plans for her wedding, the situation changed in West Mist Flat. Yao's friend Superintendant Wei sent a section chief named Chen to check up on the medical work in Ninety-nine Mounds. Chen convened a meeting of the brigade cadres then of the commune members in Ash Hollow. Liu ill-advisedly attended both, and he and Chen, croaking like crows, queried the legitimacy of Yao's pharmacy. This infuriated the other mountaineers. Chen and Liu were isolated. The villagers nearly came to blows wtih Liu because he ran Yao down as a devilish quack. They regarded him as a traitor.

Section Chief Chen adopted flexible tactics, not revealing his real mission. Sister Bayberry was in a quandary. She heard that Chen had talked in private with Yao, using threats as well as persuasion. Had asked for his pharmacy licence and his licence to practise medicine in the Wujie Mountains. Naturally Yao had no licence bearing the big red chop of the Health Bureau. He didn't panic though, knowing how well entrenched he was in Ninety-nine Mounds. Surely his old friend Superintendent Wei wasn't going to turn against him? If he did, he'd have to reckon with the local people. Obviously he had sent Chen for some other reason. Sure enough, Chen soon offered him a way out which would bypass tedious red tape. To make their medical work more scientific, in the interests of modernization he asked Yao to hand over all his secret prescriptions, especially those for contraception and sterilization, as well as his sovereign remedy, the "magic fungus". The authorities would pay for them and promptly issue him with two licences.

Yao asked for three days to consider this proposal. Sister Bayberry felt worried. Should she go to talk it over with him? She went twice to his pharmacy but each time found the door bolted. He must have gone to the mountains to gather herbs and think the matter over. Her heart ached for him. She said to herself:

"Better hand in all your prescriptions, brother. Too many people are jealous of them."

"You think it's so simple, sister? These were handed down in my family. They're how I've made my way in the world."

She seemed to see Yao shaking his head with a contemptuous smile.

Yes, it was short-sighted to advise him like that. She should have said:

"Don't let them have a single prescription, brother. Especially not your 'magic fungus'. You haven't even let me see it. . . . Besides, we've got Paipai. And I may bear you a son. . . ."

Of course she only said this to herself. Her eyes had misted over.

"Brother, people are gunning for you! Do you really have secret prescriptions? How many of them? Are they reliable? Why don't you tell me, show me?"

At once, however, she felt she had gone too far. How could she suspect a man she admired so much? He would laugh at her if he knew how upset she was.

"Bayberry! Bayberry! I've come to borrow something!"

One day at noon along came Brother Liu, whom she hadn't seen for some time. He was flushed as if from drinking. Striding briskly along he called from outside her cottage.

"What do you want, Brother Liu?"

The sight of him both pleased and embarrassed her. She had been hoping he would drop in to see her.

"A widow has better provisions than a poor bachelor. . . . I badly need two catties of snow-white bracken-root flour to make the kids some cakes."

He was chatting and laughing as if they had never fallen out.

"Sure I have some. I thought you wanted something special. I've several catties, you can have the lot."

It was seldom that Liu asked a favour. Sister Bayberry went to her bedroom, and from a vat with lime in it took out a package which she handed to him.

"Thanks a lot, sister! I'll cut you some fresh bracken root this winter. Well, I'll be off now."

"Don't treat me like a stranger, Brother Liu. I owe you so much, I can never hope to repay you.... Must you go so quickly?"

But he strode briskly out.

That afternoon she was chopping up grass for the pig when Liu dashed in again. He was pouring with sweat and covered in mud, as if just down from the mountain.

"Bayberry! Bayberry! I've some good news for you!"

"Look at you, Brother Liu! All over mud. Have you found some treasure in the hills or had some stroke of luck?"

She saw he had something wrapped up in a towel.

"Yes, sister, I've picked up a treasure.... I was digging up maize on my hill this afternoon, so as to plant saplings there, when I fell smack into a pit. Another old grave it was, like a stone chamber, with a mouldering coffin in it. We've lots of those Han tombs in Ninety-nine Mounds ... but unfortunately this one had been ransacked. Just my luck, falling into an empty tomb! Still I decided to look round for any pots, coins or copper bowls that might be left there. I saw a big black fungus growing on the coffin lid. It was giving off a blood-red light that scared me. I thought it must be a monster. I stepped back and stared at it. As it didn't budge, I went over to feel it and pinch it. It felt smooth, slippery and rather spongy. Just like a woman's breast.... Sorry, Sister Bayberry, I'm too crude.... So I picked it ... look, here it is!"

With that Liu unfolded his towel and held the fungus up in both hands to show her. Blushing, she reached out to stroke and pinch it. Yes, it was smooth, slippery and spongy. But how foul-mouthed he was, comparing a fungus to a woman's breast! Still it did smell faintly of ginseng.

"The devil only knows whether this is a treasure you've found or something quite useless. . . . Your forefathers lived well in Ninety-nine Mounds but their descendants are poor. If you go digging up graves how can you prosper?"

"Don't talk that way, sister. I suspect this is some precious medicine . . . but it's no use to me. . . ." Liu frowned. "I'll tell you in confidence, sister, because of you I've stopped going to that pharmacy in West Mist Flat. I don't hold it against you, don't blame anyone else. It's my fault for being such a useless nobody. . . . Suppose you give this fungus to Yao. No need to tell him I found it. He might think that a bit suspicious. If it's a real cure-all, better make use of it instead of leaving it in my place for cats and dogs to gnaw."

Sister Bayberry was touched. What a good man Liu was! He had announced recently that he was going to start a rival People's Pharmacy, but he couldn't have meant that seriously. She promptly agreed to send the fungus to Yao.

After Liu had left she suddenly remembered the talk about the magic fungus which grew in the Han tombs here. Suppose this really was one? How strange that he hadn't guessed.

Never mind. It wasn't an explosive or a poison, she'd send it to Brother Yao to see what he made of it. She told Paipai, just home from school:

"Paipai, take this package to your dad in West Mist Flat, and come straight back, there's a good boy."

"If he asks what it is, mum, what shall I tell him?"

"Tell him mum dug it up a few days ago in the hills from a big gravemound. I don't know whether it's any use or not."

Paipai went off cheerfully, leaving her in a flutter. She had fed the pig, cooped up her hens and ducks and laid the table for supper when he came back, flashing a torch.

"Mum! Dad was no end pleased. He hugged and kissed me. He also gave me ten yuan for you."

"Did he say anything else?"

"He said you are to go over after supper. He wants to talk to you. Told me to bring you this torch. . . . Don't stay there too late, mum, leaving me all alone here. I'm scared of the caterwauling of those wild cats in the hills. . . ."

Sister Bayberry had her arms around her son. For some reason when she heard this her heart ached. Tears came to her eyes and fell to the floor.

After dark the stars came out. The crickets in the fields set up a loud chirruping. The frogs started croaking. Sister Bayberry's mind was troubled. By the light of the torch she hurried through the fields, irritated by the raucous din as if it were aimed at her. Why couldn't they leave her in peace?

Far off at the foot of the hills flashed red and green will-o'-the-wisps, apparently all skimming in her direction. In the murky darkness below the old camphor trees at the crossroads the five stone lions lay in ambush like five warriors of old. Sister Bayberry smoothed her hair, coughed loudly and trod more firmly, keeping the torch on as she hurried past. Not until she reached West Mist Flat did she leave the frogs' croaking behind. Ahead of her dogs started barking. She welcomed the sound. Dogs did men's bidding and protected them. She trod more lightly and switched off the torch, making her way to the pharmacy by starlight. The light inside was on, and she could hear Yao bargaining with the section chief sent by Superintendent Wei. She had come at the wrong time. Could hardly interrupt them. But she stood there listening to what they were saying.

"This is a magic fungus, a sovereign remedy. Just feel how spongy it is, Section Chief Chen. Smell it. Hold it up to the light. See its red veins bright as blood! A genuine magic fungus more precious than gold, this is. You can search far and wide for a hundred years without finding one. It's a cure for all diseases, the best of tonics and a good tranquillizer which sharpens your wits as well as strengthening your muscles and liver. It increases virility and rejuvenates you...."

"Do you want to know how I came by this, section chief? I'll be quite frank with you. This magic fungus was handed down in my family for generations. My people were grave-robbers once.... Since Liberation the higher-ups have sent archaeologists here, and they say that for over two thousand years our Ninety-nine Mounds has been hallowed ground because of all the Han tombs here.... My people before me were herbalists too, who ransacked tombs to find rare remedies. That's how they discovered magic funguses, a sure cure for all diseases...."

"Here, have a cigarette, Dr Yao. Tell me what diseases this fungus cures."

It was Section Chief Chen's voice. Sister Bayberry heard matches struck.

"For instance, my grandfather once cut off 15 grams to stew with a catty of chicken for a woman over forty who was barren. Before long she conceived. Another time he steeped 25 grams in three catties of Shaoxing wine, which he buried for three years, then gave to a paralytic who'd been bed-ridden for over ten years; and in less than a month the man got up, in less than two months he went off as a porter with some salt merchants to Lianzhou. More amazing still, he steeped 50 grams in five catties of alcohol with tiger bones, rushes and sea-horse; and after it had been buried for five years he gave a dose to a rich man of over sixty. It completely restored his youth! He took a pretty concubine of sixteen and they lived happily together till their hair was white. . . . Then there was a beauty who had a tumour on her chest the size of a breast, so that her nickname was Three-breasted Goddess. He chopped up another 25 grams of this fungus, dried it on the roof then ground it into powder and added some toxic herbs to make an ointment. In less than two weeks the beauty's tumour vanished without leaving even a scar. . . . Later she offered herself to my grandfather as a serving-maid, to repay him for his kindness. . . ."

"Upon my word, Dr Yao! What you're telling me sounds incredible. . . . But how does this magic fungus grow?"

"Not so fast, Old Chen. I suppose you mean does it grow on a tree, on a vine, in the water or out of the ground. Well, the fact is it grows in Han tombs, on red sandalwood coffins. Why does it only grow there? Well, all things have their different origins. In ancient times when rich families had huge estates, if someone's darling daughter was delicate from childhood they would give her all kinds of tonics — ginseng, swallow's nest, tremella, deerhorn glue — but all to no avail. If she was fated to be short-lived, she would depart this world before being married. Then the whole clan would go into mourning. They would bury her in some auspicious plot and put in her red sandalwood coffin all the tonics left from her lifetime. As time went by, in the natural course of things her flesh would turn to dust, her bones to ashes, but the efficacious tonics in her coffin gradually congealed in the coffin lid, hanging from it like a globule of blood. . . . And countless centuries later, when the coffin was discovered by some fortunate, virtuous man, he would pick this sovereign remedy, the magic fungus. . . . My forefathers picked three of them, but only this one has come down to me. . . ."

"Well, Dr Yao, you live up to your reputation. They say seeing is believing. So this is the magic fungus!"

"Wait a bit, section chief. You can't hold on to it. . . . Let's get down to business."

"Right, Dr Yao. Superintendent Wei has been on the telephone telling me to get cracking. What business do you want to discuss with me?"

"I'll put my cards on the table, section chief. If you want this sovereign remedy, stop putting pressure on me to produce my secret prescriptions, and please go tonight to get Superintendent Wei to issue me a licence to practise medicine and open this pharmacy. Let's fix a time. Tomorrow afternoon here I'll hand over this magic fungus, for which I'll want a receipt; and I'll give you a receipt for the two licences. As for what you do with the fungus, I don't care whether you keep it, study it, or give it to your superiors. If you want to test its efficacy now, I can cut off five grams to make a powder and steep it in three ounces of liquor for you. But you'd better watch out, travelling alone at night, and not stop in some house on the way!"

Sister Bayberry had been listening raptly outside like a child entranced by some fantastic legend. Now she sensed that another eavesdropper was lurking there too.... She shivered and broke out in gooseflesh....

In a daze she tiptoed away back to the crossroads. Under the camphor trees it was too dark even to see her own outstretched hand, and all the stars were hidden. She tripped and fell at the foot of a stone lion. She could make out its gaping jaws, eyes like copper bells and claws outstretched as if to tear her to pieces .... With an effort she scrambled up. Her torch had been smashed and would no longer work. She would have to grope her way, crawling along. Heavens! All around were stone lions with bloody slavering jaws. She was surrounded, hemmed in by the fearful beasts, unable to get away from the sinister crossroads.

Footsteps sounded. Help! Had she called out? She wanted to, but couldn't utter a sound.... Have pity, you warriors of old, I'm not a bad woman, truly. Commander Han Xin, I didn't bump into your lions deliberately.... Let me go, let me go, spare my life! I've done nothing wrong, never harmed anyone or offended any spirit....

Her thoughts were in a whirl, she was distraught. But then, miraculously, her torch came on again, showing the way straight to the camphor trees. She scrambled to her feet and saw the flagstone road back to Bayberry

Gully. The bright torchlight emboldened her and she recovered some of her composure.

She walked back to the fields where frogs were croaking. That cheerful din was now a welcome sound. Vigorous and lively it put fresh heart into her. But her brain seemed paralysed. The immense sky overhead resembled an upturned sieve studded with stars like countless little eyes. Probably the rain was falling through this sieve. Was she dreaming, walking in her sleep? Everything was unreal, hazy. . . . What had happened? Had something gone wrong? Where had that black fungus come from? Was it the one that Liu had given her? The one she'd sent Paipai over with before supper? Surely not. Yao had given such a circumstantial description of how it had been handed down in his family and used by his grandfather. . . .

Just then she heard footsteps behind her, vigorous steps. They gave her a jolt. She nearly fell over again. But sobering up she recognized those steps. Liu must have caught up with her. Had he been the other eavesdropper outside the pharmacy? Had he spotted her? What a devil he was! She mustn't let him catch her. Her heart was in her mouth.

Sister Bayberry ran for dear life.

The next evening there was a hold-up on the quiet flagstone road leading from Ninety-nine Mounds out of the mountains, at the pass between two cliffs. Section Chief Chen of the district hospital was taking the "magic fungus" out in his satchel when a masked man sprang out from the undergrowth and seized it, then made off. Chen, frightened out of his wits, flopped down by the roadside not daring to chase him. There were no houses for twenty *li* round this pass, so that it had been a haunt of highwaymen in the old days. He dared not go back to Ninety-nine Mounds either. He must hurry to the district office to report this. Stranger still, when the burly masked highwayman reached Ox King Temple he was robbed by someone lying in wait by the road. By then it was too dark to see anything clearly. So one brigand was outwitted by another.

This business caused a sensation. The mountaineers had different theories about it. For all of them took an interest in that fungus. Who had sent the burly masked man? That seemed fairly obvious. But who was the second robber? They hadn't a clue. Still, all were pleased that this treasure was still in Ninety-nine Mounds. That was the crucial thing.

When news of this reached Sister Bayberry she naturally broke out in a cold sweat. The district had as yet sent no security officer to investigate the robbery. Moreover word was going round that she and Yao were to get married on the mid-autumn festival. So to show their respect for Yao and their faith in him, people started thinking what presents to send him. Some predicted that although Sister Bayberry was a widow, because of Yao's prestige their wedding would be the liveliest and grandest ever seen in the Wujie Mountains, as all the mountaineers would rally round to help out by collecting donations, slaughtering pigs and sheep, lending a hand in the kitchen, running errands, doing odd jobs, writing couplets or organizing a band. All would do their bit to make it a well-run, splendid affair.

The women of Ninety-nine Mounds stole a march

on the men by cultivating Sister Bayberry. A month or so before the wedding her cottage by Bayberry Brook seemed aglow with happiness. Neighbours called every evening to offer congratulations and bring gifts: material for new clothes, embroidered pillow-cases, a gay layette. . . . All of them, in fact, had an ulterior motive. If they got on her right side they could later ask her to put in a word for them if they needed medical treatment.

But this placed Sister Bayberry in a dilemma. She felt quite distracted. What worried her most was the fact that the "magic fungus" had been returned to her. She learned that it was made out of raw material borrowed from her. Who had brought the damn thing back? She wouldn't say. This business involved so many other people. In case security officers came to trace it, she decided to bury it under her cowshed and not say a word about it to anyone. At least this wasn't a murder case and no money was involved; so let it remain an unsolved mystery. . . . The very day after she had buried this "treasure" the fellow who had returned it started coming to ask for it to display in the People's Pharmacy which he meant to set up. He threatened to take it as evidence to the district to expose the devilish charlatan of Ninety-nine Mounds. If he did that she would be dragged into a serious court case, and whatever the outcome of it would find it hard to clear herself or prove that she had been duped. Would lose face completely. What a devil he was, so set on taking revenge.

But the people of Ninety-nine Mounds knew nothing of this. In their eyes she was now a favourite of fortune. She had no way out, hemmed in as she was by these blind, well-meaning people. Having nobody in whom she could confide, she could only swallow her tears. Suppose she were to speak out? That would never do. And she was in no hurry to make up her mind. Could she tell them that they had all been deluded like monkeys fishing for the moon in the water? Could she say: Yao doesn't have any secret prescriptions handed down for generations, doesn't possess magic powers, and that "magic fungus" is nothing but a chunk of bracken-root starch and sheep's blood?

This was what hurt most, not being able to tell the truth. For that would only antagonize everyone. If only this case could be settled in Ninety-nine Mounds without disturbing their superiors. It was out of the question to ask Liu for help, so she went to Ox King Temple to find Meng, meaning to confide in the hefty wicker-weaver and tell him what she had seen with her own eyes. But without hearing her out, Meng glared at her and shook his fist. "Sister Bayberry, you must be out of your mind! What's come over you, suspecting Yao like that? Who is he and who are you? Go and ask him for a sedative, and hurry up and get married. For goodness' sake, don't go around spreading these rumours, or everyone in Ninety-nine Mounds will think you're mad, a loony. Understand?" Meng's words dealt her such a blow her head simply reeled. Still she remained unmoved, threw caution to the winds and hurried off to find Wang. The short scrawny hunter heard her out patiently, then screwed up his eyes, pursed his lips and shook his head.

"Sister Bayberry! Why didn't you accept my five leopard skins? Now it's come to this, hold your tongue. As an outsider how can you cast doubt on something every soul in Ninety-nine Mounds believes in and a man respected by all? You'd better shut up and play dumb. Whether you marry him or not is up to you. Understand? If you go around making these accusations, you'll land yourself in trouble, you silly woman!"

Mad was she, a silly woman?... Who were the ones who were mad? Were those who told the truth silly lunatics, while those who lied and swindled others were sane and smart? But she'd used these arguments earlier on Liu. Brother Liu... why should the world play such tricks on a weak woman? Why? She'd put up with so many hardships, leading a decent life and bringing up her only son, what was wrong with that? Why should she be punished like this? It was too unjust, too cruel. She felt bitterly resentful. Well, she wouldn't appeal to anyone else. Their deeply ingrained superstitions were too much for her, were driving her out of her mind. Suppose she did go mad, never mind, she needn't try to debunk these illusions of theirs, enraging them so that they tore her to pieces.

"Mother! What can I do? I can't see any way out. I've fouled things up. I was too hard on Brother Liu, an honest hard-working fellow with good common sense; but I let myself be fooled by a charlatan, allowed him to treat me like dirt. How can I live on, now I've lost face completely...."

But Sister Bayberry had grit. She refused to knuckle under. After crying in her cottage for several days, she told Paipai he was not to go to the pharmacy any more. Yao sent messengers asking her to pick an auspicious day to register their marriage in the commune, and to choose some good woollen material in the co-op for a wedding suit. She fobbed them all off, explaining that she didn't want Yao to bear the whole cost of their wedding and meant to sell a pig and some poultry to make her own contribution. Nobody thought this in any way peculiar.

One quiet moonlight night a few days later, when all the mountaineers were sound asleep, several men and women from the foot of the mountains took out everything of value from her cottage. They did this so quietly that nobody heard them — only a few dogs barked. Sister Bayberry and Paipai went off with them. She had many relatives in her old home, and the men were such a tough lot that no one dared to go there to pick a quarrel. Besides, she hadn't broken any law. Had given up her cottage by Bayberry Brook, leaving on the table all her wedding presents marked with the names of the donors. . . . It was said that when she and Paipai reached the camphor trees at the crossroads, she had halted to gaze for a long time at Ash Hollow. . . . Then she went away, leaving behind the majestic stone lions which had stood guard through the centuries, letting passersby rest here during the day and Han Xin drill his troops in the night.

The people of Ninety-nine Mounds were scandalized by her desertion. They cursed her, calling her the ugliest names. But then they lapsed into an uneasy silence, as if the ground beneath their feet had split. Why was this? They couldn't say. There are certain things you can only sense, not speak of. What incensed them most was that their security had been undermined by a seemingly gentle young woman, actually an out-and-out rebel. Perhaps some of them wondered: Will Sister Bayberry ever come back? Who could say? She might. If some intelligent and decent fellow were to go to her old home at the foot of the mountains, offering her his People's Pharmacy in Ash Hollow as his betrothal gift, with his strong, muscular arms he might pick her up and carry her back again to Ninety-nine Mounds!

How I Became a Writer

I was born in 1942 in the northern foothills of the Wuling Mountains in south Hunan. That small village had no more than fifty households who lived north and south of some narrow fields, like two elephants standing side by side, and so the place was called Two Elephants Village. The west end was screened by a fine stand of cypresses, deep green the whole year round. A winding flagstone road ran from north to south, while from east to west flowed a brook called "Bigger than a Ditch". For us kids, in summer and autumn that brook was our "Happy River". Stark naked we learned to dive and swim dog-paddle. We had water fights and caught snails, fish, shrimps, crabs and eels, our small hands reaching boldly into the cracks of the rocks, from which occasionally we might pull out a slippery bream. We stirred up the green water till it was muddy. But it was starting with that little brook that some boys of my age later joined our glorious navy and sailed the high seas. And, even more unpredictably, one of those bare-bottomed boys took to writing stories.

Behind that little village was a big primeval forest, lush and green. In the daytime of course that was our favourite playground where we gathered firewood, pine needles, mushrooms and bamboo shoots and learned to shin up trees like squirrels to raid birds' nests. After dark we found it a scary, spooky place. The sound of wind and rain, the soughing of pines and the cries of birds and beasts frightened us into tucking our heads inside our quilts and gave us nightmares. When I woke with a start from dreams of falling out of a window, off a roof, off the top of a tree or down from the sky, the grown-ups said I was outgrowing my strength.

Climbing trees I grazed my hands and feet and tore my clothes, for which I often had my bottom spanked, my head rapped with a bamboo. Those tall tree tops which brushed the clouds and seemed to soar to the moon and stars had a great attraction for me. But actually I never once climbed to the top. The grown-ups had warned me that coiled in the crows' nests up there lay speckled snakes. The thought of that made me look down. But it's no good looking down when you're climbing a tree. It made me so dizzy, my hands and feet so limp that I quickly slithered down, ignoring the squirrels mocking me from the boughs. . . . Later, when I started writing, I often remembered those climbs of mine as a boy, the attraction they had for me and the spice of danger. It was really difficult to climb to the top.

In those days that small village near the border was culturally very backward. Only a few times a year did travelling showmen come from Henan or Anhui with their performing monkeys, and of course there were none of the broadcasts, films or modern plays that villages have today. But that mountain village had its own old culture. My home was known in Hunan for its folk songs, and the women sang and danced whenever there was a wedding. Each time a village girl married, all the other girls and young wives came to sing in her home for three days to give her a send-off.

They sang about her reluctance to leave her childhood home, her hopes for her marriage, her parents' grief at this parting. An even more common theme was aversion to feudal conventions and arranged marriages. (After Liberation musicians came to our parts to study the local customs, and they recorded six to seven hundred of these traditional songs.) Every autumn, when the grain was in the barns and the sickles hung on the walls, was the season for weddings at which such songs were sung. We kids were always able to tuck in by reaching out a row of small hands for titbits. We were able to feast our eyes on the decorated bridal sedan chair as it was borne into the village, and the bride in her red silk veil as she and the bridegroom bowed together to Heaven and Earth then went into the bridal chamber. We could also give our ears a treat by standing quietly behind the singers while they sang:

> A bride of eighteen, a groom of three
> Who wet the bed each night,
> Less than a pillow in length,
> Not up to a broom in height.
> At night he woke, for milk he cried.
> "I'm not your mum — I'm your bride!"

Another cultural activity in that small mountain village was listening to stories. Old folk told stories to pass the time and in this way taught the youngsters some culture and history. In those days, in times of peace, there was practically nothing to do in the country at night. People could relax and be quiet — there were no meetings. The only sounds were cocks crowing or dogs barking, or a sudden commotion if a thief was caught trying to steal a water-buffalo. Of course we kids had to work in exchange for listening to stories. In summer we sat on the threshing-ground in the moonlight waving rush fans to cool the old story-teller and drive away mosquitoes; in winter by the brazier we pummelled his back muscles which ached after the day's labours. As time went by my little brain became crammed with *The Canonization of the Gods, The Pilgrimage to the West, Outlaws of the Marsh* and other old stories.

Perhaps, without my knowing it, the seeds of literature were sown in my childish mind by the brook beside the village, the forest behind it, the wedding songs I heard and the stories the old folk told. Those seeds certainly fell on very poor rocky soil, and could hardly have germinated without the spring wind and rain.

I confess to my shame that the first books I read were stories about swordsmen. Soon after Liberation, when I was eleven or twelve, some dog-eared books with the first and last pages missing circulated through the countryside, most of them the adventures of swordsmen or accounts of involved court cases. I was spellbound by the exploits of those swordsmen who flew on to eaves, climbed high walls and broke into houses to kill scoundrels and save the poor, as well as by all the magic of those immortals and alchemists who rode on clouds and mist and turned stone into gold. Luckily these books did not lead me astray, because most of them were written to the same formula, and by the time the swordsmen reached a dead end the situation could only be saved by the intervention of Guanyin or some other deity.

My tastes were fairly catholic. I read a little of everything: Tang romances, Ming and Qing stories, the new literature of the May 4th period, and the critical realist works of 18th and 19th-century Europe. My favourite novel was *A Dream of Red Mansions*, which I read five or six times, sometimes reading it as a literary textbook, but never understanding it completely. It is truly a great treasury of art. Each time I read some classic it transported me into a colourful world with a whole gallery of characters, so that I felt as if drinking from a crystal fountain. Needless to say my study of great works whether Chinese or foreign was somewhat superficial. Without fully understanding them I tried to adopt their good points in the hope of producing something new myself. Later I also read histories, works on philosophy, war reminiscences, biographies of famous men and records of important world events. I tried to broaden my vision. No one poorly read and ignorant can be a good writer. I thought, since I came from the countryside, if I took no interest in and knew nothing about major current events, simply giving lively factual accounts of a few villagers, it would be hard to avoid mediocrity in my writing.

Literary writing requires nourishment which comes partly from life, partly from reading. If you are widely read in the best works ancient and modern, Chinese and foreign, you are imperceptibly influenced by them. Silently, like rain dew, they enrich and transform your mind. While trying my hand at writing I often felt that I lacked nourishment. We middle-aged and young writers today have read much less than the older generation of writers.

Just as peasants cultivate their fields, writers cultivate their lives. For life is the soil of literature. Brought up in a poor family in a south Hunan village, when I was only twelve I was faced with the contradiction between getting an education and making a living. Naturally food for my belly had precedence over mental sustenance. First I made straw sandals and sold them, then felled bamboo, carried charcoal to the market and hired myself out as a water-buffalo boy. Our village was so poor that many families took loads of charcoal to other counties to sell. In the sweltering summer the flagstones scorched the soles of your feet, and the sweat pouring off you steamed. On wet days I wrapped straw ropes round my sandals to keep from slipping. In winter the frost chapped my hands and feet so that blood dripped from the raw flesh. But it's the poor who help the poor, and we charcoal pedlars had plenty of homes to stop at to rest and wipe off our sweat — no one would be stranded half-way. If your charcoal or bamboo happened to fetch a good price, you'd buy a few pounds of meat and make a savoury stew with black soya beans, then give your mates a treat. . . . That life taught me how fine it was to earn your own living, taught me how hard this was. It enabled me to appreciate the sterling qualities of the labouring people who share their griefs and joys and help each other out.

Three years later I passed the entrance examination to junior middle school, but still went home in the winter and summer holidays. Towards the end of the fifties I interrupted my studies for a year to teach in a village school. The next year I was admitted into our district's agricultural school, from which we all went down to a poor county to go in for agriculture in a big way. In the winter of 1961 that school closed down and I was transferred to the agricultural college as a farm worker.

I lived near a small town for fourteen years, which covered the Four Clean-ups Movement and the "unprecedented great cultural revolution". I grew vegetables, tended orchards and raised saplings, grew paddy, mended farm tools and minded the store room. I learned basically all kinds of farm work. In those fourteen tumultous years at the grass-roots level I also familiarized myself with the village customs of south Hunan. The ancient flagstone street in this small mountain town, the new grey tiled, red brick houses, the old camphor tree with its fine foliage, and the crooked stilt-house all fascinated me and made me feel very close to the past. The vicissitudes, griefs and joys, the funerals and weddings of the local people and even their poultry and dogs made a lasting impression on me. I discovered that though the small town made very slow progress materially in those years, human relations changed incredibly fast. I am glad to have gone through the mill there.

Most authors take up writing mid-way in life, or begin writing in their spare time. When I published my first work in 1962, I was up against the problem of how to handle the relationship between my main job and my spare-time activities. Unless handled correctly it would lead to trouble and hold up my progress in writing. A writer must love life and his own job, otherwise he will feel isolated, unable to integrate with those around him or adjust to his surroundings and create a good environment for his work, study and writing. Because the raw material for a story is the people around you. Then, if you have any profound ideas or original views, these should be expressed in your work. A showy display of brilliance is hard for readers to accept. And overstatements and effusiveness prevent you from thinking deeply about life.

I believe that in life, the soil of literature, there is a dialectical relationship between depth and range, a focal point and the whole spectrum. If a writer produces a certain number of works of a fair standard but confines himself for years to living in one village or grass-roots unit, it is bound to restrict his view of life and his artistic vision, bound to reduce his works to mediocre matter-of-fact accounts, as he is unable to draw upon, refine and exploit many valuable materials from life. Thus writers like us who come from grass-roots units — especially if we come from villages — are confronted by completely different problems from those writers who seldom go down to the grass-roots or only make trips there to collect material. They should settle down there for longer periods, whereas we should try to see more of our country, take part in more cultural conferences, or read more Chinese and foreign masterpieces. I am keenly aware of this from my own experience. After the downfall of the "gang of four" the Writers' Association and other organizations arranged for me to travel widely in China to many famous mountains and great rivers, as well as to attend a course on literature. I was able to read more widely and listen to talks by well-known authors and scholars, to broaden my outlook on life and literature. This travel and study undoubtedly invigorated my writing.

Summing up my experience not long ago I wrote: "In the past few years I have stopped inventing stories and piecing together imaginary episodes, but instead have used the experiences of characters in real life, transforming and refining these to make them typical. This saves trouble. Drawn from life these works have the simplicity and truthfulness of life, not being as contrived as my earlier writing."

Works of literature are the saplings, or sometimes the great trees, a writer raises from the soil of life. Stories like *A Small Town Called Hibiscus* and *The Log Cabin Overgrown with Creepers* were drawn from life then altered and refined. To say "this saves trouble" is not entirely true, for this process of transmutation and refinement is actually more difficult than inventing one's own plot.

The Log Cabin Overgrown with Creepers first appeared in *October*, No. 2, 1981, a year after the hot summer in which I wrote it while staying with some foresters in the Wuling Mountains. There I heard the story of a school-leaver who had lost an arm early in the "cultural revolution" and been sent to a place called Red Hollow to help a couple of young foresters there. The husband was illiterate, pig-headed, strong and fearless. Because he suspected his wife of having an affair with the young man, after drinking one day he maimed them both for life.

At the time the story shocked me, but I paid only passing attention to it. I was more struck by the way of life of the benighted people, so set in their way, who lived cut off from the world in these lush, idyllic surroundings, going out to work all day and returning at sunset to rest, scratching a simple living from the soil with no wish for any culture or modern science from outside. . . . It seemed to me that their way of life was typical of our old nation and country. Wasn't this how we had lived for centuries before starting to modernize China? And this way of life which seemed to have disappeared from our cities and villages had in fact shaped our thinking and customs for so long that it lived on in many people's minds and manifested itself in their behaviour.

The three characters in the story about Red Hollow were each very typical. There was the ignorant, illiterate husband, a narrow-minded tyrant; his gentle wife with her strong sense of self-respect and eagerness to make progress; and the unfortunate educated youth who had lost an arm. I later incorporated them in my story *The Log Cabin Overgrown with Creepers* as Wang Mutong, Azure and Li Xingfu. They formed a small social community deep in the primeval forests in the mountains. And even this small community was a hierarchy of high and low.

Characters like Wang Mutong were familiar to me from way back. He was the product of our old society: uneducated, bigoted, narrow-minded. And he gloried in his lack of education, in his position as overlord of the forest, even though his only subjects were his wife and children and a disabled youth. Science and culture were anathema to him, as were modern civilization and democracy. Of course he had his sympathetic side too — he was hard-working. The trouble with him was not innate viciousness but the old way of life so deeply imbued with feudal ideas which he inherited.

Then there was Azure. Many people of the Yao nationality live in the Wuling Mountains, and I portrayed her as a gentle, lovely Yao girl. Born and bred in the mountains she very seldom left home; her husband would not let her go for fear of unsettling her. She was used to life in the mountains and had no extravagant hopes of her husband, satisfied if when tipsy he did not beat her too hard or make her miscarry. But as she was intelligent and eager to learn, attracted to what was good and beautiful, she was drawn to Li Xingfu, the one-armed educated youth sent by the forestry station as their assistant, and to the modicum of material and spiritual civilization he took there from outside. Innocent and chaste, she only fell in love with him later because her husband put such pressure on her and tried to isolate her. Extremes lead to their opposites. Material and spiritual culture cannot be excluded by isolationist measures or heavy pressure. Because people are naturally curious and eager to make progress, isolation tactics can only intensify the lure of a more modern way of life. So Azure's behaviour can be seen as the Chinese people's healthy urge to better their conditions.

The third character Li Xingfu, the One-hander, had a smattering of science and culture. But this was roughly rejected by Wang Mutong, who tauntingly turned down the few proposals he made for preventing forest fires. When he tried to do some useful work by classifying the forest's trees, his motives were misunderstood by Wang and the forestry station. Only Azure sympathized with him and secretly supported him. He had no designs on her, yet Wang beat him up and threatened him. So the One-hander represents the ridiculing of culture by an illiterate, the stifling of science by an ignoramus, the trampling on civilization by brute force, and the despotic suppression of democracy.

It is worth noting how the contest between these people, a contest between ignorance and culture, ended. After the forest fire Azure and the One-hander won happiness, and Wang went to another even more remote forest to carry on his ancestors' old way of life.

In recent years I have tried to avoid writing in a stereotyped, generalized way, but hitherto I have made very little headway in this respect, and I need to redouble my efforts.

Literature is the product of life. Life is its soil. And the richness or poverty of the soil determines whether a work of literature is vigorous or feeble. A great tree will not grow from barren land; only rich soil and clear water will enable it to flourish.

Looking back at what I have written over the last twenty years I feel ashamed and dismayed. But most writers seem to like to brazen things out with their readers, and so I have written this article to comfort, encourage, mock and explain myself.

About "Pagoda Ridge"

WHEN *Pagoda Ridge* was first published in *Dangdai*, No. 2, 1982 I prefaced it with the words "A song for our mountain people". *Pagoda Ridge* describes events in a production brigade in a remote mountainous area. Several enthusiastic readers have written to me saying that after reading *Pagoda Ridge* they were greatly moved by the tough and simple mountain people. It is precisely these characteristics, I believe, that have enabled working people, under the leadership of the Chinese Communist Party, to achieve revolutionary victory after a hard and protracted armed struggle and to establish a socialist China. Our socialist society possesses great vitality. However, in a country with several thousand years of feudal traditional culture, socialism is, after all, a new system and we must explore as we advance and advance as we explore. In the course of building a specifically Chinese socialist society we should not be alarmed if complications, difficulties, or even serious errors arise. All countries and peoples, without exception, must pay history's price for their liberation and prosperity. I wrote *Pagoda Ridge* to illustrate this.

I remember the spring of 1977 when I went with several colleagues to a county in the Wuling Mountains to collect old Red Army folk songs. We intended to write a few new pieces for our Chenzhou Song and Dance Troupe. While I was there I heard about a legal case in a remote production brigade which consisted of about ten or so households scattered over a distance of several miles. The brigade leader had fixed the quotas per individual household, which was forbidden at the time and had kept his superiors completely in the dark. He began doing this in 1968, when ultra-Left ideological trends still prevailed, and continued until 1977. Although the calamitous "gang of four" had already fallen from power then, ultra-Left thinking still remained, and as a result the leader was sentenced to nine years imprisonment for his nine years of "following the capitalist road". I believe his case will have been redressed now under the new policy of the Third Plenary Session of the Party's Central Committee held in 1978. When I heard about the case, I began to think about the reality of life as I knew it when I was living in those mountains. I thought too about the small town beside a river where I lived for fourteen years. During the first six years of the "cultural revolution" I wasn't able to write and could only labour in the fields. In slack seasons I would cross the river and go up into the mountains to cut firewood or pick medicinal herbs. They were mostly Chinese angelica, local ginseng or millettia which were said to be energy-giving tonics. For me and for many others it was only a way to while away the time since we couldn't do anything else. I kept myself amused then learning about Chinese herbal medicine. At the same time I was shocked by how hard life was for people in that region. The mountains were deep and high, the soil sterile and land was scarce. Even though the households were scattered through the valleys or on the surrounding ridges, people still had to assemble daily and work to a rigid schedule. In so-called "collective production through collective action" they wasted a lot of time on the way to work and back. It was a totally ritualized and fruitless way of production and of life. But everyone had to obey "to make the hard transition from socialism to communism".

In the beginning of 1979 the Party formulated the policies which allowed for much greater flexibility in the rural economy, and in particular for agricultural production to be based on individual households. These policies revitalized the countryside and have led to increased prosperity.

I wrote Pagoda Ridge during the summer of 1981 when the facts proved that the brigade leader who had fixed household quotas according to local natural and social conditions was without doubt a courageous man. Even though he had suffered tremendously, his family had been hurt and he himself imprisoned, he had saved from disaster people who might otherwise have had to become vagrants in order to survive. This is the heroic spirit of our nation, and an example of the sobriety and dedication of Communist Party members.

With the male characters in Pagoda Ridge such as Tian Faqing, Knock-out Wang and Jiang Shigong, my description centres on their loyalty, gallantry and sense of righteousness; with the female characters such as Liu Xiuxiu, Liu Liangmei and Sister Mushroom, I've stressed their outwardly mild and gentle but inwardly strong personalities, and their willingness to sacrifice their own interests if necessary. Old Crow Liu, a petty intellectual living in a mountain region, has been cast as a pathetic victim in the story. I am very familiar with these mountain people and I have put all of my love and hatred into describing them.

Now the story and characters of *Pagoda Ridge* are all past history. Yet history is a mirror in which we can not only justify and develop the present but also envisage the future.

古 华 小 说 选

熊 猫 丛 书

＊

《中国文学》杂志社出版

（中国北京 百万庄路24号）

中国国际图书贸易总公司发行

（中国国际书店）

外文印刷厂印刷

1985年第1版

编号：（英）2—916—28

00190

10—E—1765P